Praise for Denise Belinda McDonald's
Wrong Turn, Right Cowboy

"WRONG TURN, RIGHT COWBOY is a terrific book for anyone who loves contemporary tales of the West, cowboys, or suspense-filled novels. Familiar characters from the first Paintbrush novel appear, but this definitely is a stand-alone romance novel. Even though this is a fast-paced novel, it includes Denise's fun sense of humor. Denise hooked me from the beginning and kept me chained to the computer to find out what happened next. Do yourself a favor and buy this book!"

~ *Author Caroline Clemmons*

"Denise Belinda McDonald does it again, writing another captivating story that becomes an instant favorite. I really liked the fact that Quint has his own insecurities when it comes to what he wants; it adds another layer to a compelling tale. Wrong Turn Right Cowboy is the second in the Paintbrush series and will delight readers."

~ *Single Titles Review*

"Wrong Turn, Right Cowboy is a nice, easy going romance with small town warmth. Not only does Gillian get the handsome cowboy, she earns the love of the whole town. Wrong Turn, Right C⸻⸻⸻⸻d!"

~ *Blackr⸻*

Look for these titles by
Denise Belinda McDonald

Now Available:

Her Passion
Deadly Mistakes
The Inn Crowd
Trading Faces
The Cowboy Plan

The Paintbrush Series
Second Chances
Wrong Turn, Right Cowboy

Wrong Turn, Right Cowboy

Denise Belinda McDonald

SAMHAIN
PUBLISHING

Samhain Publishing, Ltd.
11821 Mason Montgomery Rd., 4B
Cincinnati, OH 45249
www.samhainpublishing.com

Wrong Turn, Right Cowboy
Copyright © 2011 by Denise Belinda McDonald
Print ISBN: 978-1-60928-203-5
Digital ISBN: 978-1-60928-156-4

Editing by Tera Kleinfelter
Cover by Mandy M. Roth

First Samhain Publishing, Ltd. electronic publication: August 2010
First Samhain Publishing, Ltd. print publication: August 2011

Dedication

For C.C.; still inspiration extraordinaire.

To: (My BFF) Sandy Behr, for being uber-supportive from day one—love you. My gals: Avery Michaels, Brenda Chitwood and Geri Foster for being the best cheering squad—and *always* making me laugh. Yellow Rose 'Buds, love y'all bunches. The Faulkners, just because. Amie Stuart, for always challenging me to keep going. Chicas—write on.

Again to Oscar and Imogene Head who gave me my love for all things horses and cowpokes—miss you both!

Alan and our wonderful (noisy) boys, thanks for always keeping things chaotic and fun.

Tera Kleinfelter—super-editor—thanks for all you do! You rock!

Chapter One

"Are we there yet, Mom?"

Gillian Harwood glanced over at her daughter, Heidi, and tried not to lose her temper. The trip from Mobile, Alabama to Billings, Montana was a long, tedious drive. She'd thought Heidi would settle once they crossed the state line, but no, she'd whined every fifteen miles since they left Sheridan, Wyoming, wound tighter and tighter with each mile.

"Soon, hon." Gillian bit the corner of her lip to keep from smiling. She didn't think her teenager would appreciate it.

"How much longer?" Heidi, sixteen going on twenty-six, had sulked ever since Gillian announced they were moving across country. Now that they were almost there, she all but bounced in her seat she was so restless.

Gillian flipped down the visor to block the late afternoon sun. "Ten minutes."

"You said that already. Twice." The gum in her mouth smacked like crazy.

"Then why do you keep asking?" Gillian smiled when Heidi stuck out her tongue. "You're such a brat." She chuckled. "Another half-hour or so. I think." Gillian ran her hand down her daughter's head. "Then we don't have to get in the car again for a month. How does that sound?"

She popped a huge pink bubble. "Super!"

Gillian pulled onto the dirt farm road. "I think we missed a turn somewhere." Dust flew up around the Volvo.

"Mom, maybe you should slow down. There's so much crap you can't see far ahead."

The road grew bumpier.

"This sucks. Why'd we have to move to Montana?" The teen crossed her arms over her chest and sunk in her seat.

"I'm sorry, hon." Gillian's hands tightened on the steering wheel as she gave Heidi a quick look. "You know I didn't ask for this."

Heidi's eyes grew huge and round. "Look out!" She pointed in front of them.

Gillian slashed her gaze forward in time to see a man on a horse smack dab in the middle of the road. "Holy..." She slammed on the brakes with both feet and pulled the wheel as far to the left as possible. The car swerved then fishtailed, followed by a resounding thud before it lurched to a stop.

"Heidi, are you okay?" Gillian asked as her daughter screamed, "You hit him!"

"Are you hurt? Look at me." She tried to reach for Heidi but the seatbelt was pulled taut and locked. Pain shot across her forehead, but she was more concerned with her daughter.

"God, Mom. I think you killed him." Heidi was fumbling with her seatbelt just as the airbags deployed and smacked them both in the face. "Ow."

"You have got to be kidding me." Gillian pushed the fabric away from her. It seemed like an eternity, but the bags started to deflate. Heidi was again working to unlatch her seatbelt. "Sit still and look at me." Gillian managed to snag Heidi's chin. "Your nose."

The teen swiped at her nose and paled at the sight of blood on her sleeve. "Yick." She swiped once more. "I'm fine. I think you hit the horse. We need to check on him." Her seatbelt popped free and she wrenched the door open.

Images of a dead horse and rider flashed before Gillian's eyes. "Get back here." She tried to grab her daughter's arm, but got nothing but the airbag fabric. "Heidi, I don't want..." She pushed the airbag back as far as possible and wrestled her own seatbelt off. She hustled out of the car but stopped short when she saw the man half under her car.

His strawberry blond head turned toward her. The man all but growled at Gillian, "Grab her." His gray eyes flared.

"Who? Heidi? She's okay. Are *you* hurt?" She drew closer. "This is not happening." One of his legs was under the front end of her car. "Ohmygawd, I'm so sorry."

He wrestled with his leg, but stayed pinned. "Grab her, dammit."

Gillian jumped. "Heidi's fine." *Why is he worried about my daughter?*

"My horse," he said through clenched teeth. "She's spooked. Don't let her get away."

Gillian glanced over her shoulder. A huge, brown horse with flared nostrils pawed at the ground and stared back at her. "Let me help you up and you get her." She grabbed at his arm and tugged but he didn't budge.

He slanted his head and let out an exasperated breath. "I'm stuck under the car."

Blood rushed to Gillian's ears and a moan escaped.

He could sue for this. There'd be a court case. A searchable database. The world tilted. Spots danced before her eyes. They'd have to change their names to stay off the radar for good this time. She took a couple of deep, calming breaths.

"I'm fine, just stuck. But, please, grab the horse before you spook her anymore."

The pounding in her chest eased a little. "He's fine," she said to herself.

"I've got her." Heidi walked up, leading the horse by the reins.

Gillian's gaze volleyed between her new hood ornament and the horse. Maybe if she just backed her car up, he'd pop free. And while they were in the car... If she were quick enough, they could leave and no one would know.

"Can you..." The man grunted, breaking Gillian from her thoughts.

As bad as life could get, she couldn't just abandon the man. He might be hurt too bad to make it home on his own. "Can I what?"

"My boot's stuck under the tire. Help me pull."

Gillian nodded and moved closer. She kicked off her heels—while helpful when standing next to her daughter, not conducive for dislodging a man from the front end of her Volvo. She reached for him, hesitated for a moment then straddled his leg and snagged a handful of denim.

"On three." He looked at her; his gray gaze sent a shiver down her spine. "One, two—" he gave her a quick wink, "—three."

The pair yanked once then twice. The third time, she thought it would jerk free, but it wasn't until the fifth pull that his foot came loose. The momentum unwedged the man from the tire and tossed Gillian right up against him, seating her firmly in his lap. "Oh."

Dust kicked up all around them.

The man looped his arms around Gillian to keep her from tumbling them both flat. His short, strawberry blond curls bounced around his head. A small smattering of freckles disappeared as red blotches covered his cheeks.

His heart beat a heavy tattoo against her palms. She swallowed hard. "Are you okay?"

The man stared at her for a long moment, his gaze raking across her mouth. "Fine." He then not-so-gently shoved her up off of him and onto the hard-packed ground. "What the hell is wrong with you?" He righted himself and dusted off his dark jeans.

"Me?" Gillian tried to stand gracefully, not liking his towering height standing over her—and yelling—but with the awkward position he'd left her in, she couldn't do much more than tilt her head back and stare up at him. "Do you mind?"

She scooped up her shoes and held her hand out for help up. His large, calloused hand circled hers. A little zip of electricity shot up to her elbow, almost making her lose her grip. He pulled her to her feet effortlessly—and immediately released her hand.

He huffed out a breath. "Are *you* okay?"

She wiped the dirt from her capris. Without her heels, she barely came up to his shoulder and had to crane her neck to look up at him. "Yes, thank you. I—"

"You can't just come barreling down the road like that. You could have killed someone."

"I...we're lost." She thrust her hands on her hips and stepped closer to him. "How the hell was I supposed to know you'd come out of nowhere?"

"There's a road right there." He pointed off to his left.

"And I am supposed to know this how?"

"If you weren't trying to break the speed of sound."

"Please. That car is nearly seventeen years old, has over a hundred and forty thousand miles on it." She waved her hand at the Volvo. When she glanced over her shoulder at it though, something didn't look...quite right.

11

It sat lopsided with smoke coming out from under the hood. "My car." She dropped her shoes and hurried over to the silver sedan. "Aw, man."

"That's what happens when you run over a fence post. A post that kept you from running all the way over me, by the way."

Heidi cleared her throat. "Uh, Mom?"

"Mom?" The man frowned and shook his head. "You're her mother?"

Quint Walters must have hit his head when she ran him down. The little bit of woman who tried to make roadkill out him barely looked out of high school. Not old enough for a teenage daughter.

"Sir? What's her name?" The younger woman held tight to the horse's reins.

Quint scrutinized the teen. She was the spitting image of her...mother—all platinum blonde hair and blue eyes—just supersized. While "mom" was all of five feet tall and maybe a hundred pounds soaking wet, the teen stood damn near eye to eye with him and was built like an athlete.

"Mallow." He turned his attention to his Appaloosa. "Short for Marshmallow." He patted the horse's neck then ran his hands down each of her legs, inspecting her to make sure she hadn't been injured when she'd bucked him. "Thatta girl." He glanced at her hooves and checked to make sure she hadn't thrown a shoe. He released a heavy sigh when he found no problems.

Quint scanned the road and found his Stetson. He hobbled over to the misshapen felt hat and snapped it up from the road.

"You're limping." The teen followed him. "Mom, he's limping."

He bent the edges of his hat until it somewhat resembled what it should look like. He plopped it on his head and reached for the reins. "Thanks…"

"Heidi." The girl smiled a dazzling, toothy grin. "And she's Gillian. Harwood."

Gillian glared at Heidi.

"What? I know I'm not supposed to 'divulge'—" she made air quotes with her fingers, "—information willy-nilly, but considering you almost killed him…" She shrugged.

"I didn't almost kill him." Gillian waved at the smoke coming from her car. "Are you hurt badly, Mr…?"

"Quint. Quint Walters, no mister." A thousand questions flashed through his mind. Not least of which, why couldn't they divulge their names? Witness protection, on the run from the police?

Out on the back end of the Skipping Rocks Ranch wasn't the place to ask. "I just twisted my bum knee. It'll be fine after I ice it."

Relief washed over her face. "Do you have a cell phone we could borrow?"

"Won't matter."

"Beg pardon?" Her gaze narrowed on his.

He shook his head. "No service out here. Up closer to the house or back in town…" He shrugged.

Gillian ran a hand through her hair. "What now, then? The car obviously isn't going anywhere."

"We walk." He turned and guided Mallow up the road.

"Walk?" the two females asked in unison. He glanced back as they both examined the fields around them.

Quint stopped. "We could wait for someone to drive by."

They both sighed and leaned against the car.

"But this is a private road and I'm the only one who drives it most days."

The teen's head flopped back against the roof of the car with a loud thwack. He wondered if this was normal or if she had a flare for the dramatics. His aunt's two girls were still just young enough and out of reach of teen-itis so he wasn't sure. And his sister's twins were thankfully rough and tumble boys and yet to start walking.

"We could wait for someone to come looking for me. But it's my day off and I won't be missed until sometime tomorrow."

"Got it. We walk." Gillian bent and scooped up her heels from the road. "One second, please?" She hurried to the back of the sedan and fumbled around in the trunk, her lithe body tempting to even the most celibate man—like he'd sworn himself to recently. He couldn't help but peek when her shirt rode up. Nothing but creamy skin, whereas most city women— and this woman was definitely a city woman—he knew had some form of body art to draw the eye, Gillian needed none but her perfectly rounded derrière. "Hon, will you get my purse?"

Her words shook him out of his leering and he cleared his throat. He looked to make sure the teen hadn't caught him ogling her mother, but she was wound up in a pout, hugging a dark brown teddy bear to her chest and didn't seem to be paying him any attention.

Heidi's lip poked out. "Fine." She slammed the door shut and shoved the bag on her shoulder.

When Gillian joined them, she'd slipped into a pair jogging shoes and had a larger bag looped over her shoulder. She unfolded a map. "Where exactly are we?"

Quint chuckled before he could help himself. "You won't find it on there."

"Why not?"

"Well, darlin'. That's Montana."

"Yeah." She shifted the bulky bag on her shoulder.

"You're on the outskirts of Paintbrush." Quint looked over his shoulder.

Gillian scanned the map.

"Wyoming."

Chapter Two

"I came as fast as I could." Quint's Aunt Zan barreled through the back door of his small house. "Tell me what happened."

She pulled up short when she saw Gillian and her daughter huddled together on the leather sofa.

"There was an accident out on Old Matherly Road." Quint walked out of the kitchen to hand Heidi a rag for her nose and an ice pack for the welt on Gillian's forehead.

"Thank you." Gillian took the bag and settled it on her the purple bump. She volleyed her gaze between Zan and Quint. Her voice faltered slightly as she continued. "I ran my car into a fence."

His aunt's eyebrow raised and she glanced at Quint. "Why are *you* limping?"

"Mallow and I were between her and the fence."

His aunt gasped. "Is she..."

"Mallow's fine. She threw me and got the hell out of the way. They got the brunt of the injuries, Gillian and Heidi." He motioned at them. "One sec. Zan, can I see you in the kitchen?" He grabbed his aunt's arm before she could comment and dragged her along with him.

"Let me have a look at you." Zan was only a handful of years old than he—they were more like brother and sister than aunt and nephew—but she still fussed over him as much as his own mother.

"I'm fine. Look, I called Dr. Hambert's office but he's out on a call at the Tullman ranch."

Zan smiled. "Did Lizzie have her baby?"

"I don't know. Can you look *them* over?" He motioned back to the living room.

She frowned. "Me?"

Quint leaned against the counter, tried to relieve some of the pain in his knee. "You have medical knowledge."

"I don't even have my license yet." She narrowed her eyes. "And even if I did I am a vet tech. Not for humans."

"Please." He glanced over his shoulder to make sure they couldn't hear him. "Something's going on with them."

Her shoulders stiffened. "What do you mean?"

"I don't know." He was probably making too much out of a few off-hand comments, but there was something that tugged at his gut and he couldn't shake the feeling. "Just do me a favor. Please."

She huffed. "Fine. But you have to babysit for me."

"Deal."

She held up two fingers. "Twice."

"Whatever." Quint smiled down at her.

"Let me have a look at your knee first."

"I told you, it's fine." It hurt like a sonofabitch, but he'd wrenched it many times before and other than taking it easy for a few days and icing it down, there wasn't much to do. "Heidi's nose has been bleeding on and off. I don't think it's broken but I know her mom would feel better if they knew for sure."

While Zan looked after the teen, Quint sat near Gillian on the large leather sofa. "I called Manny, the mechanic. He should

17

be out to get your car by the end of the day."

"That long?"

"He's at least thirty miles away on a job and has two other folks he has to tow."

Gillian glanced at her watch. "May I use your phone?"

"Sure." Quint braced his hand to push up and go grab the cordless.

"Sit. Tell me where it is and I'll get it."

"Kitchen counter."

Gillian took a deep breath and dialed the number for her new boss in Billings. When the woman picked up after the third ring, Gillian's nerves hummed as she said, "Mrs. Taylor, hi. It's Gillian Harwood."

"How was your trip?"

"That's why I'm calling. We've had a little setback. I'm in—" She leaned around the kitchen wall. "Where are we again?"

Quint stopped rubbing his knee and glanced up at her. "Paintbrush."

"Paintbrush, Wyoming."

"Is everything okay?"

"Yes, ma'am. Well, not exactly. I'm going to need to get some work done on my car." She'd been counting on this job. Hoping to set down roots for her and Heidi as far away from anyone who knew them as she could.

"How soon will you get here?"

She closed her eyes. "A day or two tops," she said and all but held her breath.

"See you then."

Gillian released the pent-up breath and replaced the phone

to its handset. She'd taken a big chance moving so far away from what they knew for a tentative job offer, but she hadn't had much choice. If Rick Damon caught up to them... She shuddered to think what would happen.

"Excuse me."

Gillian jumped. "Yes?"

"I'm Zan. I don't think we were properly introduced. Quint's manners have never quite developed." A genuine smile spread across her face. "Do you mind if I have a look at that bump?"

There was something familiar about the woman but Gillian couldn't put her finger on it. She was a few inches taller than Gillian and had freckles everywhere. She couldn't have met her. She and Heidi lived a pretty sheltered life and had never really left Alabama until they had to pick up and move away. Still there was something familiar...

"I don't bite, I swear." She smiled.

Gillian nodded and relaxed—if only marginally. "Is Heidi okay?"

"Yes. I think the bleeding has stopped. It's not broken. She'll have a nasty bruise for a day or two."

"Thank you for coming out here."

"Just wait until you get my bill."

The blood drained from Gillian's face.

"Oh, hon. I'm just kidding." Zan patted Gillian's arm. She took a hold of Gillian's chin and turned her head this way and that. She looked into her eyes; the scrutiny would have made Gillian squirm if she hadn't had such a firm grip. "No broken skin. Some ice should make it go down pretty well. Pull your bangs forward and no one will even notice. If you start getting headaches or anything, have..." she paused, "...have Quint call Dr. Hambert again for you." She winked at Gillian. "Quint, I gotta run. Doc's waiting for me back at the Cates' ranch."

Quint hollered his goodbyes from the living room.

"Nice to meet ya." Zan paused for a second as if she might have something else to say but instead turned and headed out of the small house.

In the living room, Heidi had her bruised-but-not-broken nose buried deep in her book. "You doing okay, hon?"

Heidi waved absently at Gillian. Quint was rubbing his knee again.

"Do you mind?"

He frowned. "Do I mind what?"

"If I have a look at your knee."

"I don't..."

"I'm a masseuse. I do, did, therapeutic massages." Gillian pushed a strand of hair behind her ear and moved closer to the club chair he sat in. "How did you hurt it? Originally, I mean."

"Old injury. Baseball. Catcher."

"I've worked on sports injuries before." Gillian squatted in front of Quint. "I promise it won't hurt."

"I guess." He shifted in his seat, stretched his leg out fully in front of him.

"Hon, can you hand me my bag?" Heidi shoved the large bag at her mother. "Roll up your jeans, please."

Quint toed off his boot and shoved the denim up over his knee.

"Sandalwood or musk?"

Quint swallowed hard. "Beg pardon?"

"I have sandalwood- or musk-scented oil."

"Aw, hell, Maybe not." Quint pulled at his jeans. It was almost too much to bear having her squat in front of him.

"Mom's pretty good. You should let her try." The teen barely looked up from her book.

"Fine." Quint gave in. Gillian snagged the closest bottle and poured some oil in her hand. She worked it around for a minute or so. He flinched when she set her small hands on his knee. His gut shouldn't tumble with her barest touch; she'd almost mowed him down not an hour earlier.

Despite being a teeny-tiny thing, her strong hands fit around his knee. It did hurt a little but it lessened by degrees as she worked. He couldn't think of anything but the pain or lack thereof because if he thought of her porcelain skin and big blue eyes he'd be lost. And God forbid he acknowledged how much he wanted to bury his hands in her hair and draw her to him, he might embarrass the pair of them.

After ten minutes or so she stopped. Quint opened his eyes—he didn't even remember shutting them. "Wow." He rotated his leg around, worked his knee. "Pain's gone."

"Told ya," Heidi said around a huge wad of gum in her mouth.

Quint started to ask where she'd learned to be a masseuse, but a knock sounded at the front door. He shoved down his jeans leg—and all the thoughts swirling through his sex-deprived brain—and answered the door. "Hey, Manny. You're early." Quint wasn't sure why disappointment spread through his gut.

"Where's the car at?" Manny pushed a greasy ball cap back on his head.

"Out at the end of Old Matherly Road." Quint ushered the man inside. "Can I get ya a drink?"

"Naw. Ran by the diner on my way here." Manny eyed Quint's lone boot over by the sofa then looked down at his sock covered foot.

"She ran up over a fence post." Quint snagged his boot and stuffed his foot back into the worn, leather roper. "Airbags deployed. Don't think it was leaking any fluids when we left it."

"Will you be able to get to it today?' Gillian came up behind the two men.

"What is the year and make of the vehicle?"

Gillian rattled off the details.

Manny glanced at his watch. "I can start work on it tonight, but it'll take a couple of days to get airbags for it. I don't keep those in stock. Are you up for a visit or are you passing through town?"

She blanched at the question—something was definitely going on with the Harwoods.

"I'm only asking 'cause we don't have rental cars here." Manny shifted and adjusted his coveralls over his paunch. "But I can get someone to run you over to Sheridan and get something."

She nodded. "Oh. We're passing through." She darted her gaze to her daughter and back, then gnawed on her lower lip. "Um, could we ride into town with you? We need to find a place to stay until the car is ready."

Quint stifled the urge to invite them to stay with him. He didn't know a thing about either of the two women. The last thing he needed was to get in the middle of whatever issues they had going on. "I'll head out there with you and get that fence fixed up."

"For two nights?" The woman wrote down something in a ledger.

"Yes, ma'am." Gillian was pleased there wasn't a

computerized system. She hadn't really thought that far ahead when Manny had dropped them off. She'd been ever so glad to get as far away from Quint Walters as possible. The tall, handsome man stirred up emotions she'd thought she capped a long time ago.

Why she'd offered to work on his knee... Touching the man was just about the stupidest thing when she already had all the flutterings running though her nerves. She'd done countless massages in the four years since she'd opened her small practice. Never once had one fantasy after another bombarded her. Never once had anything past a professional level accompanied the automatic ministrations. But the moment her hands covered his knee...

"Mom." Heidi nudged her.

The clerk must have spoken to her, judging by the look on her face. She named off a fee that wouldn't put too much of a dent in Gillian's cash on their short stay. Not that it could be helped. She didn't even want to think about the cost of the car repairs. Hopefully, it wouldn't deplete their cash completely before she could get to Billings, Montana and start her new job.

"Did I see Manny dropping you off?"

"Yes." Gillian nodded.

"Car trouble?"

"Yes."

"Where about?"

Gillian frowned. She wasn't used to having to give a run-down of the what's-what in her life, but from her mother's stories of growing up in a small town outside of Mobile, she knew small town culture was different. "The edge of the Bowmans' Skipping Rocks Ranch I think they said." She'd largely tried to ignore the men talking as they hooked her car up to the back of the tow truck.

"They?"

"Manny and Quint Walters."

The woman's faced morphed. Her dark brown eyes softened and a smiled curved her unpainted lips.

"I'm hungry." Heidi, the sullen teen, had returned.

They had stopped for a quick snack late in the morning, but she'd expected to be in Montana by lunch and hadn't grabbed anything extra. Halfway through the afternoon and they hadn't eaten for hours.

"There's a diner just up the way. Best pot roast this side of the Big Horn Mountains." The hotel manager reached over the counter and proffered a room key on a large plastic tag. "Name's Ruby. If you need anything, just let me know."

"Thanks." Gillian took the key—they didn't even have magnetic swipe cards, but an actual old-fashioned key—and smiled. She snagged Heidi's elbow and dragged the teen behind her out the door. "Let's get settled in our room and we'll go get something to eat."

At the room the pair stood at the threshold. Beige walls with a lone mirror over the small dresser accompanied a pair of beige-topped double beds. "Homey."

"Homely." Heidi shuddered. "Norman Bates is prolly hiding in the walls." She walked over to the bed and set her stuffed bear up against the pillows. It was a raggedy toy, but something she'd had since she was tiny child. When they'd run, it was the only keepsake to remind her of home.

"It's temporary." As it had been for the last year plus months. Gillian's heart gave a little twinge. "But we can make the best of it." Once their bags were stowed, Gillian turned to her daughter. "Let's eat."

The small main street in the middle of Paintbrush, Wyoming could have been the set for any old west movie. The shiny new pickup trucks were the only thing that put it in the twenty-first century rather than back in the days of outlaws and saloon gals. When she pushed through the doors into the diner she found Zan at the counter holding a little girl with another on the stool beside her.

"Oh, hi." She shifted the toddler in her arms and swiveled to face the two new patrons. The little girl was the spitting image of Quint. Gillian's heart did a stutter step.

The little girl's face lit up. "Daddy."

Gillian expected to find Quint behind her. Instead a brown-eyed cowboy walked over and took the girl in his arms. "How's my little sprite doing?"

A wave of relief shouldn't have washed through her, but still the tightening in her chest loosened and she took a deep breath. "Zan, right?"

"Yep. This is my husband, Jacob Bowman."

Gillian's eyebrows raised. "Of the Skipping Rocks Ranch?"

A slight blush tinted his cheeks. "Yes, ma'am." He leaned over and ruffled the hair of the other little girl too intent on a bowl of chocolate ice cream to look up longer than to smile.

"Mom, food." Heidi at least whispered. She kept her hand over her nose, hiding the largest part of the bruise.

Gillian looked past the Bowman's to the waitress. "Can we sit wherever?"

The dark-headed waitress flashed a quick smile. "Yes, ma'am. I'll be right with you."

Gillian bid the Bowmans good evening. She and Heidi sat in a booth in the far corner, away from the couple and hopefully any further conversation. No talking meant no questions.

A young man came from the back and bussed the table next to them. The boy looked to be around sixteen or seventeen.

Gillian wanted to laugh as Heidi sat a little straighter and toyed with the end of her ponytail—still covering her nose. When the waitress came over to the table she said something to him. He rolled his eyes and groaned something indistinguishable. Gillian had experienced the same thing many, many times before. When the waitress sidled up to their table she asked, "Your son?"

The woman nodded and smiled. "Ryder. Every inch a sixteen-year-old. How could you tell?"

"I get the same looks from my daughter." She motioned to Heidi. And in doing so proved her point when the teen rolled her blue eyes and slumped low on the vinyl seat.

"You're her momma? Why, you two could be sisters."

Gillian's smile fell. So many times she'd get that comment. Yes, she was fourteen when Heidi was born, but she didn't want to explain details that were better left alone. She'd lied about her age for so many years, it rolled off her tongue without any hesitation or defensiveness. "I'm older than I look."

"Sorry. Didn't mean to overstep." The waitress sighed and leaned a hip against the table next to them. "My daddy's is always saying, 'Missy Lunsford, you need to quit chatting up every person that crosses your path. One of these days you're gonna run outta words to say.'" She laughed. "I can't see that happening any time soon. Anyhoo. What'll it be?"

Gillian relaxed with Missy's easy nature. Gillian and her daughter ordered. Neither spoke as they waited for their food, both lost in their own thoughts, but both looked up when a group of men came in the front door and settled at the counter next to Zan and her family.

"Hey, you're not limping." Zan hugged Quint.

Despite the woman's husband clapping the man on the back—clearly having no issues with the Quint—a fierce pang of jealously shot through Gillian.

Then she heard her name.

"...might have wrecked the fence and tore up her car but she was pretty good with her hands."

Heat crawled across her cheeks and she mimicked Heidi's sunken posture in the booth. Zan whispered in his ear and his gaze whipped around and zeroed in on her. Quint gave her a real quick head nod and turned back to the counter. He and the group quieted down and as best as Gillian could tell paid not one whit of attention back to them.

The food came and she and her daughter ate in silence. She'd grown used to the ways of a sixteen-year-old. She didn't like it, but had learned not to take it all personally anymore. She thought back to her high school days. How vastly different her world and Heidi's were.

Missy came by a couple of times before finally bringing a check. "Is there anything else I can get y'all?"

"No, thank you. This was all wonderful." She hadn't tasted good old-fashioned cooking since her own mother died twelve years before. She wasn't a horrible cook, but her culinary skills couldn't compare to the food Heidi had all but devoured.

The woman hovered by the table longer than necessary. "Yes?" Gillian tried not to squirm in her seat.

Missy eyed her for a long minute then grabbed a chair from the table next to them and sat at the end of the booth. Before she could speak, Heidi rose. "I'm gonna go out front, 'kay?"

"Just stay close."

The teen rolled her eyes but nodded and headed to the front door. She gave a quick, shy wave to Quint and pushed through the double glass doors.

"This is a little embarrassing. I couldn't help but overhear Quint telling his aunt about your fixing up his knee earlier today."

"Excuse me? His aunt?" Gillian glanced up at the people clustered around the counter. As far as she could tell, Zan was still the only woman with all the men.

"Zan." Missy laughed. "Yeah, threw us all at first she being only a few years older than him. But yeah, Zan is Quint's aunt."

The resemblance finally fell into place. They both had the same freckled complexion despite the different hair color. Also, something about the way Quint and his aunt carried themselves. She should have caught it back at his house. But she'd been a little jealous. Not that she had any reason.

"Anyhoo," Missy kept talking. "I hate to impose, but seeing how you're stuck here until Manny gets your car up and running—"

Gillian flinched.

"—it's a small town, hon. People know each other's business." Missy patted her on the hand much the same way Zan had earlier that day. "Quint said that's where your daughter got her shiner, crashing into his fence. Around here, folks see bruises like that on a girl and they get all worked up. Anyway, I was wondering about your massages."

The food sat heavy in Gillian's stomach. Did she have enough cash on hand to buy some clunker to get her and her daughter the hell out of Paintbrush and on into Montana?

Missy ducked her head. "My daddy would never ask you himself, he'll probably tan my hide for mentioning it, but he's got a bad shoulder. Hurt it last year getting thrown from a horse. Dr. Hambert said that he should go up to Sheridan to get it looked at, but Daddy's pretty much set in his ways and won't do much more than pop an aspirin or two."

"And you want me to..."

"Could you do what you did for Quint?"

Gillian sighed. It wasn't like she had much else to do until she got to Billings. "Sure. Where?"

"He's splitting his time between the Cates' and Jacob's ranches. Oh, but shoot, you don't have a car. Hmm." She tapped her lower lip and looked up at the ceiling. "Tell ya what. I can get Daddy to come over tonight. Why don't you and your daughter stop by. Y'all can get some supper and you can have a look at Daddy's shoulder."

Gillian couldn't help but grin at the woman's bright smile. Everything about Paintbrush should make her wary. A small town where folks noticed—and talked about—other folks' bruises. Everyone knew everyone else's business. But there was something odd. Gillian breathed deeper. And folks were just...nice. Add to that, they were miles off course so even if Rick found out where they were headed—and she hoped to God he never would—they weren't there. Maybe he'd give up and leave them the hell alone.

"Would that work for you?"

Gillian nodded finally. "Sounds good."

Missy wrote out directions to her house a few blocks over from the diner. "Seven okay?"

"We'll be there."

Missy smiled, patted her hand again and took the cash Gillian had laid out for her.

"Where are we going?" Heidi shoved her hands in her hip pockets.

"Missy invited us to her house tonight."

Heidi's eyes widened and she straightened. "Are you serious?" She glanced around the diner. "Come on. We gotta go."

"What? Why?"

"I have to find something to wear."

Chapter Three

Gillian's hands shook as she rang the bell. Despite being in a public-service-type job, she didn't really associate much with other people. Sure, she was there to help out Missy's dad, but eating with folks she barely knew... She should never have agreed.

Heidi tugged at her shirt.

"Hon, you look beautiful. Quit fussing."

The teen stuck her tongue out at her mother just as the door opened. The dark-haired teen who opened it ducked his head. "Hey." He turned and hollered, "Mom, they're here." It took him a minute but he finally moved to let the pair in.

Missy came from the back end of the house. "Ryder Lunsford, don't keep them just standing there." Missy waved them all the way in. "Hey. I was afraid you might not come."

"Why?"

"Stuck in a small town waiting on your car to get fixed. Got to be a little strange to just pop over to someone's house for some supper."

Gillian smiled and lifted her bag. "And a massage."

"Come on back." Missy looped her arm through Gillian's. She was only a few inches taller, but she had so much presence she seemed to tower over Gillian. She wore her dark hair pulled up in a twist with a huge clip. It didn't look like she had on a lick of makeup, not that she needed it. Her lightly tanned skin and dark lashes gave her a summer-girl look.

They walked down a short hallway to a wide open living area with an attached dining area. Photos covered the walls; one in particular caught Gillian's eye.

"Is that Cade Holstrom?" The actor-slash-country singer was the hottest new thing to hit Hollywood.

Missy nodded. "We went all through school together. He grew up right here in Paintbrush."

"Until he got all famous and citified." An older man, dressed in faded denims and a worn flannel shirt smoothed a few gray hairs over a wide bald spot. His boot-covered foot tapped a steady rhythm on the linoleum floor. "His momma taught him better than to run off without so much as a howdy from time to time."

"Enough, Daddy."

"Manners. S'all I'm saying."

Missy rolled her eyes—mimicking her son's to a perfectly perfected T—then leaned into Gillian and whispered, "What's your daughter's name?"

"Heidi."

"Heidi, sweetie, Ryder has some friends playing with his Wii if you want to go on back. Here you can take this." She handed Heidi a plate full of cookies. "Don't worry, they don't bite. Unless your hand's a little too close to the plate."

"Daddy," Missy said once Heidi headed down the hall, "this is Gillian. The woman I was telling you about. Gillian, Hank Calhoun, mayor of crotchety town."

"Aw. Don't know why you think I need some hocus-pocus to make my shoulder right."

Gillian moved a little closer to the man. "Tell you what, Mr.

Calhoun."

"Hank. No one calls me Mr. Calhoun."

Gillian smiled at him. "Hank, let me have a little look at your shoulder. Maybe see what I can do. If it hurts I'll stop and no harm done." She held out her hand. "But if it feels even a wee bit better, I get to come back tomorrow and work on it a little more."

Hank eyed her hand for a long moment then shook it. "I guess it couldn't hurt." He released her hand and shifted in his seat. "But I'm not taking off my shirt."

"That's fine." Gillian set her bag down. "Turn around and straddle the chair for me, okay?" Most times when people came to her for help, they came because they wanted to. Very rarely did she have a reluctant client.

Hank nodded and did like she asked. "Lean forward a bit." She posed to show him how to drape his arms over the back of the chair. Once he was in place, she carefully, slowly set her hands on his shoulder. He jumped a little at first, but once she started working, his entire body relaxed.

Missy came over twice to see if her father was sitting still. She'd smile and go back to cooking.

"All done, Hank."

He sat up straight and rolled his shoulder. "Well, I'll be damned."

"Daddy."

The older man blushed. "Sorry." He ducked his head and a tint colored his cheeks.

"No problem. That's a pretty good compliment." She walked the few steps into the kitchen. "I need to get him some water." Missy filled a large glass and handed to her. When she returned from giving it to Hank she asked, "Can I help you with anything?"

"Naw. This is all pretty much automatic now." Missy removed a large pan from the oven. Garlic permeated the air. "Will you go back and get the kids?"

"Sure."

"Just follow the noise."

Noise was an understatement. The kids had some game turned up so loud it rattled the pictures on the walls at times. Being that it was only she and Heidi for the past twelve years, it was often too quiet. She knocked but didn't think anyone heard her. She eased the door open. Two boys and four girls lounged around the spacious room. One girl danced on a pad in the middle of the floor corresponding with cues from the game. It took Gillian a minute to recognize her daughter.

When the song ended Heidi laughed and turned toward Ryder. "Your turn. Oh, Mom, hey. Did you see me? I got the highest score."

"Good going, babe."

At the word "babe" Heidi's smile fell a scant degree and her eyes rolled.

"Dinner's ready."

"Thanks, Mrs. Harwood." Ryder tapped one of the girls on the shoulder and she pulled ears buds loose. "Chow's on."

"Cool."

Gillian dashed aside to get out of the way of the teens' mass exodus to the dining room. By the time she caught up to them, they were all seated around the table and had already dug into generous portions of lasagna.

"Here ya go, girl." Hank handed her a plate with twice the amount of food than she could eat in one—possibly even two—sittings. "My daughter's the best cook in all of Wyoming."

"Daddy, hush now and eat your supper." Missy waved at

Gillian. "Here, come sit over here by me. We'll never be able to talk over them." The teens were discussing the merits of Metallica jumping into the Guitar Hero scene. Heidi glanced over at her mother and shrugged, but the smile stayed firmly in place.

It had been too long since Heidi could just be a teenager with nothing more to worry about than zits and boys.

"You okay, hon? You look a little down. You're not a vegetarian, are ya?"

Gillian gave a swift mental shake. "Not with my addiction to cheeseburgers."

Missy snorted. "You don't look like you've ever had a cheeseburger in your life. You weigh all of a buck-twenty. With change. I should be sticking to my salad, but I can't resist gooey cheese and tomato sauce."

"I'd kill for your curves. If I didn't have all this dang hair, I could pass for a ten-year-old boy." Gillian paused. Hank said something under his breath about women and fickle wind. She laughed and took a bite of the pasta. "This is wonderful. Do you do the cooking at the diner?"

"Lord, no. Clara would tan my hide if I so much as turned a burner on." She leaned close to Gillian. "One night when she was feeling a little puny, she told me to lock up when the last customer left. Well, wouldn't you know it, Dustin Wood comes in—he's a trucker whose route goes right through town twice a month—he's beat and hungry as all get out. I couldn't turn him away. I whipped him up a batch of Clara's pancakes. But I made him swear never to tell."

"Did he?"

"Not so far as I know. But he hasn't ordered them again. I think he prefers mine." She leaned back in her seat and smiled.

"Done, Mom. We're gonna run down to the diner for some

35

ice cream." Ryder stood and carried his plate to the sink. His friends followed suit, but Heidi stayed, picking at the remnants of food on her plate.

Gillian leaned toward her daughter. "Do you want to go too?"

She shook her head. "Can we go back to the room now?"

"Sure, sweetie." Gillian grabbed Heidi's plate and carried the two over to the sink. "Missy, thank you for a wonderful dinner. I think we're going to head back now and rest. Hopefully, we can get the car back tomorrow."

"Oh, sure." Missy moved in close to Gillian. "Is everything okay?" She motioned to Heidi with her shoulder. The teen gave a quick wave as Ryder and his gang left.

"Moving across the country's just been hard on her." Gillian wouldn't—couldn't—elaborate. She couldn't remember the last time they'd truly let anyone into their lives. They didn't have a relative to speak of. They had very few close friends and even then, Gillian kept them walled off from most of the rest of the world to protect Heidi.

"I'd like to say I understand, but I've lived in the same place my entire life, as did both my parents and their parents." She patted Gillian on the shoulder. "I'll be at the diner first thing in the morning so come on by and have a cup of coffee with me."

Missy refused Gillian's offer to help clean up the dishes. At the front door Hank stopped them and offered to drive them back to the motel.

"You don't have to."

"Nonsense." He slapped a straw cowboy hat atop his head. "'Sides, I gotta head back home anyhow and I go right through town."

"Then we would be grateful."

After all of two minutes to ride a few short blocks, Hank

dropped them off. He thanked her again for his shoulder being right as rain—as he said several times during dinner—then waved and headed to his home.

Night had fallen and even though she wouldn't admit it to Heidi—not about to risk scaring her daughter—it was darker than she'd expected and she would have been a little bit spooked to walk, even the short distance, in the darkness.

As she was pushing the key into the door, a dark shadow dislodged itself from the door by the front office. "There you are."

Both Harwood women shrieked.

"Sorry, sorry. Didn't mean to scare you." Quint stepped into a stream of moonlight. "I thought you two might be missing this." He held up Heidi's backpack.

"Ohmygawd." She took it from his outstretched hand. "I thought I left it in the car. Where was it? You didn't go through it did you?"

"Heidi." Gillian swatted at her daughter but missed.

"I don't want some *man*—" she exaggerated the word, "—going through my things. That's not right."

"Heidi." Gillian tried to smile when the teen rolled her eyes, but her nerves were still a little frayed.

"Thank you, Mr. Walters." Heidi pushed through the door and into the room when Gillian finally got the lock undone despite her shaking fingers.

Gillian pulled the door closed again and turned on Quint. She shoved her hands on her hips. "You can't sneak up on people like that."

"I didn't exactly sneak." He'd been waiting for the better part of an hour. At first he thought maybe Manny had gotten the car fixed and they left before he could see Gillian again. It was stupid to be so...mesmerized by a woman passing through town.

"You didn't exactly not sneak."

Quint frowned. "Yeah, that one was a little hard to follow."

Gillian ran her hand through her hair. "Thank you for bringing that out to her. I'm sorry you had to come back all this way."

"It was no problem." Quint leaned his shoulder on the doorframe. "Are you okay? I was worried about you."

"Why would you be worried?" She crossed her arms over her chest. "I'm a grown woman."

"In a strange town."

She glanced around the street behind her. "Y'all are strange?" She pulled her bag tighter on her shoulder. "Should *I* be worried?" A hint of a smile crooked up the corner of her mouth.

"Strange to you, woman." Quint wasn't sure he liked the hitch in his stomach or the way his fingers itched to toy with the end of her hair where it lay across her cheek.

"We're fine. We just got back from Missy Lunsford's."

He smiled. "She'd feed the world if she could." His urge got the best of him and he tucked a few loose strands behind her ear. Gillian leaned into him ever so slightly.

He lowered his voice to just above a whisper. "I really did want to make sure you're okay. Is everything—"

"Ready to go?" Ruby came out from the main office two doors down.

Quint tried not to flinch when Gillian's stance instantly grew rigid.

She gave him a tense smile. "Thanks again for returning

Heidi's bag. Have fun."

The quiet of the door snicking shut was almost worse than if she'd slammed it. He raised his hand to knock, even though he had no clue as to what to say or even why he'd bother with a perfect stranger in town for as long as it took to get her car fixed.

There was just something...

"Dominique's awaits." Ruby tugged on his sleeve. "Tonight's karaoke night."

Quint groaned and followed Ruby to the parking lot on the far side of the building. "Let's take two vehicles. I have to get up early in the morning and work on the fence some more."

Ruby glanced back over her shoulder toward the set of rooms and shook her head. "Trouble in the form of a perfectly petite pixie with a past."

"What makes you say that?"

"You're kidding, right?" They reached their two parked trucks and Ruby leaned against hers. "She paid cash."

"That's not so mysterious. Most of the people in town pay cash for everything."

Ruby shook her head. "She has all the men jumping around like it's branding season. Half of them haven't even laid eyes on her yet."

Quint waved away her words. "Back to the 'past' part." Unease skittered up his spine. "What makes you say that? Did she tell you something?"

"Nope. Wouldn't answer any questions." Ruby crinkled her nose.

"She doesn't know you from Adam." Quint rolled his neck and shoulders to loosen some of the tension. "You're prying into her business?"

Denise Belinda McDonald

"I wouldn't call it 'prying'. Just being friendly." Ruby narrowed her eyes. "Aren't we a little too interested in some woman who mowed us down earlier this afternoon?"

He barked out an uneasy laugh. "She didn't mow me down."

Ruby's eyebrow rose up into her hairline.

"Kinda mowed. More like a weed-whacked really."

"You aren't going soft on me now are ya, Walters?"

"Naw." Quint squeaked out the words. He cleared his throat and tried again. "Naw. You hungry? Let's go."

Quint's fingers tapped the steering wheel the entire ride out to Dominique's. Nervous energy tingled every nerve ending. Why was he getting worked up? She'd be gone tomorrow. He shook his thoughts away, parked his truck next to Ruby's and joined her by the front door.

All night though, Ruby gave him pointed looks, but never said anything. He'd been too distracted to hold up much of his end of the conversation.

It'd been over five years since he'd moved to Paintbrush. He'd dated a little here and there but no one, *no one,* had ever elicited any feelings near the spark that rocketed through him every time he came near Gillian Harwood. It was almost a mean joke. She'd be leaving as soon as Manny got her car fixed up.

As if conjuring up the man, Manny strode in through the front door and took one of the last seats available.

"Be right back." Quint tossed his napkin on his barely touched food.

Ruby nodded as she scanned the binder with songs for karaoke night.

"Hey, Manny." Quint sat next to the garage owner.

"Walters." He slugged down half the glass of tea the

40

waitress set before him. "Oh, better." He swiped his mouth with the back of his hand. "Ooo-wee that little lady did a number on her car."

"Fixable?"

"Yep. Gotta order a couple of parts from Laramie. Gonna be a few days."

The flutter in Quint's gut sped up. "Hmm."

"I talked to your aunt the other day."

"Which one?" When he'd followed his Aunt Zan to Wyoming, it had been a temporary stop in his search for what he wanted to be when he grew up. But once he got situated in Paintbrush, the lifestyle and feel of the town suited him—and having Zan and his great-aunt Bonnie had been an added bonus. Growing up within ten miles of most of his family his whole life, he'd gotten used to having someone to turn to when need be.

"Miss Bonnie. Her and Gene were passing through town."

Quint smiled and nodded. "Getting back from seeing Gene's new grandbaby in Denver."

"Yep. Proud as a peacock that one." Manny leaned back as the waitress set his food in front of him. "Care to join me?" he asked Quint.

"No, sorry." He tilted his head toward the table with Ruby still pouring over the song lists. "I'll let you get back to your dinner." Quint clapped the man on the shoulder. "You have a good one."

Quint whistled on his way back to the table. His week was looking up.

Chapter Four

"How much?" Gillian tried not to visibly gulp at the amount.

Manny repeated the sum. "I'm sorry. We don't get a lot of call for Volvo parts around here. Any kinda of pick-up or tractor..."

"I understand." Gillian ran a hand through her hair. "I appreciate what you're doing." Her shoulders tensed. "That'll wipe out most of my money." She hadn't meant to say it aloud.

"We take credit cards." Manny's smile was soft and genuine.

Gillian swiped her sweaty palms on her tan capris. "I don't have any."

"What?" His smile fell and he looked at her as if she'd just said she kicked puppies for a living, instead of not using plastic to pay for things.

She had her reasons. All valid, not one of which she'd share with him. Instead, she said, "My momma taught me, if I can't pay for something outright, I don't need it." True enough, though she omitted the fact that someone could be tracked by their purchases. "Usually this isn't a problem."

"Smart one, that momma of yours. I tell you what." Manny finished wiping his hands on the pink rag and tucked it in his back pocket. "It doesn't take me all that long to actually get the work done once I have the part. And it's coming from the same place I have a couple more orders that I need for another job. We could call it even for..." he named off a figure less than half the original amount quoted.

"I can't ask you to—"

"You're not asking. I'm offering." Again his smile returned. "But it may take an extra day to wait for them to ship all of my other parts together. How about it?"

An extra day of hotel cost versus the huge fee? If he was willing... "Deal. And thank you." She shouldered her bag and stepped out into the bright morning sunlight. She and Heidi had had breakfast at the diner, and she'd hoped to be able to call Mrs. Taylor and give her an updated arrival time.

"How long will she hold it?" Gillian spoke aloud to herself, then gnawed on her lower lip. Things could be worse. Thanks to their unexpected layover, no one knew where they were. She moved to step off the curb just as a shrill noise sounded to her left.

The door of the fire station was open and men scurried to board the small engine. If she wasn't mistaken, Quint jumped up on the rear as the fire truck pulled out. Sirens clattered.

Once they passed, Gillian headed back the few blocks to the motel. The siren didn't lessen as she expected but kept echoing through town. She picked up her step. She turned the corner, a block away from the motel. The engine sat at an odd angle across the intersection. Men scrambled, pulling hoses from the huge truck.

The back of the motel was smoldering.

"Heidi."

Gillian took off at steady run. She pushed through the onlookers. "Heidi?" It eked out as a whisper. Before she could scream, someone called her name.

"Gillian. Over here."

Stationed between a group of trucks, Missy stood with her arm wrapped around Heidi's shoulder.

A shuttered breath wracked though Gillian. She wasn't entirely sure how her knees held out for the short walk to her daughter's side. "What happened?"

"Don't know yet." Missy snagged Gillian's hand.

Her first instinct was to pull away. She wasn't used to physical contact. But until her nerves steadied Missy's kindness was a welcome warmth.

"Are you okay, hon?" Gillian tugged on her daughter's ponytail.

"Yeah." Heidi tightened her arms over her chest. "I was reading and smelled smoke." She sniffed. Her face scrunched up.

"It's almost out." Ryder ran up to the group. "Maintenance shed out back behind the motel's on fire. But they got the flames pretty much out. Granddad told me to get outta the way."

Gillian looked at Missy. "Hank?"

Missy nodded. "Volunteer. There're only two full time firemen so most of the rest of the men in town volunteer. Quint and Daddy were in town picking up their lunches for later. It was lucky they were here when the fire broke out."

Gillian tried to picture Hank laden in fire gear. She shook her head. It didn't come to mind. Quint however... His curly hair stuck in wisps to his sweaty scalp. Turnout coat slapped over his shoulder and red suspenders across rock-hard pecs. Muscular arms carrying the heavy axe.

As if her mind conjured him up, Quint Walters rounded the corner of the motel. Soot covered his face. His hair stuck out every which way. And he held a huge plastic Santa in his arms.

"Everything okay?" Missy released Gillian's hand.

"Yep. We got it put out." Quint poured a bottle of water over his head and shook off the excess, then looked at Gillian. "The fire didn't spread. But you may want to air out your room for a while. It'll probably smell pretty rank."

She nodded. "Do you know what happened?"

"Not yet. It looks like someone may've been smoking out behind the building and tossed a cigarette."

Gillian didn't miss the sly glance toward her daughter. Were they not surrounded by half the town—that and the fact that she'd be revealing far too much to him—she'd have told him how off base he was. Something she hadn't shared with anyone—ever.

Ruby pushed her way through the throng of folks milling about. "What happened?"

Something in the way she asked, and looked at Heidi then Gillian gave Gillian a start. *Does new in town equate to instant culpability?*

"Not sure yet. The chief is gonna have to sift through it all." Quint raked his hand through his hair again.

Once the hubbub died down, the townspeople dispersed and headed to their respective jobs and daily activities. Gillian grabbed Heidi's hand and made it halfway to their room when Hank caught up to them—he moved pretty quick for looking so raggedy after the fire. Ryder was fast on his heels and almost skidded into the older man when he stopped.

"Miss Harwood."

"If I can call you Hank, you can call me Gillian."

He gave her a quick smile. "Gillian, I was hoping I could get with you again for a quick touch up." He lifted his shoulder. "I tweaked it a bit working on the fire."

"Sure."

Gillian glanced at her room. That might be a bit awkward.

"Um…"

"Spit it out, girl. I ain't got all day."

Gillian couldn't help but smile.

"Granddad." Ryder licked his lips several times. "Quint said I could come out later to help you and Jacob set up the new stalls for the horses coming at the end of the week."

"I could hitch a ride out with Ryder and work on your shoulder." She smiled at the boy.

Hank rubbed the stubble on his chin. "Might could work."

"If that's the case, why doesn't Heidi come on out too? I bet she'd like to see the horses." Ryder shoved his hands in his pockets and kicked a rock loose. "Could be cool."

Gillian wanted to say no. She didn't want Heidi to get too attached to Ryder. They'd be leaving in a couple of days and she'd seen the way her daughter had been looking at him—but if the dreamy glaze that came over the teen's eyes was any indication, it may already be too late.

At the same time, she needed to let Heidi be a teenager as much as possible. "If it's not too much trouble…"

Gillian walked the length of the corral. She'd finished Hank's shoulder and he'd hightailed it off the ranch saying he had some business in town. Zan had taken her daughters to work with her when her regular sitter had called in sick. Jacob headed out right after Hank to pick up the girls, leaving the ranch with few options. Gillian was hoping she could find Ryder and Heidi and get out of there before she ran into…

"Hey. I've been looking for you." Quint pulled his hat from

his head and smacked at the dust on his jeans.

Super. She pasted on a wan smile. "Found me."

"Manny called."

She frowned.

"I was up at the house and he was looking for you, heard you'd come out here."

"Small town?"

Quint chuckled. "Something like that. He got the part for your car. Said he'd have it finished by tonight."

Her stomach fluttered. She couldn't decide if it was joy or disappointment. "That's wonderful." She and her daughter could move on with their lives.

Gillian swiped at her forehead. Clouds had rolled in and lowered the temperature, but whenever Quint was around her temperature rose. Her gaze scanned the corral, barn area and all the way up to Jacob's house a hundred yards away.

"Lose something?"

She headed toward the house where Ryder'd parked his truck. "I was just looking for the kids."

"They left."

Her step stuttered. "Pardon me?"

"Steven called."

"Who?"

"The vet's son, Steven. The lot of them went out to the pond out past town to swim before the storm hits. After the rain it'll be days before they can get back out to it."

"And Heidi went, too?"

"Is that a problem?"

"Yes. No. I guess not. I would like to have known she was leaving." And leaving her stranded on the farm with a man who made her body ache in places she hadn't realized she had.

"They said they'd be back for you in a couple of hours." A smiled crooked the edges of his mouth. "I bet Hank could take you back to town, if you don't want to wait."

"He's gone." Gillian dropped the heavy shoulder bag at her feet and rolled her shoulders. She glanced around the corral.

Quint settled the straw hat back on his head. "I'll be happy to drive you back to town."

Thank goodness.

"As soon as I finish up the fence. About an hour's worth of work. I'd let you borrow the truck, but I won't be able to get back to town. Plus, I've seen the way you drive and it's a little too daredevil for my taste."

"There's no other vehicles?"

"If you don't count Emily's bicycle—which still has training wheels by the way—nope. There are a couple of tractors, but despite what you might think, folks around here frown at driving them through town."

Gillian eyed him for a long moment.

"Only about an hour. I promise."

She could wait—not like she had a choice. But she'd have to watch the muscles in his sinewy forearms dance as he wrapped the wire around a staked post. She'd about come undone watching him for all of five minutes while she looked for the kids. An hour or so of it? No thank you.

Gillian pulled her bag back on her shoulder and headed across the hard-packed ground to sit on the front steps of the Bowman's home.

"Hey, where ya going?" He caught up to her side.

"To sit. And wait for you to finish."

The squeak of hinges echoed in the yard.

"Shit." Quint ran back to the corral. "I left the damn gate undone."

Gillian turned and in a flash a dark animal ran out of the small enclosure.

Quint snagged a rope and took off after the loose animal. Jacob would kill him if anything happened to the foal. The Bowmans were new to breeding horses, but had already made a decent name for the ranch.

He cursed with every step he took across the back pasture following the direction of the tracks. If he'd had a horse saddled and ready he'd have been able to catch the foal within moments. But on foot...

After half-an hour, he tracked the horse to the hillier part of the ranch. In a copse of trees, the skittish creature stood half-obscured by the brush. Quint crept quietly to the edge of the trees. He fashioned the end of the rope into a loop and swung it around over his head. If he missed, the horse would take off again and it might take hours to find him.

He took a steadying breath and released the rope. It landed around the horse's neck. Quint nearly released the other end when a loud gasp sounded behind him. He glanced back at Gillian.

"That was wonderful. How'd you do that?" A huge smile crossed her face.

He closed the distance between himself and the horse. He patted the colt's neck and spoke softly for a moment before he turned back to Gillian. "Why'd you follow me?"

"I wanted to make sure you caught it. And in case you needed me for anything."

"Him, not it." He held the rope aloft. "Will you hold this for a second?"

49

The smile slid from her face. He'd forgotten her wariness around the animals. What exactly had she expected to do if she was too afraid to hold onto a rope?

"Just for a second. Please?" Quint let go of the rope when she reluctantly took it from him. He snagged his work gloves from his back pocket and shoved his hands into them. "You should have waited back at the house."

She released a heavy breath when he took the rope back. "I don't mind."

"Then I guess you don't mind keeping me company." They walked back toward the ranch. The little colt trailed behind the pair. "So, where ya from?"

Gillian laughed. "Do people still use that line?"

"You know us country folks. We're a little behind city slickers like yourself."

She smiled up at him. "I think you're doing just fine."

"So, you'll tell me?"

She shook her head. "Nope."

"If I guess? Will you tell me when I get it right?"

Gillian sighed. "Sure, why not?"

Quint slowed his pace. "How many?"

"How many what?"

"Guesses do I get. I mean if you give me forty-nine, I WILL eventually get it."

"There are fifty states." Gillian pushed at the hair on her face for the fifth or sixth time.

"Here." Quint whipped a bandana from his pocket and shoved it at her. "You can keep the hair off your face." He could smell her perfume. It wafted up around him as the breeze grew stronger. The sweet scent tickled his nose and sparked thoughts of soft skin and long, lingering kisses. He had the biggest urge to grab her hand and intertwine their fingers. Anything just to feel her. Maybe then pull her to a stop and drop a heavy kiss on that challenging mouth of hers. Instead, he held onto the rope with both hands to keep the temptation at bay.

Gillian's soft laughter pulled him from his thoughts. "You giving up already? Or did you not know there are fifty states?"

"Yes, I know there are fifty states, but I think we can pretty much rule out you being from Wyoming. And since you didn't know where Montana was, I'm going to give that one a pass as well. So now we're down to forty-eight."

"Okay, smarty pants. Four then. What do I get if you can't guess?"

Quint's pulse raced. "A kiss?"

"And that's MY prize?"

It's a win-win for me, he thought. "Absolutely. Best prize in the whole state of Wyoming."

"Ha!" Gillian crossed her arms over her chest. "That work on the girls around here?"

"Can't say that I've tried to steal a kiss before."

"They fall at your feet that easy, huh?"

Quint stopped her with a hand on her arm. A strand of hair pulled loose from the bandana and danced around her face in the growing wind. He couldn't resist the urge and tucked it neatly back into place. "I'm not exactly sure what kind of guy you take me for."

When Gillian didn't pull away, Quint took it as a sign and leaned forward. Before he could even feel the heat of her breath a shock of lightning streaked through the sky and they jumped apart.

"I..." A huge clap of thunder jolted him in his boots.

Gillian screeched and grabbed Quint's sleeve. "Sorry."

Heat ran up Quint's arm even with her fingers not touching his skin directly. It pooled low into his belly and spread through the rest of him.

The little horse pulled against the rope.

Quint tried to soothe him as small droplets of rain fell. "There's a little shack up over the hill." He held tight to the rope with one hand and took Gillian's hand in the other then led the pair toward the shelter. As the topped the hill, the sky opened up.

"You call that a shack? It's so dilapidated the wind may topple it onto us." She pulled back against his hand as the colt pulled against the rope in the other. "It won't even keep *me* dry much less all of us."

"There was more of it the last time I was out here." Quint grabbed her by the shoulder and steered her under the open slatted roof. The rotting shelter did little to protect them as the rain beat down with an unrelenting pace.

Gillian shook, the cold, wet rain already soaking into her clothing. "I'm so sorry about this."

"Not your fault. If I'd've made sure the gate was closed all the way... If anything I owe *you* an apology.

"You're gonna have to hold this again." Quint handed her the rope and she took it with little hesitation. He shucked off his work gloves then removed his heavy denim shirt. "Squeeze in." He held the shirt over their heads. "You're gonna have to get in closer if you wanna stay outta the rain."

Gillian hesitated for moment. Another lightning strike zigzagged overhead and she edged her head up under his chin, got as close as humanly possible without actually touching him—which, despite his overwhelming need to touch her, was for the best.

Quint made the mistake of glancing down. Gillian's transparent shirt rose and fell with every breath. Dark, tight peaks poked at the thin fabric.

"You need to stop that."

"Stop what?"

"Breathing."

Gillian started to laugh, but as a shudder ran through Quint she sobered quickly. "I thought you didn't like me much. You're always teasing."

"Darlin', I like you just fine. Too much, in fact."

Their eyes met as lightning slashed through the sky.

"Oh, hell." Quint ducked his head and captured Gillian's mouth. Rain soaked the pair as he lowered his arms around her to pull her tight up against him, his shirt falling to the ground.

She settled one hand on his bare chest; the other gripped the rope harder, digging it into her palm. Quint's heart beat steadily. The sandy hairs tickled her fingers.

His hands tightened around her, trapping her hand between them. Even as the water pelted her face and neck, she could think of little else but the kiss. Being stuck out in the middle of freaking nowhere with the sexy-as-hell guy made all her anxiety flee. All replaced by heat and a passion she didn't know she was capable of feeling.

Quint's hand slid up her back and into her hair. He slanted her head and delved his tongue in, deepening the kiss when she sighed.

He tasted of coffee and something sweet.

A sharp tingle ran up Gillian's spine. She wanted so badly to lean back and look into his eyes, but was too afraid to break the kiss. Afraid she might not ever feel this heat again. Because once she stopped there would not be a repeat.

Quint's lips left her mouth far too soon. She wasn't expecting him to then lave her earlobe. Nibble on her neck. A shudder ran through her and she fought to free her hands. Once she could, she slid them around Quint's back—all the while hanging onto the rope. Her nipples rubbed against her cotton top. Sensations, too many to count, flooded her system, threatened to weaken her knees, but his powerful arms kept her upright and pressed to him as if life depended on it.

A tear came loose and ran down her cheek. Gillian wasn't sure if it was from the tender way Quint ran his hand over her hip—something she had yet to ever feel before—or the knowledge that she was pretty damn sure she'd never find a man who'd make her feel this way again, even if she looked for the rest of her damn life. Whatever the reason, it didn't matter. The thrill and the pain comingled in her heart, made it ready to burst. Thank God for the rain hiding her confusion.

Lightning slashed through the air, hit not too far off from where they stood. The pair pulled apart.

Quint wiped a hand through his hair and pushed the wet locks off his face. "Jesus H. Christ. I have heard of bells, but not explosions."

Gillian tried to smile, but was still a little too overwhelmed to do much more than run her fingers over her swollen lips.

"We can't stay out here. We're better off hoofing it back to the ranch. Do you think you can?"

She nodded.

"Are you okay?" Quint cupped her face, ran his thumb down her wet check.

Again she nodded, not willing to risk her voice, couldn't take the chance it might quaver and Quint would know for sure what he did to her.

"Okay. It may be a little tricky up ahead. The rain will have washed away part of the culvert." He snagged his wet shirt off the ground and slid his arms into it then took hold of the rope. He held out his other hand to her. "Do not let go, okay?"

"Okay."

Quint gave her a quick, but sensuous kiss before he dragged her behind him.

"You still doing okay?" he yelled over the roar of the rain. He had to give her credit. She kept pace with him and didn't complain once.

"Yes."

They only had one obstacle to tackle before they were home free. They needed to get to the end of the culvert soon or they'd be stuck out here for a while. If they could reach it before any more of the trail washed away they'd be fine. He wouldn't tell her he was scared shitless about actually reaching it in time.

He probably should have waited for someone to come looking for them, but with the storm worsening, they wouldn't be able to get the trucks out this far. And no way would Jacob risk taking the horses out during this downpour.

They made it around the worst part, but still had to follow the edge of the culvert for a bit before they could reach the trail to the ranch. "Not far now."

"You said that already." A wan smile tilted up the corners of her mouth. "Now I know how Heidi..." Her hand slipped from his.

Quint turned expecting to find her at his feet, tripped by the rocky terrain, but she was gone. Just vanished.

"What the... Gillian?"

With the foal pulling tight against the rope, he took a step forward. The rocks underfoot gave way. It was all he could do to keep from going over the edge himself. Once steadied, he dropped down on all fours. The stiff woven fibers bit into his palm as he leaned forward and looked over the edge of the lip of dirt. "Gillian?"

She moaned. He was about to slide down after her when he saw a pale hand waving at him.

"Here. I'm here."

"Are you hurt?"

"No, just had the bejesus scared outta me."

"You and me both. Can you climb back up here?" Quint saw a flash of clothing in the darkness.

She cursed. "Yeah, no. I don't think that's gonna happen."

"Why? What's wrong?"

"Too short." She waved up at him, her fingertips barely cresting the edge. "I don't think I can pull myself up."

"Are you shitting me?"

Her laughter rose over the roar of the rain. "I would not shit you."

"I'm coming down."

"Wait." Gillian yelled up at him.

"What for?"

"I hear something."

Quint laughed. "How can you hear anything over this rain?" He stilled and tried to catch whatever it was that made her pause. Finally, a low rumble echoed through the culvert. "Gillian, give me your hand. Now." Fear skittered up his spine. "Hurry."

"What's the matter?"

"Water's coming." Quint flattened to the ground and

stretched his hand out to her. "Reach."

Water dripped into his eyes as the edge of the culvert gave way in little increments. Gillian stretched her hand toward Quint.

He snagged her wrist with one hand and twisted the rope around the other hand so as not to lose hold of the colt. He snagged Gillian's other wrist with the rope wrapped around his hand. The rumble grew louder. With his elbows, he shifted to a crouching position. He'd more than likely leave deep bruises on her pale skin, but the alternative... He couldn't even think about it. "I'm sorry."

"For?"

Quint yanked her as hard as he could and dragged her up over the edge of the culvert. The momentum sent him onto his back and plopped Gillian down on top of him, her right arm wedged between them.

She released a low, guttural moan before her eyes slid closed and her head went limp onto his chest.

"God, Gillian." He set his head back to hold them both as still as possible. Water pelted his face. He'd imagined himself wrapped her in his arms, but not like this. "Hey? Can you hear me?"

She didn't answer. He rolled her off of him and examined her wrist—it puffed up pretty quickly. He slipped his shirt back off and wrapped up her wrist. As he finished tying it, Gillian stirred.

"You know, if you wanted me to carry you, you could have just asked rather than fainting on me."

"Very funny, cowboy." Gillian tried to crook the corner of her mouth up in a smile.

Quint helped her sit. "Can you stand?"

"In a second. My head's still spinning." She pushed the wet hair off her face. "I've heard people can pass out from pain, but I always thought it as hokey. Who knew?"

"Anyone who's ever busted themselves up by not staying put." Quint helped her to her feet. "You doing okay?"

"I think so." The world still spun slightly and she wobbled a bit but she wasn't about to let on how incredibly her wrist throbbed. Knowing him, he actually would scoop her up and carry her back the rest of the way. "Thanks for not saying I told you so or anything."

They walked in silence the last stretch of the way. When they got within eye sight of the corral Jacob headed toward them. "What happened?"

Quint handed him the rope still tethered to the horse's neck. "I left the gate open and had to hunt him down." He motioned toward the foal.

Jacob narrowed his eyes at his wife's nephew but didn't say anything. His gazed turned to Gillian. "You?"

"I followed to help. And fell." She held her wrapped arm aloft. Her teeth chattered but she bit down hard so neither man could see.

Quint detailed to Jacob what had happened—all but the kiss. He conveniently left that part out.

Waves of dizziness washed over her. "I think I need to sit down." She started to sit right out there on the wet ground, but two strong arms went around her and scooped her up.

"We need to get you up to Dr. Hambert's." Quint shifted his hold.

He wasn't even breathing hard when he settled her into the front seat of the truck even though he'd trekked from the corral to the side of the house where the truck was parked, all the while carrying her. This after schlepping however far they'd gone with the horse.

Gillian leaned her head back against the seat and fought to keep the shivers at bay. "Thanks."

Quint didn't look at her. "Nothing to thank me for. You should be spitting mad you got tangled up in this."

The rocking motion of the truck and her waning adrenaline lulled her.

In her world, before she and Heidi had taken off, it was every man for himself. Someone falls and your biggest challenge is how quickly can you step over them and get the hell away. But Quint had done everything he could to keep her safe. It wasn't his fault the earth had eroded and she'd fallen. If anything he should be *spitting mad* she'd mucked up everything he'd had to deal with.

Her eyelids slid shut. The pain in her wrist had subsided— or maybe just numbed. "Thanks for not leaving me."

Chapter Five

"I hope you're not right-handed."

"No, left." It took a moment for Gillian's brain to connect. "It's broken?" Her stomach lurched much like it had when she'd fallen.

"Yes, ma'am." Dr. Hambert made a note in a file and turned off the X-ray lightbox as his nurse dug in a cabinet. "We'll get that set in no time. Luckily, no surgery is needed."

You have no idea how lucky.

"We have red, white, green or hot pink." The nurse held up a package of cast wrap. A sweet smile crooked the corner of her mouth. "What color would you like for your cast?"

Gillian blew out a heavy breath. "Why not hot pink? Make it fun."

"Super." Her smile grew. "I need to go grab a couple more rolls. I'll be right back."

"Is she always that cheerful?"

"'Fraid so." The doctor nodded. "Best thirty-eight years of my life."

Great, she'd just insulted the doctor's wife. First the fire, then getting stuck out in a storm with Quint. One more complication and she might just cry—which was why she hesitated to ask the most obvious question. Though, in her line of work, she pretty much knew the answer, but she still had to ask. "How long will I have to wear the cast?"

"Six to eight weeks."

She groaned and dropped her chin to her chest. Tears filled the corners of her eyes.

"Okey-dokey." Mrs. Hambert returned with two extra packets of hot pink cast wrap. "This won't hurt a bit, I swear."

Gillian looked up and the woman's smile faltered. "Aw now, hon. It's not as bad as all that." She rubbed Gillian's knee. "You'll feel better in no time."

If only that were true. Gillian sucked in a huge sob and pasted on a watery smile for the older woman.

Half an hour later, Gillian had a set cast, a sample of pain killers and a promise to check in with a doctor as soon as she and Heidi got settled in Billings.

She doubted she'd still have the job as a masseuse once she made the call to her potential boss. Waiting a couple of days for a car repair was one thing, waiting a couple of months—which would hit right as the season started—was surely out of the question.

Mrs. Hambert helped Gillian to the waiting room.

"Mom. Ohmygawd. It's broken?"

"Um, uh, yeah." She held her casted arm aloft then groaned as a throbbing pain radiated up her arm.

Mrs. Hambert snagged her elbow and brought it down to her side. "Enough of that. You need to keep it still." The woman fashioned a sling around Gillian's shoulder and helped her settle the cast snug inside.

"Thank you. How much do I owe you?" She rooted around in her bag. Between the medical bill and the work done on her car, she'd be lucky if they had enough money to last out the week.

"Don't worry about that right now, hon." Mrs. Hambert snagged Gillian's bag and handed it to Heidi. "You just get back to your room and rest up a bit. Call on me in the morning and let me know how you're doing."

"Really? Are you sure?" Small towns were a different breed all together.

"Um, Mom." Heidi shifted from one foot to the other. "Since your arm is all messed up..."

Here it came. Heidi was going to ask about how she'd be able to work, how she'd be able to support them, feed them. Fear trickled down her spine. "Yes?"

"Mr. Manny delivered the car while you were in with the doctor. Can I drive back to the motel?" Heidi held her clasped hands in front of her. She poked out her lip as she had back when she was three and asked for another cookie. "Pretty please?"

Driving. Leave it to a teen to see the Small Picture. Gillian tried to smack her forehead and nearly pulverized her face with the cast. If it weren't for the sling, she might have made contact. When she settled her arm at her waist, she nearly tipped herself over. "Room's spinning a bit."

Mrs. Hambert patted her shoulder and wrapped her arm around her waist. "Pain killer's kicking in." She gave Heidi a long look. "You do know how to drive, don't you?"

The teen beamed. "Yes, ma'am. Mom taught me all spring and I got my license last month."

Gillian wasn't sure if the meds were making her ears tingle or if Mrs. Hambert clucked her tongue. She leaned in to Gillian. "There's not much traffic this time of the day. But just say the word and I'll find someone to get y'all home."

Not much traffic? Gillian snorted which turned into a

giggle. There weren't more than three cars going down the main street at any given time—and that was during lunch. "I think Heidi'll do fine."

A foggy blanket engulfed Gillian's thoughts. She had to concentrate to form a coherent sentence. "I think we can make it. Thanks though."

"Okey-dokey. Make sure you call me tomorrow."

"Abso-toodly-lutely." Gillian tried to salute, but again the cast and sling slowed her.

Heidi giggled a little too loud when she jingled the keys. "Let's go, Mom."

"We're home in one piece. We're home in one piece." Chalking the harrowing ride the few blocks from the doctor's office back to the motel up to the meds, Gillian repeated her new mantra even an hour after they'd gotten back to their room.

"What'd you say?" Heidi plopped down on the bed.

"Nothing." The pair watched TV for a while. Gillian dozed off in the middle of one of her favorite movies. She woke with gritty eyes and an awful taste in her mouth. The remnants of the smoke still lingered in the room, permeating everything. "Strange, that fire, huh?"

Heidi set down the magazine in her hands. "I think Quint wanted to blame me."

"That's just crazy. He doesn't know you well enough to know how wrong he is." Gillian thought back to the awful day when she'd nearly lost her entire world. Her sister had been killed, the house set ablaze with Heidi still inside. It was a miracle the four-year-old had survived, physically unscathed. Mentally, it took years of therapy before she could be in the vicinity of a fire without quaking in fear. There was no way in hell she'd go near open flames, much less deliberately set fire to something.

Gillian was so sure Heidi had nothing to do with the fire it hadn't even crossed her mind to question the teen. Unfortunately, telling Quint the hows and whys would lead to more questions and she didn't know when or if she'd be ready to share that information with anyone.

"No worries." Gillian, one armed, pushed herself up to a sitting position. "Will you mute the TV, please? I need to call Mrs. Taylor."

Heidi shut off the set and turned to her mother, but didn't say a word.

"So, when can we expect you?" the woman asked after Gillian identified herself.

"I have a little problem."

"Is the car still not fixed?"

"The car is fine." Gillian took a deep breath. "I, uh..." *Just spit it out*, she chastised herself. "I had an accident and broke my wrist this morning. The doctor said it'll be six to eight weeks to heal."

"Are you okay? I mean other than the break?"

That was why Gillian liked Mrs. Taylor. No yelling, no blaming, but instant concern for her. "A few bumps and bruises." She went on to explain what had happened getting caught out in a storm—she left off the whole kissed-a-hot-cowboy part. And how it had stirred so many emotions and feelings she'd never expected. And then the fact that he'd taken off as soon as he'd dropped her off at the doctor's office—and hadn't bothered to check in since. Not that he owed a single thing to her. And if she kept saying it, it might not sting so horribly.

"That's scary."

Gillian blinked. *How did she...* She meant the storm itself, not the one raging inside her.

She might have agreed it'd scared the bejesus out of her if she had given herself time to really think of it, but for her sake and that of her daughter, she didn't dwell on the close call.

"I understand you can't hold the job for me." Gillian was hoping Mrs. Taylor would say, "Don't be silly, of course we will." But when the woman didn't Gillian continued, "I'm really sorry to put you in a bind."

"Not so much a bind really. I'm just disappointed you won't be joining us. Tell you what..." There was a long pause. "When you're back to one-hundred percent, call me and we'll see where the resort's at. Maybe if business does better than projected..."

"Thanks. I appreciate it." She hung up the phone at sat still for a long moment. Tears stung the back of her eyes, but she was determined not to cry in front of her daughter.

"What did she say?" Heidi gnawed on her lower lip.

"To call back when the cast comes off."

"That's, good, I guess." She looked down at her hands and asked, "What are we going to do right now?"

Gillian snagged a pencil from her bag and tried unsuccessfully to wedge it inside her cast. Anything to distract her from the turn of their life. No job. Renting a motel room day by day. Money running out. She did have another bank account she could gain access to and get funds, but it was a "just in case" account. Her depleted wallet was a few dollars shy of just in case, but not there just yet. They would have to run again the moment she accessed the account. She just couldn't risk the chance that it could and would pinpoint their location—to *anyone* monitoring it. She needed to formulate a plan of action. Again.

They had a slew of other states they had never even been to, much less lived in, so the country was wide open to possibilities. Finding a job with a broken wrist would be a challenge. And then there was high school. Heidi still had two years left before she graduated.

Maybe Gillian could hold off having to make a decision until the cast came off. She might be able to get her job or any job at the resort and everything could go back to the way they'd planned. She just had to wait it out.

Gillian dropped the pencil back into her bag. "You know what? We can do just about anything. We have the summer to figure out where we want to land."

Heidi's eyes brightened. "Really?"

"Grab my bag, please, sweetie." They were headed down to the diner for a light dinner, but one-handed Gillian was making no fast progress getting ready. She twisted the laces of her sneakers this way and that. A knock at the door stopped both in their getting ready.

"I got it." Heidi tied her hair back with a pink ribbon.

Gillian grunted in disgusted. "Damn laces." Three unsuccessful tries at her sneakers. "I give up." She tossed the shoes aside and was slipping into a pair of flip-flops when Heidi called her to the door.

A couple in their late-sixties stood side by side. "Hello." The woman smiled and toyed with the strap of her purse.

"Yes?"

"We're looking for Gillian."

"That's me." Her shoulders stiffened. The last time she'd had someone on her front porch looking for her, she'd packed up her daughter and headed for parts unknown. She leaned into the edge of the door with her shoulder. She raised her eyebrows expectantly.

"Where are my manners? I'm Bonnie Carmichael. And this is Gene Twofeathers."

"Nice to meet you both." On top of the nerves, Gillian's stomach growled and she hoped Bonnie would get to whatever point had brought her to the motel. "Is there something I can do for you?"

"Zan told me where to find you."

Gillian relaxed scant degrees. "Bowman?"

"Yes." Her smile broadened. "She's my niece."

"And that would make you Quint's aunt as well." When the woman nodded, Gillian held the door open wider. If she were going have a social call, she might as well sit. "Can I invite y'all in?"

"Why, thank you."

Gene removed his cowboy hat when he followed Bonnie in and sat at the small table in the corner. Not once uttering a word.

"Oh, my. What happened to you?" She pointed to the hot pink cast.

Gillian fidgeted. "My own clumsiness."

"Well." Bonnie glanced at Gene. "That changes things a bit, doesn't it?"

"I don't mean to be rude, but I'm not sure what you're talking about."

"Zan told me what you'd done for my nephew's knee. And Hank Calhoun's shoulder. I'd been hoping that maybe you could have a look at Gene's back. It tightened up on our way back from Jackson Hole visiting his new grandbaby—it does that every now and again, but will usually work itself out. This time though it's just not letting up."

The man sat stiff in his seat.

"But seeing how you're—" Bonnie again pointed to the cast, "—I guess doing what you do is next to impossible." The older woman frowned. "I'm sorry to have wasted your time." Bonnie and Gene stood.

"Wait. Please."

The couple sat.

"You'd wanted me to work on Gene's back."

Bonnie nodded.

Gillian glanced at the older man. Pain tightened his handsome features. She tugged at her lip. She'd taught a few classes back in Mobile. "What if I show *you* how to do it?"

Gillian gave Bonnie Carmichael a crash course in therapeutic massage. She also recommended several books for the couple. She might not be able to help them directly but between the copious notes the woman took and the books, Bonnie'd be able to muddle through Gene's stiff back, hopefully.

They'd only been gone a minute when Heidi started tapping her foot. "Mom. C'mon." She stood by the door with her bag. "I'm star-ving."

Gillian's stomach growled again. Enough impetus to get her butt in gear. They opened the door to find it raining again. "Damn cast." She closed the door back and glanced around the small room. "Grab the trash can next to the TV, hon."

Heidi handed her mom the little, black receptacle. Gillian set the two empty Coke bottles on the dresser and removed the bag.

"You're not serious." Heidi frowned and scrunched up her

nose.

"You want to eat don't you?"

The teen crossed her arms over her chest and nodded.

Gillian fashioned the bag up over her cast, but she was afraid it might leak. "Will you go grab the one from the bathroom trash too?" When her daughter brought the second bag, she repeated the odd glove-like covering then tucked into a light denim jacket to keep the bag secure. "Let's eat."

The pair walked the few short blocks to the diner. Several heads turned and waved at them when they pushed through the door. Gillian's growling tummy went from hungry to something akin to familiarity.

"Hey. Y'all find a seat somewhere. I'll be right with you." Missy waved and hurried to one of the tables with a coffee carafe.

Gillian ushered Heidi to their regular—being the second time they'd sat there—booth. She glanced around the room hoping to see Quint, a little shocked he hadn't checked on her once. You kiss a girl, watch her go into a washed-out gully then break her wrist and hightail it for parts unknown.

She couldn't blame him.

"Hey, hon." Missy stepped up to the end of the booth. "You stopping in to get something to eat before you head on out?"

"Actually, no." Gillian tapped a teaspoon on the tabletop in a nervous staccato.

Heidi snagged the spoon from her hand and whispered, "Cut it out, Mom."

"No?" Missy frowned and clicked the pen closed, but held her hand poised over the pad. "You just stopping in to say bye?"

"Sorry, sorry." Gillian chuckled. "We're here for dinner. Not sure when we're leaving, just yet, so no goodbyes. Just food."

Gillian and Heidi rattled off their orders.

Missy turned to go but paused. "Crazy about Jacob and Quint, huh?"

Gillian's stomach flipped over. "Wh-what do you mean?"

"That storm washed out part of Jacob's fence. They'd've lost half the herd, if Quint and Jacob hadn't gotten to it when they did."

"That's terrible." Gillian picked at the plastic bag over her hand.

"What's that?"

"A cast?"

"You broke your arm?" Missy pulled up a chair to the end of the booth. "I'd heard something happened up at Jacob's place, but... You broke it?"

"My wrist. Yes." Gillian held the jean jacketed, plastic bag covered, hot-pink casted arm in question up.

Missy frowned. "What about your job? How'll you be able to give massages?" She motioned to the cast.

"I won't." Gillian's chest tightened. "And they can't hold the job until my arm heals."

Missy leaned forward, set her elbows on the table and rested her chin on her hand. "What are you going to do?"

Gillian pasted on an over-bright smile—she'd been serious when she'd told her daughter they could go anywhere or do anything, but deep down it scared the hell out of her. She hadn't been without direction since she was fourteen. "We may just make it up as we go along. Or at least until it's time for school to start."

"Sounds exciting."

"I know, right." Heidi mimicked Missy's stance. "But we could also just stay right here." She glanced back over her shoulder to where Ryder and his group of friends sat at the counter. "Paintbrush isn't so bad."

"You'd want to stay here?" Gillian hadn't expected that.

"We could." The teen shrugged and sat back in her seat. "It's as good a place as any."

"What about work?" Missy persisted.

Gillian tried to wedge her finger into the cast, despite the plastic rain protection, but she couldn't quite reach the itch. "I'm not real sure."

"There you are." Bonnie and Gene stepped up next to the table. "I tried your room and hoped you might be here."

Gillian's eyebrows rose. "Did you need something else?"

"We were talking on the way out and started wondering about…" She asked several specific questions about working on Gene's back.

While Gillian explained a few of the different aromas and pressure points to Bonnie and Gene, Missy had gone back to the kitchen with their orders. After a few minutes, she returned and set the plates in front of Gillian and Heidi. The teen dug right in, but Gillian finished up writing out a couple more suggestions for Bonnie and her beau.

"That's great. I am so sorry we interrupted your supper. 'Night." The couple stood to go and Bonnie huffed. "There's my no good great-nephew."

Quint came in all but drenched and sat at the counter. Gene slapped him on the shoulder and Bonnie gave him a quick kiss on the cheek. They exchanged a few words. Once or twice he glanced over toward them, but he hadn't so much as waved or smiled at her.

Why had she thought he'd be the least bit attentive? Didn't his running off show her she'd been a nuisance? Not a potential date.

She shook off her thoughts. A date was the absolute last thing she needed while they were stuck in Paintbrush regardless of how long they stayed in Wyoming.

When Missy hurried past, Gillian waved her over. "Can we get our check?"

"Miss Bonnie got your meal. Gave me a pretty good tip too if I do say so."

"She shouldn't have..."

"Hon, you can go over there and tell her no thank you. But I can tell you now, you'll hurt her feelings."

"O-okay." Gillian wiped her mouth again with the napkin.

"That's so cool." Heidi smiled. "Can I get dessert?"

"It's broken?" Quint's gut dropped.

"You didn't stay at Dr. Hambert's long enough to find out?" Bonnie glowered. "Quinton Walters."

He hadn't put that look on his aunt's face too many times as a child, but he still got the gnawing in the pit of his stomach from disappointing her. "No, ma'am. Jacob lost half the fence in the storm. I had to leave as soon as I saw she was settled in with the doctor."

Thanks for not leaving me. Her words still haunted him. What did she take him for? Why did he now feel that was exactly what he'd done?

"I guess you can have a pass. But the least you should do is check up on her. Gene just pulled up out front." She stared at him for one moment longer then turned to go.

"Aunt Bonnie, how'd you know Gillian?"

His aunt shrugged. "Small town, hon."

"Shoulda known." Quint smiled and waved her off as she rushed out of the diner and into the waiting car.

Missy set Quint's food in front of him and his stomach rumbled. She held a tray with two huge banana splits. "Our little friends are gonna stay a while." She motioned to Gillian and Heidi.

Quint lowered his fork without putting so much as a single bite of food into his mouth. A smile spread. "You don't say?"

"Yep. Seems she's no good to that spa with a broken wrist."

His smile faded as quickly as it came. "It's really broken?"

Missy lowered the tray a little and inclined her head toward him. "You didn't know?"

"Aunt Bonnie said, but I thought she was giving me a hard time for not staying with her at Dr. Hambert's office." Quint stood. "Tell you what." He set his plate on the tray next to the desserts. "Let me take this for you."

Missy gave him the biggest smile he'd seen in a long time.

One summer at a Dave and Busters back in Dallas flooded back to him as he hoisted the tray of food. The two Harwood girls were chatting about shoes or some girlie crap and paid him no attention as he set the ice cream in front of them. When he set his plate down they both looked up and gasped.

"Quint. Hey." Gillian licked her lips.

He'd give anything to taste them again, but with her daughter right there, he needed to get his thoughts in check. "May I?" He stood right next to the bench where Gillian sat. When she finally scooted over to let him in, he slid in beside her and settled his plate in front of him.

"Thanks for watching over my mom," Heidi said almost begrudgingly.

He smiled over at the teen. "Not a problem."

"Next time though, could you try to bring her back in one piece?"

Gillian snorted. Quint leaned back laughed. "Deal."

His stomach growled again.

"Eat. Before your food gets cold." Gillian tapped his plate with her spoon.

Quint picked up his fork and did as she commanded. Not that he could have waited much longer—he was famished.

It seemed like a good idea at the time, coming over to sit with the two of them. That was until Gillian dug into her banana split.

"Oh, this is heavenly." She licked a spot of chocolate syrup from the spoon. He hadn't seen a woman enjoy anything as much in so very long.

Her eyes closed as her tongue darted out to swipe at a small glob of strawberry from the corner of her mouth.

Quint's fork clanked with a resounding echo on the edge of his plate.

Heidi didn't even look up from her ice cream. Gillian blushed.

"I'm..." His voice cracked and he had to clear his throat. "I'm so sorry about your arm. And your job."

"Mom, I'm gonna go talk to Ryder." Heidi left the booth before her mother could breathe much less get a word in.

"Not your fault." She ducked her head. "I mean, it was, but...still. Not on purpose."

His stomach turned over. He'd never broken a bone in his own body, much less someone else's before. If not for the damn gate being loose... He'd screwed up majorly this time. "Is there anything I can do?"

"Oh, you've done enough, thanks." She smiled but it didn't quite reach her eyes.

"I feel horrible."

"To be honest, with that water rushing toward me, I'd take a broken wrist to the alternative any day." She shook herself.

That was an image Quint didn't need implanted in his head. "Are you staying here? In Paintbrush?" He held his breath and waited. And waited.

Finally Gillian set her spoon down. "At least for a few days. I don't have a whole lot of options." She glanced around the room and leaned toward him. "Can I tell you something?"

Quint leaned over too, their shoulders touched. "Absolutely."

"I'm terrified." Gillian's eye glazed over with unshed tears. Her hand trembled on the tabletop. "I have never been without a direction or a plan since I was fourteen. Never had to worry about what came next. I..." She blinked several times, sat up straight and took a long drink of water. "I'm sorry. I shouldn't have laid that all out on you."

Quint settled his hand over hers. "I don't mind. Everyone needs someone they can talk to."

"Still, I—"

"Hey, guys." Ruby bumped his leg sticking out from the booth. "I've been looking for you, Quint. I heard about all the ruckus up at the ranch today."

If Quint wasn't mistaken, Ruby's eyes narrowed at Gillian. As if it were her fault rain came and washed away creek beds and knocked down forty-year-old fence posts.

"Nothing that hasn't been taken care of." Quint shoved his plate forward. "Did you need something?"

"Naw. But since I'm here, Gillian, did you want to settle up your bill? You're leaving today, right?"

Gillian gulped. "Actually, I—"

"Yes, she's checking out." Quint wiped his mouth with his

napkin. "How much does she owe you?"

Ruby crossed her arms over her chest. A smug smiled turned up the corners of her mouth. "Just the keys. She paid up in advance."

"She'll get you those keys as soon as she gets back and packed up. Right, Gillian?"

"I guess so." She narrowed her eyes at Quint.

Ruby walked off with a little more bounce in her step.

"Mind telling me what that was all about?" Gillian tried to cross her arms over her chest, but the bulky cast made it next to impossible as she tucked and untucked her arms several times before giving up and settled her hands in her lap.

Quint fought hard not to laugh. He cleared his throat and said, "No point in you staying up at the motel, seeing how your budget just got tighter."

She batted her eyelashes at him. "And Heidi and I are gonna do what? Sleep in my car?"

"Nope. You're moving in to my place."

"I beg your pardon?" Gillian shook her head, blinked her eyes, but the room didn't morph into some kind of weird dream. Quint still sat with his hands folded on the tabletop. No smile tipped up his full luscious lips. No jest crinkled his slate gray eyes at the corners.

"We can't stay with you." The temptation alone would drive Gillian insane.

He eyed her for a long moment. "As enticing as that sounds, I didn't say with me."

Heat ran through her cheeks. "Oh. I, uh. Okay."

"I said 'my place'. I have a house in town. It's sat empty for over a year now. You'd actually be doing me a favor."

Is that what the spider said to the fly before it got stuck in the web? *You'll actually be doing me a favor. Testing out the strengths of the strands.* She shook her head. "Yeah, I don't know. I appreciate it but—"

Quint held up his hand and stopped her. "It's furnished. Sort of. I keep the water and electricity on." He leaned toward her. "You never know when a stray Walters will come to town."

"I wouldn't want to take up something your family—"

"Nonsense." Quint eased back into his seat. "Why pay for a motel room while you try to decide what you're doing? I know money has to be a little tight right now. And like I said, you'd be doing me a favor. Having it occupied will cut down the chances of someone cleaning me out."

Like the chances of that happening were anywhere over nil.

He picked up his cup and finished off the remaining iced tea. "But if you really don't want to, I'm sure Ruby can extend your billing." Quint stood to go.

"We'll take it."

Chapter Six

"What are you doing?" Zan handed Quint her two year old. "Two people in the diner heard you offer the Harwoods use of your house. Is that a good idea?"

He kissed the top of the little girl's head and tickled her belly. Why did he have to have this conversation? "I'm being neighborly."

"She's not a neighbor. We don't know anything about her."

"Zan." Quint settled the child on his shoulders and followed his aunt across the back yard to the corral where Jacob was gentling the new colt. "When did you get so..."

She turned and stared at him. "*So*...what?"

"I'd choose your words carefully," Jacob warned. "Your aunt is a little persnickety today. She failed her last test."

"I didn't fail. I got a B. Shoulda been an A," Zan mumbled. She set her five-year-old up on the fence. "Watch Daddy, sweetie." She ran a hand through her short spiky hair. "You haven't so much as whispered in the direction of any of the women in this town for anything other than a free meal here and there. Gillian Harwood shows up with a teenage daughter in tow and you can't get within two feet of her without something catastrophic happening and giving folks stuff to talk about."

"I didn't break her wrist on purpose. It was an accident.

That incidentally probably saved her life had she stayed down in the culvert." For the hundredth time, his stomach rolled at the thought.

Zan shook her head. "And she didn't run over you on purpose either, but she still hit you with her car."

"Almost."

She grabbed her daughter around the waist and righted her on the fence. "What's next? One of y'all gonna end up in traction?"

"Funny." Quint snuggled up next to the toddler. "Your mom is quite the comedienne."

"Momma funny." The two-year-old clapped her hands together.

Zan huffed. "Don't you get my daughter involved in this."

"Told you," Jacob hollered from the corral. "Persnickety."

Zan stuck her tongue out at her husband. "Why your house though?"

"She lost her job, Zan, because I broke her wrist. No job, no money. No money, no way to pay rent." He lifted his head up to the cloudy sky. The rain had stopped but the humidity hung heavy in the air still. "As long as I am staying out here at the ranch the house is sitting empty."

"Which is why you should sell it," she said so low he suspected it wasn't for his ears.

"You find me a buyer in the town and I'll happily sell it."

Zan had the decency to blush.

"I might as well let her use it. It's the least I can do until she can find some way to make a living with her wrist all jacked up. Worse case, she's in the house until the cast comes off and she can get back to her massage thingies." His mind flashed to those capable hands—not that he had any right to think about her that way. Not to mention why he'd want a virtual stranger to hang around for as long as possible. Zan might be right. He didn't really have any business giving this woman run of his home in town. But when you injure someone and wreck their immediate future, it puts you in an obligatory state you can't quiet explain.

"As long as you know what you're doing."

Quint eyed his aunt for a long moment. "I'm not doing anything."

She smiled. "But being neighborly."

"Exactly."

"Wow. This is the biggest house we've ever lived in." Heidi set her backpack on the kitchen table while she still hugged her bear.

The three bedroom, two bath house was at least twice as big as anything the two had had in over five years. "This is temporary. Remember." Gillian could get too comfortable in this house. Something she and her daughter could *not* afford to do. Anywhere.

Heidi ran off down the hall. "Found my room."

Gillian went in search of the teen. She was in the first room off the hall. Decorated in warm colors and dark wooden furniture, it was a little masculine for the teen, but four walls and a door was something she hadn't had all to herself in some time. Again, guilt washed over Gillian. When Heidi grew into an adult, would she be able to understand all the trials they'd gone through, or would she resent her mother for the untraditional years of living they had?

At the moment, the smile on Heidi's face was enough to give Gillian hope her daughter would be okay. "Good choice."

The room tilted. "Whoa." She settled her hand on the doorframe to keep from swaying. The ever present ringing in her ears since her fall grew. Nausea rolled through her and sweat beaded up forehead despite the chills.

Heidi frowned. "You okay?"

"I'm fine, hon. The meds the doctor gave me just make me a little woozy at times."

The teen took Gillian by the elbow and walked her a few paces down the hall to the other two bedrooms. "Which one's it gonna to be?"

Gillian pressed her back against the wall. "Give me a minute."

"Mom, I think you need to go lie down for a bit." She rubbed Gillian's shoulder. "You need to a pick a room or I will pick one for you."

She smiled at her daughter. "Since when did you become the mom?"

Heidi stood and wrapped an arm around her mother. "When you turned green." She guided her mother into the master bedroom and over to the huge sleigh bed. "Why would a single dude have something like this and live in that small shack like he does?"

"He doesn't live in a shack."

Heidi scrunched up her face and tilted her head to the side.

"Okay, a little bit of a shack. But I'm sure it's so he can be close to the ranch and the horses and—" she waved her left hand, "—and stuff."

"Still..."

The room tilted again. "Whoa."

"Into the bed and lie back." Heidi helped Gillian crawl under the covers. "I'm going to go get you a drink. Then you're gonna nap. No arguments. Got it?"

"It's barely seven o'clock."

"Mom. Bed. Now."

Gillian pulled the blanket up to her chin. "Yes, ma'am."

Quint knocked on the front door. Of his own home. It was odd not to walk right on in.

"Hey, Quint." Heidi popped a huge bubble of gum after she opened the door. "Mom's in bed."

He pulled his pocket watch out and glanced at the time. The sun hadn't even started to go down yet. "Is she okay? Should I get the doctor?"

"Naw." She shook her head and talked around another huge bubble. When it popped and covered her mouth and nose, she removed the pink gum from her mouth to pull it loose and said, "The meds are just whacking her out a bit. She turned three shades of green and wobbled back and forth." Heidi snorted and sounded just like her mother.

"Maybe I should..." He motioned back to his truck. The last thing he wanted to do was become a nuisance.

Ryder bounded up the porch steps, a couple of other kids followed in his wake. "Hey, Quint." He tucked his hands into his pockets. "Hey, Heidi, we're all going over to Steven Jensen's house. We're having an X-Men movie marathon."

She glanced at Quint, her eyebrows raised in question. He leaned forward and whispered, "Lives a block over."

"Gotcha, thanks." She turned back to Ryder. "I don't know." Her shoulders slumped and the smiled slid from her face. "I should prolly stay with my mom."

"I could stay for a while." Quint volleyed his gaze between

the teens. "I don't have plans tonight. And I'm sure you'd rather see Wolverine rather than babysit your mom."

Wide smiles spread across both teens' faces.

"Super." She shoved a glass of water in his hand. "Tell her for me, will ya?" Heidi, Ryder and the other two teens were down the porch stairs and halfway to the Jensens' before he realized what he'd just offered to do.

Why did the sudden need to run skitter through every inch of his body?

Condensation from the water glass ran down his fingers as the cool, air-conditioned air feathered over his face. "Wasn't born in a barn, boy."

Quint closed the door and headed toward the back of the house. He peeked into one room then another until he found Gillian in his bed. All tucked up like a sick child. But she wasn't a child. She was a woman, all woman, with curves in the right places and one hell of an ability to kiss.

Why looking at her in his bed made him uncomfortable...he wasn't ready to examine where his thoughts headed. He'd traded places with Heidi as nursemaid. Not some letch getting an eyeful whether she knew he was watching or not. As she slept. In his bed.

He was never more thankful for hanging on to the house rather than putting it on the market. Affording the pint-sized pixie a place to stay, his decision was one of the best he'd made in a very long time. When Jacob had started his own ranch, Quint had moved into the small, foreman's cabin to stay close for when he was needed. He hadn't seen any reason to move all his furniture out—not that it would have fit in the close quarters.

Especially the large sleigh bed. With one beautiful woman bundled up under the covers.

His groin tightened. Maybe he was a letch. Regardless, he had a duty to his patient.

Focus, man. He pushed through the bedroom door. "Knock-knock."

"Heidi, I must be hallucinating." Gillian kept her eyes shut and tugged the blanket up. "I'd swear I heard Quint's voice."

He chuckled. "Is that a good thing or bad?"

A lush smile crept up at the corners of her pink mouth. "Mmm, very good."

Heat crawled up his spine and spread low in his abdomen. He was in a perpetual state of arousal when he was near her. "I'm glad you think so."

"Hmm?" Gillian propped open one eye and peered up at Quint. "W-what are you doing here?"

"Playing nursemaid." He handed her the glass of water, then took it back and set it on the nightstand. "Let me help you." He tried not to think of the little zip of electricity that shot up his arm as he helped her sit upright and handed her the water again. "Drink it all."

"Yes, sir." She finished the drink in one long swallow and handed him the empty glass. "All done." She swiped at her mouth with the back of her hand then fussed with her matted hair. The blanket pooled at her waist revealing a light-colored T-shirt. It was cockeyed and tight across her chest.

He tried not to audibly gulp and distracted himself by sliding the fat club chair over to the side of the bed. "How's the arm?"

"Still attached. A little achy. A lot of annoying." Her words slurred slightly. "Those are some powerful meds."

Quint smiled. "They cause hallucinations and everything."

Gillian laughed quietly and burrowed back under the

covers. He reached out toward her and arranged a couple of pillows under her cast to cushion it. "Comfy?"

"Mmm." Her eyes slid shut.

If she moaned one more time, Quint might come undone. He'd broken the woman's wrist and not only had she not railed at him, she'd thank him for not leaving her.

He frowned. Such an odd thing to say but under stress and duress there was no telling what flashed through people's minds.

"You still here?"

Quint shifted in the chair. "Yeah."

She yawned. "You, Quint Walters, are a good guy." Her voice weakened. "Can you promise me something?"

"What's that?"

"Promise me you'll keep Heidi..."

With his elbows on his knees he leaned closer to the bed. "Keep Heidi what?"

"Hmm?" Gillian snuggled on the pillow. "Keep her safe."

He blinked several times. Strange request. His instant reaction was to run like hell and stay as far away from Gillian and her daughter. But his rational brain kicked in. She wasn't asking him to become a father. Was she? "Safe from what?"

"If anything happens to me. We have no one else."

His chest tightened. Sure sounded like impending fatherdom. What did he know of her? Did she have some fatal disease? He couldn't wrap his mind around that. She and her daughter seemed to be "hiding". Maybe there was some real boogey-man out there they were avoiding. "Are you expecting trouble?"

Gillian didn't answer him. Deep, even breaths lifted her shoulder as she slept on her side.

Quint sat staring at Gillian for a couple of hours. So many questions bombarded his every waking thought. Twice he'd deliberately bumped the bed and tried to rouse her, but she was out. The night crept in before she finally stirred. Her cast clunked on the headboard when she stretched.

She turned her face to him and her eyes fluttered open. "Oh." She laughed quickly. "I thought I had dreamt you up."

"Nope."

"I had a weird dream with you in it so I wasn't sure."

His eyebrows rose. "Really? What were we doing in this dream of yours?"

"Nothing like that." She smiled over at him. "You have a dirty mind. We were square dancing."

"I can honestly say I have never been square dancing in my life." He chuckled. "So you were definitely dreaming."

She rubbed the tip of her nose. "I hope I didn't snore or talk in my sleep."

"You did talk a little."

A red tint darkened her cheeks. "Nothing embarrassing, I hope?"

Quint debated asking her about what she said, but more than likely it was sleep-talk. After falling into the culvert, breaking her arm and losing her job all sorts of insecurities could be plaguing her. "Naw."

"Have you been sitting watching me sleep the entire time? I think that's taking nursemaid duties a little far."

He snagged a magazine from the floor and held it up. "I caught up on my—" he flipped the magazine around and held in a grimace when he saw the cover, "—teen fashion."

Gillian's eyebrows rose and she nodded. "Gotcha."

"I have a proposition for you." He cleared his throat as a zip of electricity ran up his spine. "For Heidi really."

Her eyes widened slightly before she narrowed them at him "Go on."

"I, we, Jacob has been needing some help out at the ranch and I thought Heidi might be perfect for it."

"A job?" Gillian sat up quickly in the bed. "You want to give my daughter a job?"

"Sure, why not?" Quint leaned back in the chair and set his left ankle on his right knee. He toyed with the edge of his jeans.

"She's never held a job before."

"It's not like I'm asking her to do my taxes. It's mucking the stalls and feeding the animals on Jacob's ranch. He boards several horses along with his own livestock. He always needs an extra hand around." He shrugged. "Ever since she went riding with Ryder the other day, I've been thinking about it. She had a blast out on the ranch. It would give her something to do. Keep her occupied."

He hazarded a glance up. Gillian had a crocked smile. "And her thoughts less occupied with a certain teenage boy."

Quint fought his own smile and waved. "A minor added bonus, though he works on the ranch too. But at the very least there'd been a couple more eyes on them at all times."

A blush colored her pale cheeks. "You're a sweet man."

Quint gripped his chest. "Why would you say such a thing? You wound me so."

Gillian giggled. "I have a feeling you'll get over it pretty quick." She ran her finger around the edge of the cast. "Stupid thing is so annoying."

Quint dropped his foot to the floor. "Will you let her? Work at the ranch?"

"If you're serious, I don't see why not. When?"

"Tomorrow if she can." He stood. "I should probably go. Sounds like the worst of the meds have passed." He glanced at his watch and tucked it back into his pocket. "The kids should be heading home pretty soon. Ryder has work in the morning."

Gillian stopped messing with the cast. "Oh. Okay." She pulled back the covers and exposed her bare legs. "I'll walk you to the door."

Quint swallowed hard. It took every ounce of control to snag the quilt and cover her back up. "Not necessary. I know the way." He waved. "Take it easy."

"Take it easy?" Gillian flopped back onto the pillows. "As if I could."

Every inch of her flamed with desire. She'd wanted nothing more than to beg the man to crawl into the bed with her. Fear had kept her from asking. Fear he might say no. She didn't think she could handle that kind of rejection.

Worse yet, fear he might say yes and she would spontaneously combust or lose control. Control that for her entire life she'd only been out of once, which had landed her in Wyoming.

The front door slammed. "Mom!" Heidi ran into the bedroom, eyes wide, huge grin on her face. "You said yes?"

"Calm down." Gillian laughed. "You spoke to Quint?"

The teen jumped up and down and nodded. Her ponytail swayed back and forth.

Gillian took a deep breath. The idea of other people watching out for her daughter held great appeal. Especially men like Quint and Jacob. They'd keep a close eye on her. And at the same time, Heidi would have the normalcy she'd craved for the past year. "If it's something you want to do."

"Abso-freaking-lutely."

"Mouth."

"Mom." Heidi rolled her eyes.

"He wants you to start tomorrow if you can."

"This is so cool." Heidi flopped into the club chair and plopped her long legs over the side. "Did he say why?"

"What do you mean?"

The teen toyed with the end of her ponytail. A frown pulled down her mouth and she shrugged. "I don't know. Is it normal for someone to be so nice for no reason? First the house and then the job offer."

Gillian's chest constricted. A girl her age shouldn't have so much doubt. There were many good people in the world. The Harwoods just hadn't run across too many of them in their limited life experiences.

Gillian leaned toward Heidi and held out her hand. When the girl clasped it, Gillian squeezed it then held on tight. "Hon, I'm sorry that you even have to ask. I know it's been hard."

Heidi released her hand and huffed. "No big deal." She stood. "I better go find something to wear."

"I don't think the horses care that much," Gillian spoke to her retreating back.

For the millionth time, Gillian wondered if she was doing right by her daughter. She hadn't had anyone to confide in or a shoulder to cry on for so long she could never be sure.

Then, once Rick got out of prison, life had been so chaotic and frightening, staying as far out of his reach as possible had superseded everything else. When they'd landed in the middle of nowhere—and no one knew where they were—they could breathe, if only for a little while.

If she could give Heidi as much normalcy as possible, she'd try.

Her eyes fluttered shut.

Quint hadn't slept much, tossing and turning the night away with one thing on his mind: Gillian Harwood. Sure, he'd come up with the job for Heidi spur of the moment. But he and Jacob had talked about finding another teen to come out to the ranch and work part-time with Ryder. As the ranch grew, they'd need more and more folks.

Jacob had jumped at the idea. It would give him a little more time with the business end of ranching and boarding.

When his phone rang right after breakfast, and he'd heard Gillian's voice, for a minute, he thought he might still be asleep. Had he been dreaming, though, she'd have been curled up next to him, not letting him know they were on the way to the ranch. He'd just hung up with Gillian, when the phone rang again.

"Just couldn't live without me," he said.

But instead of Gillian answering it was his dad. "Hello to you too, son."

"Dad." His excitement and anticipation evaporated quickly. He set his empty plate in the sink and moved into the living room. "How are you doing?"

"Better than you, I think. Your aunt told me about your accident."

Quint groaned and mumbled, "Big mouth."

"She didn't mean to tell me. She thought you already had."

He balled his fist at his side. "I'm fine. No big deal."

"Someone tries to run you over—"

"It was an accident. Her car got the brunt of the damage. And Gillian wasn't *trying* to run me down. Hence the term *accident*."

"You're on a first name basis with the woman who ran you down?"

Quint scrubbed his hand over his face. The man never listened to a word he said. "Did you need something, Dad?"

"I spoke to Craig. A spot has opened at the firm."

"Dad."

"Hear me out. He could bring you in on a temporary basis and once you complete your degree you could move up to junior partner in three years."

"Thanks but no thanks. I'm happy where I'm at."

"As a ranch hand?"

"Your sister's husband is a ranch hand."

"Jacob owns his own ranch."

"Now he does. But not when they met." Quint tucked the phone in the crook is his neck and grabbed a clean shirt from the laundry basket next to the small sofa and folded it. "You didn't have a problem with ranch hands then."

"You have so much potential, son."

"And I'm squandering it away in a hole of a town in the middle of nowhere. Yeah. I know." He folded another shirt. "We've had this conversation."

His father sighed. "If history repeats itself, you'll get bored eventually and quit, just like everything else you've done. I just have to bide my time."

"I'm glad you have so much faith in me." Quint dropped the next shirt back into the basket. "Look, I've gotta go. Tell Mom hi for me." He hung up before his dad could comment.

Quint sat in the leather club chair and ran his hands through his hair as he took a deep breath. He shouldn't let his dad get to him, but always, always when they spoke, he was right back there in high school, his algebra average teetering on failing and him missing out in the state championship. Forget the fact that he'd maintained a B in every other class. He'd only played ball to make his dad happy. Sure, he was okay at it, but it didn't give him the thrill that working with horses, working on a farm did.

His dad seemed to forget that his great-grandfather had eked out a decent living for his family working his farm.

Half an hour passed as he sat there. "Pity party over, man." He stood and snagged his straw cowboy hat then headed for the corral.

Heidi and Gillian stood at the gate. Heidi rubbed Mallow's nose while Gillian eyed the horse skeptically. She turned and looked at him. "Oh, hey." The keys jangled on the end of her fingers. "What time should I pick her up?"

"Um, I can bring her home." Ryder stepped out of the barn.

Quint had watched how the teens kept eyeing each other. He should check with Missy and ask if she'd like him to talk with the boy.

Gillian frowned. "Okay." She backed away. "I guess I'll see you."

"Hang on a sec, will ya?"

She nodded.

Quint motioned the teens to follow him into the barn. "Ryder, show Heidi the basics. Where we keep the feed and the other supplies." Once he had Ryder and Heidi working, he went looking for Gillian. Things whirled around in his head, things he wanted to say to her, ask her. But after his conversation with his father, he didn't know up from down.

What the hell was he doing?

He didn't know this woman from Eve, and as his father pointed out, her introductions left him sprawled on the ground and his foot wedged under the front of her car. It was a miracle he and Mallow weren't hurt worse.

Then the damn flood where he broke her wrist. He shook his head as he crossed the corral back to Gillian. He'd felt so damn guilty he'd moved her and her kid into his home—vacant though it may be—and offered the girl a job. Hell, he'd even hinted to Manny just that morning that he could use someone to help him out at the garage. When the older man had pointed out there were no new prospects in town, he causally reminded him of the newest transplants. He'd done everything short of carrying a banner in front of the man's garage with the words "HIRE GILLIAN".

If kissing her hadn't all but melted his spurs he'd just blow off everything and treat her like any other gal in town, with polite indifference. But something in him couldn't push back and let well enough alone. Which scared him more than anything else.

When he came back to Gillian's side, she lowered her voice and glanced toward the barn where the two teens had their heads bent close as they fiddled with a couple of curry combs. "I thought the whole point of offering Heidi the job was to keep her occupied and her mind off of Ryder."

"I never said they wouldn't be working together."

Gillian released a heavy sigh. "I don't think this is such a good idea."

He should just hand the teen back over to her mother. But the clawing feeling of Gillian leaving town and never seeing her again tore at his gut. "Give it a day or two. See how it works. I guarantee they'll be too busy to even think about each other."

She gnawed on her lower lip and leaned to look past him and at the barn. "Fine." She turned abruptly and walked to her car without a backward glance. "But if anything goes wrong, it's your head."

Chapter Seven

Gillian stood at the counter and looked in her all-but-empty wallet. "Last twenty dollars." She paid for the small bag of groceries.

"Morning to ya, Ms. Gillian."

She glanced behind her. Manny, the garage owner, stood with his hands tucked into his dark coveralls. She flashed him a quick smile. "Hi."

"Can I help you with that?" He snagged her groceries before she could answer.

"You don't have to."

"I don't mind." He shifted the bag into his left arm and waved her on in front of him. "I came looking for you."

A flutter tickled her stomach. "Me? Why?"

"I heard about you missing out on that job of yours." He motioned to her cast. "I was kinda of hoping I could offer you a job."

A job? First Heidi, now her. This town was too good to be true. "What? Why would you do that?"

He chuckled. "Well, I need some help around the garage. And I'm thinking you might be needing a job."

They walked down the sidewalk side by side. She tilted her head toward him and narrowed her gaze. "Again, I can't help but ask why."

He held her gaze with his as they walked. "You don't trust too easy, do you?"

She smiled. "No, I guess I don't."

"That's a shame, but I'm not gonna pry." He shifted the bag. "But let me tell you, this is a small town. We look out for each other." Manny looked away. "It's a sincere offer. I do need the help if you're wanting to work for me."

"I don't know."

"What I'm needing is someone to answer the phones and maybe double-check order forms and billing, office type work that I end having to do in the evenings. With an office worker, I wouldn't get so far behind. How 'bout this. We can try it a bit, for..." He offered her a decent sum. "Maybe like a trial period. A couple days, maybe the rest of the week until you know for sure if it's something you want to do."

She frowned. The echo of conversation with Quint earlier that morning played through her head. "Can I think about it?"

"Yes, ma'am. Take all the time you need."

What's to think about? the little voice in the back of her head shouted. Until her arm healed, she couldn't get a job as a masseuse anywhere. She'd actually looked around the small town and had not seen one inkling anyone was looking to hire. Paintbrush was so small it didn't even have an employment agency. So it was either move on to a larger town or accept Manny's offer.

They reached her home and Manny handed her the groceries. "Thank you. For carrying my stuff. And the job offer."

"No problem, ma'am." He turned to go.

"Hey, Manny." She waited until he stopped halfway down the walk. "I'd love to give it a try if you're willing to take a chance on me."

95

A smile broke across his weathered, old face. "Yes, ma'am. Can you start first thing in the morning?"

"How do I look?" Gillian had dug through her clothes and came up with a pair of navy pants and paired it with the only businesslike shirt she had, a lemon yellow oxford. The shirt had been wadded up in the bottom of her suitcase. Luckily she'd found an ironing board and iron in the linen closet. "Heidi?"

"Hmm?" The teen glanced up from her bowl of cereal. "Old."

"Brat." Gillian tugged at the hem of the shirt. She didn't have anything overly-dressy. But working in a garage she wasn't sure that she needed to worry. "What're your plans?"

"After a day at the spa, I figured I'd go shopping down at the mall and then lunch at Spagos."

"Sounds good." Gillian smiled. "Have fun at the ranch. And tell everyone I said hi."

"Who's the brat now?"

She kissed the top of Heidi's head. "Wish me luck." Gillian walked the few short blocks to the garage. Coffee and motor oil wafted on a breeze through the open bay door.

"Right on time." Manny came out from the office and handed her a ball cap with "Manny's Garage" emblazoned across the front. "For you."

"Why, thank you." She tucked her hair behind her ears and pulled the cap on. "What can I do first?"

"Go grab yourself some coffee." He jerked his thumb toward the office door. "There's some pastries on the counter if you haven't had any breakfast."

Manny gave her a tour of the small building—an office that held a desk, cash register and a filing cabinet, a restroom, and two garage bays. A small shed in the back held parts and extra supplies that lined the walls. He showed her his filing system and a quick rundown on how to work the three-line phone system more advanced than she'd expected in a small middle-of-nowhere town. Still, with one mechanic for the entire town—cars, trucks, tractors and all—he had a pretty brisk business.

"We service the sheriff's vehicles whenever need be. Later this week I'll be doing a once-over of the entire fleet. And by fleet, it's two deputy cruisers and the sheriff's SUV."

She stiffened at the mention of the sheriff.

Manny paused in the middle of popping the hood of an old pick-up. He eyed her for a long moment. "You got something against the sheriff? Or vice versa?"

She pasted on an over-bright smile. "I haven't broken any laws." *That I'm aware of.*

He nodded. "That's good." He rested his forearms on the edge of the truck and held a wrench with both hands. "If you ever need to talk..." He trailed off and held her gaze for a long moment before he leaned under the hood. "Like, I said, small town. We look after each other."

She'd never before let anyone into the cloistered life of the Harwoods. She and her daughter had been a duo for so long... It'd be nice to unburden herself. She wasn't ready yet, though.

Despite her and her daughter finding jobs and the normalcy she craved, they were in a make-believe world. Cocooned by a false sense of security that could pop wide open at any moment. She had to keep reminding herself not to get lulled into thinking they were anywhere close to home-sweet-home. A bag of clothing still sat in the closet by the front door for any potential hasty retreat.

She shook her head and reached for the phone as it rang. "Manny's Garage..."

"Lunch." Missy set a paper bag on the desk in front of Gillian.

"How did you..."

Missy smiled. "Heidi came in for lunch with Ryder." She opened the bag and removed a Styrofoam container. "Three people in for breakfast mentioned it. And Manny told me when he picked up the pastries this morning." She smiled then opened the container to reveal smothered chicken, mashed potatoes and seasoned broccoli. She waved the food under Gillian's nose and set it in front of her. "Still hot from the oven."

Gillian's stomach growled.

Missy shoved a fork in her hand. "Eat."

Gillian took a huge bite of the chicken. When she swallowed she asked, "Are people around always so nice to new folks in town?"

Missy folded her arms and leaned back. "We don't get a whole slew of new folks here. But when we do and we like them, yes, we like to be neighborly."

"This is a bit more than neighborly," she said around a mouthful of broccoli.

"Hon, you don't trust too easily, do you?"

Gillian snorted. "You're the second person to ask me that."

"I'm guessing 'cause it's true." Missy stood. "I've got to get back. Why don't you and Heidi come over for dinner tonight? You'll probably be whipped after working all day."

"Thanks. I think we just might."

"Manny's lunch is in there too. Make sure he eats. Before it gets cold, please." Missy waved as she exited the small office.

A few minutes later her new boss came in. "Did I see Missy

leaving?"

"Yes, sir."

"Aw, now don't go calling me sir. I might get a little too full of myself. Everyone in town just calls me Manny."

"Will do." Gillian reached into the bag for another container. "Your lunch."

"Good. My gut feels like it's been running on empty for days."

Gillian fought off a laugh. That morning he'd eaten at least six of the pastries—and that was just since she'd come in. No telling how many had been in the huge box originally. While he was digging into his food she studied him.

Growing up, she'd always imagine what her dad would have been like if he'd stayed—maybe not Gus Harwood per se, from what her mother said, he was no picnic—but a dad who would have loved his children unconditionally. Been there for them and them alone. Someone to man-up and be the father he was meant to be, not run the minute he got a whiff of some pretty thing who would crook her finger at him. Her dad was anything but what a father should be.

Manny, however, fit the bill to a T.

He cared about the folks around him. Just in the few hours she'd worked for him, she'd seen him give a discount here, wave a fee there and promise to drive out across town later that night to check on an elderly neighbor. Just because.

On the surface, he looked like any small town garage owner: oil-stained hands and coveralls. His gray hair was wild at best and usually covered by a greasy garage cap. But his eyes, his dark brown eyes gave him a warmth that just radiated. They were gentle when he spoke to you, alive when he smiled and a little bit sad when he pulled into himself, sitting quietly.

Like he did while he ate his lunch.

They ate in silence for a little while. Manny got up and grabbed them both bottles of water. "I hope I'm not overstepping here, but you kinda remind me of my late wife. She was as fragile as an injured bird when we met."

The food in her stomach grew heavy.

"She had a nightmare of an ex. Liked to beat her for sport." He took a long draw on his water.

"You think I'm fragile?"

"Not so much that. But you have the same look of wariness on your face. Kinda like you're always looking over your shoulder." He shook his head. "You and your daughter pick up and moved across the country—"

"How did you..." She settled her hands in her lap to keep him from seeing how they shook.

"Alabama plates on your car." He shrugged. "Obviously, I heard about the job or lack thereof. Small towns."

"I've heard that." She smiled briefly.

"I'm guessing all you have is what was crammed into your car. Which I have to say, wasn't much. Anybody who goes so far from home with that little bit of belongings... They're either on the run from the law or hiding from something bad."

Gillian released a heavy sigh.

"Like I said before," Manny rested his forearms on the edge of the desk, his hands linked over his food, fingers twined, "I won't press you for details, not unless you want to share. But for my own peace of mind, I have to ask, are you in danger?"

She swallowed hard and shook her head. "Not me."

"Your daughter?"

Gillian dropped her gaze to her clasped hands. "Very much so."

"Her daddy?"

"No. He left the picture long before she was born."

Manny nodded. "Can't say that I quite understand what you're up against, but know that there are many good folks in this town that will bend over backwards to help you and yours."

"Th..." She cleared her throat. "Thanks." Her hands shook so badly she didn't dare finish her lunch. She'd revealed more to Manny than any person she'd know for the last few years. Relief and fear warred in her.

Her first instinct was to grab Heidi the moment she walked in the door, pack her up and head to parts unknown. They were getting too involved with the residents of Paintbrush, Wyoming.

Quint Walters's faced popped into her head. The many times they'd moved over the past year, she'd never once missed a soul. Not since they'd left all they knew behind in Alabama. But leaving, Paintbrush and Quint... Her chest tightened and the fear of not seeing him again was stronger than staying in one place. For now.

It didn't make sense.

Since the moment she became Heidi's mother, she'd always put her daughter first. Never had time to think of dating, much less romance, but Quint Walters made her want things.

She didn't need the hassle.

Manny finished his lunch and tossed his trash in the bin.

"Mind if I jump on your computer for personal use? I haven't checked e-mail in forever." *Like in over a month*, she mentally added. They'd been moving a lot since school had gotten out for summer break. No place felt right so she and Heidi kept on the road.

"You go right on ahead."

Gillian logged into her e-mail account. Only two people had

the address and then they only sent her messages, updates really, about Rick Damon and the case the Mobile prosecution was building against him.

Several SPAM messages filled her inbox. Nothing from back home, but one address she didn't recognize from a month earlier. The subject line simply said, "Hello."

When she opened the message her blood ran cold. It read: *"You can't run forever. I will find you. I always get what I want."*

She didn't have to read a signature to know Rick had somehow found her address. She logged out and backed away from the computer. "He can't know where we are." She paced the small office. The date of the e-mail was two weeks old. If Rick Damon had found out where they were, he'd have been there already. No warning. No time to run.

"What's got you so worked up, girl?"

She jumped at Manny's voice.

"Bad news?" He swiped his hands with a rag and tucked it into his back pocket.

"Can I ask you a question?"

He nodded.

"If you're checking e-mail, can someone find out *where* you might be checking it from?"

He eyed her for a long minute. "I can't say for sure. I'm sure government type people can. Regular folks, it would take some doing, I'd guess."

She sat heavy back in the chair she'd vacated. "My daughter's in trouble."

Manny sat back in his seat across the desk from her.

"My sister always had the worst taste in men. She was dating a real peach of a man when Heidi was little. Rumor had it, at the time, that he was a drug dealer. No amount of talk though could get my sister to see him for who he was.

"One day she came home all freaked out. She was crying and I could barely understand. I finally got out of her that her boyfriend shot a man. Right between the eyes, she said."

Manny settled his elbows on his knees.

"It was enough to scare some sense into her. She went to the police and became the prosecution's number one witness." Gillian picked at a piece of tape stuck to the desktop. "Rick was having none of that. He snuck into the house while my mom and I were at work and killed my sister." She swiped at a tear on her cheek. "Heidi was there. Saw the whole thing."

Manny cursed. "Sorry. Go on."

Gillian ran her finger around the edge of her cast. "He was convicted of a couple of drug charges—stuff they'd had on him for a while. I think they were trying to get him to turn over on someone else, I don't know exactly, but he never did. They didn't have enough evidence to get him on the first murder. They didn't even try him for Becca's murder."

The phone rang and she reached for it.

Manny waved her hand away. "The machine will get it."

She nodded and took a deep breath. "A little over a year ago, he was released from prison. Time served. It scared the hell out of me, but the authorities swore we'd be safe, that he wouldn't be stupid enough to come looking for Heidi—but she doesn't even remember that night. He had no reason to come looking for us." Her entire body shook. "He started calling then. I told the police and started a protective order.

"Then one day I found him on my front porch. Just sitting there. I wasn't taking any chances. I packed up our things and we left." She took a deep breath. "We've been moving around for the last year. This is our fifth town. As luck would have it, I had a job offer in Montana. We got lost and you know what's happened since."

"And you got an e-mail from him?"

"It's a couple of weeks old, but yeah."

"Does he have any way of knowing where y'all are? Did you tell any friends where you're staying?"

"No. When we left Alabama, we left all of that behind." She rubbed the tip of her nose. "I met a woman in Kansas when we were living there. Her cousin was opening a spa as part of a ski resort in Montana. Since we didn't actually end up there, outside of Paintbrush, there's not a soul who knows where we are."

"Good." He rose from his seat. "Would you be willing to talk to Sheriff Reese?"

Her stomach pitched again. "I don't know."

"He's a good guy."

She nodded. "I believe you, but I don't think I'm ready."

"Thank you for trusting me."

"Thank you for listening." She rose up on her tip toes and gave him a quick hug as the bell sounded, announcing a new customer to the shop. She was thankful for the interruption. "Back to work." An odd calm came over her after telling Manny, sharing her worries with someone else for the first time. Even Heidi didn't know most of it. She'd been through years of therapy and never remembered the night Becca died. She knew the basics thanks to TV reports and overly-chatty neighbors, however, she'd mentally shielded herself from most horrific parts of it. The therapist said she probably never would remember the worst details.

And for that Gillian was ever thankful. Some things a child didn't need to remember.

She shook herself and dove into the paperwork set aside for

filing. Anything to take her mind off the past. The rest of the day went by in a blur. By five thirty, her neck and back ached—in a good way. "Do you need me for anything else?"

Manny closed the bay door to the garage and locked it. "No, ma'am. We're good to go."

The pair exited together and Manny locked the front door. "Can I drive you home?"

Home. Despite everything, Paintbrush was starting to feel like home.

"No thanks. I'll walk."

He paused. "If you need anything, absolutely anything, you give me a call." He handed her a slip of paper with his home phone number.

"You're a good guy."

He shook his head. "Nothing I wouldn't do for anyone."

"Which is exactly what makes you a good guy." She waved. "'Night."

"What's for dinner, Mom? I'm starving." Heidi ambushed Gillian the moment she walked through the door.

"I hadn't really planned anything."

"But I'm *star*ving." Heidi's shoulders drooped and she rolled her head back on a moan. "*Star*ving."

"I heard you the first time." She batted her daughter's ponytail. "Missy invited us over."

Her head popped up. "What did you tell her?"

"Maybe." Gillian kicked off her sneakers. "Do you want to—?"

"Yes, give me ten minutes to get ready." Heidi dashed down the hall.

Gillian slipped her feet into a pair of rubber flip-flips and settled into the sofa. Ten minutes could easily become thirty.

Surprisingly, it was only twenty minutes. "Ready. Come *on*, Mom. We don't want to be late."

Gillian laughed. "Grab my bag for me, will you please?"

"Can I drive?"

"We can walk."

"But, Mom." Heidi flipped her lip down in a full pout. She threaded her fingers together and pulled her hands up in front of her pleading. "Pretty, pretty please."

Gillian bit her lip to keep from smiling. "I guess so."

"Yee!" The teen jumped up and down and yanked a huge key chain from her pocket.

"Pretty sure of yourself there."

"I was hoping."

"Let's go."

Gillian let Heidi drive several blocks past the Lunsford home and back. Even though she'd gotten her license in the last state they lived—just before they fled—the teen had had little chance to actually practice.

"Easy." Gillian braced her good hand on the dash as Heidi pulled the car to the curb in front of Missy's house. She tried to smile and tell her daughter good job, but she was afraid it would come out more like a grimace and a squeak.

The teen bounded from the car. "Come on, Mom."

Gillian's knees shook slightly as she exited the car.

"Hey, y'all." Missy had the door open before they got to the top of the porch steps. "Dinner is just about ready."

"Can I help you with anything?" Gillian set her purse on the sofa and pulled up short when Quint Walters stood. "Hadn't expected to see you."

He glanced toward the kitchen where Missy had gone. "Ditto."

"Ryder," Missy hollered from the other room.

Ryder came tearing down the hall and skidded to a halt when he caught sight of Heidi. His cheeks blazed and he straightened then relaxed his body in an almost boneless teenage stance. "Hey."

"Grab Heidi on your way," Missy yelled again.

Heidi shrugged at Gillian and followed Ryder into the kitchen.

"How have you been?" Quint tucked his hands into his back pockets. "I heard you got yourself a job with Manny."

"That old small town thing again, huh?"

Quint nodded slowly. "Yep."

She frowned. Several scratches dotted his cheek and he had a welt over his eye. "What happened to your face?"

The corner of his mouth crooked up. "I'm afraid I was born that way."

"Funny, but no." She stepped forward and touched the bruise above his left eye. "This."

He held her gaze. "We were working on a roof and I stepped off the side." He said it nonchalantly, but his words were a little clipped and tight.

"Geez." Gillian's heart sped. "Are you okay? Are you hurt anywhere else?" She ran her hand over his shoulder.

He took several shallow breaths. "Ribs hurt like hell."

Gillian gentled her touch and probed his side. She couldn't believe he was standing there as if nothing happened. "What did Dr. Hambert say?"

Quint looked away. "I didn't see him."

She snagged his chin and turned his gaze back to hers.

"What? Why?" She tilted his head this way and that. "Look me straight in the eye." When he did, she examined his pupils. "You could have a concussion." She ran her fingers over the scratches on his cheek.

"I'm fine." Quint stilled her fingers. "Hazards of the job." He held onto her hand. "But thanks for being concerned."

A shiver ran through Gillian.

"Dinner."

The pair broke apart quickly and turned in tandem toward their hostess.

Missy's eyebrow twitched as a smile tugged up the corner of her mouth. "Y'all ready to eat?"

"After you." Quint settled his hand at the small of Gillian's back.

The shiver grew tenfold.

Three place settings adorned the table. Gillian straightened a napkin. "Who are we missing?"

"The kids wanted to eat outside on the patio with Daddy. I—" The phone rang before Missy could finish her sentence. "Hello?" She listened for a minute. "Sure. Five minutes."

She replaced the receiver. "I apologize, but I have to fill in for Jen at the diner. You two enjoy your dinner." She set a huge vat of chili in the middle of the table. "I'll tell Daddy and the kids bye on my way out."

"Do you think she set this up?" Gillian sat at the table.

"After inviting us both?" Quint helped slide her chair in. "I doubt she'd leave. She'd never know if her evil plan worked."

Gillian laughed. "You're probably right. Should we go out and join Hank and the kids?"

"Naw." Quint sat beside her. "Let me have your bowl."

Gillian hesitated. "Don't strain those ribs."

"No worries, I told you I'm fine. How was your first day on the job?"

She handed Quint her bowl and let him fill it for her. "It was good." Her stomach did a somersault. She had honest to goodness work. Not to mention, she'd practically had a therapy session too—not that Manny was Dr. Phil, but he was a great listener. "Manny's a nice guy."

"That he is." Quint winced as his side bumped the table.

"Are you sure you don't need to see the doctor?"

He shifted in his chair. "Positive. But if you think you need to look at it for peace of mind, knock yourself out." Quint stood and held his hands aloft.

Gillian eyed him for a moment. Was this a trick?

When she didn't so much as move, he un-tucked his shirttails and lifted the edge to expose a deep purple bruise covering almost his entire left side. It took all her willpower to focus on the abrasion rather than the fit and firm abs. It wasn't like she hadn't seen his bare chest before. She swallowed hard as her eyes followed the light sanding of hair that trailed down into his denim.

Focus, girl. Gillian rose to her feet, too. "Looks nasty." *But how does it taste?* Her mind went from one extreme to the other in a millisecond. She cleared her throat. "This may hurt a bit." As gently as she could she tested his ribs with her fingers.

He sucked in a deep breath.

"Sorry. Didn't mean to hurt you."

"Didn't hurt, darlin'," he said under his breath.

Gillian pretended she didn't hear him and quickly finished her examination. "I still vote for a visit with Dr. Hambert."

"Duly noted." He released his shirt and settled at the table. "Hungry?"

"Always." Two bites into the chili and Gillian's eyes watered. "Holy hell. What does she put in this?"

Quint took a bite and swallowed. "*Habaneros.* They're a little warm."

"A little?" She grabbed a roll and alternated bites of bread with the fiery chili. Quint hadn't even broken a sweat.

They ate with little chit chat. Just as they were setting their dishes in the sink, Hank came in with a handful of bowls. "I'm gonna take the kids up to get some ice cream. Would y'all like to join us?"

"No thanks. You go on ahead." Quint took the dishes from the older man.

Hank nodded and was gone.

Gillian tried to cross her arms over her chest, but with the cast it came across more as if her arms were at war with each other. She stopped fidgeting and ran her finger over the back of her chair. "What if I wanted ice cream?"

Quint gave her a slow head-to-toe once over. "You don't look like you've ever had ice cream."

A shiver ran down her spine. "Why?"

"Why what?"

"Why are you always using such cheesy lines?"

Quint rinsed off the last dish and settled it into the washer. "You ever seen Wyoming stars?"

She got dizzy with how quickly he jumped from one subject to the next. "They're different from other stars?"

He nodded. "Absolutely."

"If you say so, I'll take your word for it."

"I can show them to ya."

Gillian shook her head. "No, that's okay."

"Scared?" Quint tossed the dishtowel to the sink.

Gillian snorted. "Of you?"

"Of the dark. I am far too charming to scare you away."

She leaned forward and looked deep into his eyes.

"What are you doing?"

"I thought your eyes were gray, but you're so full of shit that I almost expect them to be brown."

He blinked several times. "You noticed the color of my eyes?"

"*Gaw.* You are the most insufferable man."

He smiled broadly. "I have heard that before."

"I'll just bet you have."

Quint held out his elbow to Gillian. "Can I interest you in a walk under the magnificent Wyoming stars to get some dessert?"

Gillian stared at him for a long moment. She should go back to her house, lock the door and do her very best to forget about the very sexy cowboy who tempted her at every turn. But more than anything she wanted to go walking blanketed by the beautiful night sky with said cowboy.

"What the hell." She slid her hand into the crook of his arm. A little electric charge zapped her, like a zing of awakening. The first time she'd felt it, it could have been a fluke. The second, a coincidence. Every time since then... It was hard to ignore, but she'd been good at compartmentalizing things.

"This way, m'lady."

Chapter Eight

The last time Quint had to work at wooing a woman, he had braces. Not that he was a ladies' man, necessarily. But Gillian challenged him in every area, especially in the one-on-one, man/woman areas.

He loved a challenge.

The pair walked in silence for a couple of blocks. She left her hand looped with his arm. He could have walked and walked all night, just to have her beside him, with him—despite the pain in his side. On Main Street, they walked past the diner.

"Aren't we…" Gillian glanced back over her shoulder.

Quint clicked his tongue like he did with the horses. "Not a very patient woman."

She gave a quick, nervous laugh. "A confused woman."

Two shops farther and he turned to the door.

"The grocers?"

"Last time I checked they sold ice cream." He snagged a hand basket at the front door, shifted his other hand to the small of her back and guided her back to the freezer section. "What's your favorite flavor?"

Gillian volleyed her gaze between the glass door and Quint.

"You do like ice cream, right?"

She laughed again, this time with no nervousness or

tension. "Yes."

"Okay. Pick a flavor or two. I'll be right back." He hurried around the shop and grabbed a few essentials. All the while he ignored the way his heart raced at the remembrance of his hand on her back, her hand on his arm, the sweet scent of her hair when he'd bend down to speak just to her.

He returned and she had one pint balanced on her cast and held another in her hand. "I picked. I couldn't decide between these two." A huge smile spread across her face. "What's in the basket?"

"Supplies." He nodded toward the front of the store. "This way. Follow me."

Once Quint paid for dessert, he and Gillian walked a couple more blocks to the picnic tables at the elementary school playground. The few streetlamps close by gave just enough light for romantic seclusion.

"Now can I see what all you bought?"

Quint set the bag on the picnic table. "We're having dessert."

"Yeah, I kinda got that. The ice cream was the first giveaway."

"Like I said, impatient." He removed plastic bowls and spoons as well as napkins. He set down a pint container in front of each of them, then also pulled out whipped cream and an assortment of sprinkles. "I wasn't sure what you liked."

She smiled up at him. "All of the above."

They spent the next few minute concocting their desserts.

Gillian licked the back of her spoon, slanted her head back and moaned. The woman liked her ice cream.

Quint's crotch tightened. He had to clear his throat before he could speak. "Open your eyes."

113

"Hmm?" Her eye lids fluttered open and gazed heavenward. "Oh, wow. You weren't kidding."

Head still back, she blindly dove her spoon into the ice cream for another bite. "I don't think I've ever seen so many stars before."

I've never seen anyone so beautiful. The words were on the tip of his tongue, but instead of scaring her off good he simply said, "Told ya."

She lowered her gaze and squared it on him. "You get a kick out of that, don't you?"

Watching you in the moonlight? Wanting to touch you? "Um, what?"

"The 'I told you sos'. Are you ever wrong?"

Wrong at underestimating her power over him? Yes, he wanted to admit. But he was nowhere ready to tell her how she tore him up inside. "I thought I'd made a mistake once." He shook his head. "But I was wrong."

She pointed her spoon at him. "Cute."

"I try."

"A little too hard," she said quietly.

Quint pretended he didn't hear her. He'd never had the urgency and desire for a woman swell up in him all at once. It was confusing. The more he pushed and tried, the more she seemed to retreat. She was as skittish as a mistreated mare. With a horse, you took your time to gentle them. With Gillian, it felt like a clock was hanging over their heads. He wanted to make the most of their time together. And if he was lucky, make their time together last as long as possible. He wasn't ready to lose her.

He shook off the heavy thoughts.

They finished the ice cream—all of it—he'd never seen a

woman so petite pack away so much double-chocolate-brownie ice cream before, and didn't so much as apologize for her appetite—just one more thing he liked about her. He tossed the trash in a nearby can and held out his arm again for their walk back to Missy's.

Quint couldn't remember the last time he'd been so content. Sure, moving to Wyoming had been one of the best things he'd ever done for himself, but it was still tough trying to work your way through what you want to be when you're grown and settle into that life. Walking with Gillian though and every decision he'd made was timed perfectly, and he couldn't ask for much more.

"That was the best dessert. I don't think I have ever had better."

Warmth spread through his chest. "For me, too."

As they were passing the diner, Hank and the kids came out. "Oh hey, were y'all coming to join us?"

"Yeah, but I guess we're too late."

Gillian snickered but didn't comment.

Quint waved the trio on in front of him. "Y'all lead the way back to the house."

Both teens narrowed their eyes at Quint and Gillian but neither ventured a comment. They stayed half a block ahead the entire way back to the Lunsford home. Quint waited until the door closed behind the trio to pull Gillian to a stop. "Thanks."

She frowned. "For?"

"Letting me treat you to dessert."

"I should be the one thanking you." She leaned against the front door.

"Yes, you should." He smiled down at her. A spot of

chocolate winked at him when the corner of her mouth tilted up. "You have a little..." He motioned to his mouth with his thumb.

"Oh, geez." She swiped at her mouth but missed the spot.

"Here, let me." Quint raised his hand. Instead of wiping away the smudge, he cupped her cheek and leaned forward. He lapped at the corner of her mouth with his tongue. Then he settled his mouth over hers. He'd longed to kiss her again. She tasted of chocolate and want. The perfect combination. A shiver wracked through her and he repeated the process. "Mmm, tastes sweet."

The door opened behind them and Gillian nearly fell in. "Mom!"

Gillian jumped. "I, uh..."

Heidi shoved her hands on her hips. Her toe tapped the ground in an impatient rhythm.

Quint looked between the pair of Harwoods and laughed. "A bit much. It's not like you've never seen your mom kiss a guy before."

"Actually—" she turned her glare to Quint, "—I haven't."

He would have laughed if Gillian's cheeks hadn't turned an alarmingly shade of crimson. "Never?"

"We...um, we should get going. Good night." Gillian snagged Heidi's wrist. She dragged the teen down the walk behind her.

Quint stood, mouth agape like a damned old fish, and watched the Harwood women walk to the car at the curb and get in. The teen looked back longingly at the house, but didn't fight when her mother told her to get into the car. When the taillights were nothing more than pinpricks, he shook himself and knocked on the door.

"Hey, where'd Heidi and her momma get themselves off to?" Hank leaned out the door and looked around Quint.

"They left."

The older man frowned.

"I'm gonna head out too. Tell Missy thanks for dinner when she gets back home."

"Will do. Oh, hey. Gillian left her bag here. Will you take it to her?"

Quint raised his hand, poised to knock again when the door whooshed open. His fist sat frozen a mere inch from Gillian's nose. "Uh, you forgot this." He held the bag out to her, but she just stared at him.

"Who is it, Mom?" Heidi bounded to the door behind her mother. "Oh. It's you." She scrunched up her nose.

"Be nice." Gillian swatted at her daughter as she vanished behind the door. "Thank you. You didn't have to come all the way out here."

"It was on my way home." Quint set the bag down inside the door.

"No, it's not. The ranch is in the other direction."

Quint stared at her for a long moment. "Why have you never kissed a man in front of your daughter?"

Gillian's eyebrows pulled down and her shoulders stiffened. "None of your business. Thanks for the bag." She swung the door closed, but Quint stopped it with his booted foot.

"You're a strange woman. Hard to figure out."

Her gaze narrowed. "No one asked you to."

Quint didn't stop her the second time and the door snicked shut.

When he pulled up next to his small house on the Skipping Rocks Ranch, Ruby's pick-up sat in his spot. He pulled up in the slot next to it and let the truck idle for a moment. Hands gripped on the steering wheel, he let his pulse settle after the rollercoaster with Gillian.

Ruby got out of her truck when he shut down his engine.

"Did I forget some plans?"

She shook her head. "Nope. I thought I'd just stop by and say hi." A long denim skirt swooshed around her legs as she followed him in through the front door.

When was the last time he'd seen her in a dress? Had he ever seen her in a dress? Hell, until that moment, he didn't think he'd ever even seen her bare legs—sure he knew she had legs under her jeans, but…still… It was a little weird. He gave a quick mental shake. "Would ya like a beer?"

A smile stretched across her face. "'Kay."

With beers in hand, they settled in his living room. She sipped from her bottle, then said, "So, I kinda expected you home tonight. After that nasty fall."

"Missy invited me over to dinner."

Ruby frowned. "She was working at the diner tonight."

He took a long draw and nodded. "She got called up to work just as we were sitting down to eat."

Quint's mind shifted to Gillian as it had so much since she'd come to town. He'd been damn lucky he hadn't embarrassed the two of them when she examined his bruise. Her hand, careful and gentle had all but stopped up his breathing. He'd had to run through a mental list of his daily chores to keep his hormones at bay—always so close to exploding without any prompting. If desire hadn't been laced with the pain, he didn't know how he'd have been able to

118

control himself. Then later, the kiss.

God, he almost begged for more. Until her teenage daughter growled at him.

"Did your mom ever kiss one of her boyfriends in front of you?"

Ruby sputtered her drink. "What?"

"Before she married Guy. She dated right?"

She nodded slowly. "Yes."

"Did she..." He waved his hand in a slow circuitous motion.

"Kiss men?" Ruby blinked. "Yeah, I guess. I didn't really keep a score sheet. What's with the weird questions?"

"Nothing. Something I saw on TV."

She laughed. "Whatcha been watching?"

He tried to make his laughter sound relaxed and normal, but it fell flat.

Ruby scratched at the beer bottle label with her thumbnail. "I heard Cade Holstrom is coming back to town for a week."

"Hank mentioned it." He crossed his ankle over his knee. "It's been a while since we've seen him."

Ruby nodded. "Yep."

Quint nodded. "Yep."

"Do you have plans for Friday night?"

If he worked up the nerve to ask Gillian to go out with him he would. "Nope."

She shifted in her seat and turned toward him. "Me neither."

"You know what?" Quint pointed his bottle at her. "You should give Eric up at the Cates' ranch a call. He's been hinting around about asking you out."

Ruby smacked her beer down on the table. The resounding

119

crack echoed through the room. "I should be going." She stood. "I have a couple checking in first thing tomorrow morning."

"Oh, sure." Quint stood, too. "Walk you to your truck?"

"I think I can manage."

"Hmm." When the door shut, he fell back into his chair. He fingered the phone on the table next to him. He'd give Gillian another day before he asked her out on a for-real date. Just the two of them. No interruptions or disapproving teens. "Now, I just have to convince her to say yes."

"Mom, is there something you need to tell me?" Heidi flopped on the foot of Gillian's bed.

"You were actually left by aliens on our doorstep. Becca took one look at you and traded her favorite pair of gold hoop earrings. Just for you."

The teen's blonde eyebrows rose up into her bangs. "Funny. You should take your act on the road."

"What's that noise?"

"Don't try to change the subject, Mom."

"No, seriously." Gillian rose from the bed. "Can't you hear that?"

Heidi twisted her head in the direction of the sound. "What is it?"

"It almost sounds like growling." The humming vibration grew louder.

"In the house?" Heidi slid off the bed and snagged Gillian's shirt. "Wait for me."

The two person conga line crossed the bedroom toward the bathroom.

"Maybe we should call someone." Heidi dug her finger tips

into Gillian's hand. "It sounds like a monster."

"Don't be ridiculous." Gillian said the words to calm her daughter's fears but it did little to ease her own. "Stay right here." She left Heidi in the doorway and edged into the bathroom.

The roaring grew. Before Gillian got more than a foot into the small room, the faucet shot up into the air and water spewed everywhere.

"Ah!" Gillian rushed out trying to keep her cast dry. "Go call Quint. His number is by the phone in the kitchen."

"I'm not used to having hysterical women call me in the middle of the night." Though he'd sure raced like hell to get to town after the phone call.

Heidi stuck her tongue out. "I was hardly hysterical."

"'Oh, Quint, you have to hurry'." He raised his voice in falsetto. "'It's raining in the house'."

"Thank you for getting here so quickly." Gillian added another wet towel to the growing pile.

"Would you stop that?" Quint guided Gillian to the chair for the third time. She couldn't sit still. "If you get your cast wet..."

"I haven't up to this point. You can't do this all by yourself."

Quint snagged Heidi's ponytail, but didn't yank too hard. "I have help. And seeing how it's my shoddy plumbing that got us in this predicament in the first place." He shrugged.

"I can't just sit here."

He smiled down at her. "I've noticed."

"Do you know how gross the two of you are?" Heidi made a gagging noise. "There's nothing worse than old people flirting."

Quint flattened his back up against the wall and grasped his chest. "Did she...just...call me old?"

121

"Puh-leeze." Heidi's eyeballs rolled heavenward—for the umpteenth time.

"My uncle used to say if you keep rolling your eyes like that they may get stuck up in the top of your head. Then where would ya be?"

Whoop, the round orbs rotated again.

Gillian laughed from her perch on the chair.

Quint peeled himself off the wall. "Back to work." He mopped up the remainder of the water and took all the wet towels out to the back porch to dry until they could be properly washed. He'd lost his helper five towel runs in. She'd lain down on the bed and immediately fallen asleep. As he finished up alone, he'd slowed down considerably and his ribs screamed in pain. Initially, adrenaline kept the pain at bay, but now... He groaned. A little louder than he'd meant to.

Gillian slumped half-asleep in the chair stirred. "Done?" She sat up when he walked past her.

"For now." Quint rubbed his chin with the back of his hand and tried not to breathe too deeply. "I can't turn the water back on until I get a couple of parts from the hardware store."

"I'll wait."

"Darling, maybe you forgot in your sleep-fogged brain, but this is Paintbrush. The town doesn't open until eight a.m. There's no Wal-Mart to run up to in the middle of the night." He glanced at his watch. "This early in the morning."

She swiped at her matted hair. "Right. Forgot."

"'Kay." He yawned. "I'll be back."

She stretched, pulled her arms up over her head. A peek-a-boo of skin flashed at him before she settled her hands on her lap. "Stay."

Those darn hormones rioted again. Between the pain in his

side and cleaning up Old Faithful in the bathroom, he'd managed to tamp them down. But those four little letters—almost whispered from a sleepy Gillian—pushed them back into overdrive. "I, uh, what?"

"No point in you driving all the way back out to the ranch and then back out here. You won't get any sleep at all."

Didn't have to ask him twice. "Okay."

She leaned her head back on the chair. Her eyes drifted shut. "I'll make up the sofa for you." She didn't move.

"You asleep?"

"Hmm. Naw." She didn't so much as open her eyes.

"I'll make up the sofa."

"Sounds good." She slumped into the chair a little further.

"You can't stay there." He nudged her foot.

"Sure."

Quint chuckled. Pain be damned, he shifted Heidi on the bed and pulled down the cover for Gillian. She hardly weighed anything. Her breath feathered his neck the short walk from the chair to the bed. Every fiber of his being screamed at him at how perfectly she fit up against him. Sure, he'd carried her after the rainstorm but situations being what they were, his head was anywhere but lusty then.

As the morning strolled slowly in, he casually carried her the few feet to his bed. He wanted nothing more to crawl into bed with her—had her daughter not already been there snoring away.

He imagined what a life with Gillian could entail and an odd longing built in his chest. His gaze shifted to her daughter. He'd never thought of kids—he had nothing against them but that was something far off, in the future. A woman with a teenage daughter should scare the bejesus out of him. And it didn't. Further proof that he needed to find a way to keep this woman in his life.

Wrong place, wrong time, however. But he would make the right time and the right place. He had to.

He settled her next to Heidi then ran back into the bathroom to snag a bottle of Tylenol he'd seen. Quint stood with his hand on the light switch. "Good night, darlin'. See you in the morning."

"Ahhhhh!"

Gillian jumped from the bed and raced down the hall. "What the..."

"What's he doing here?" Heidi pointed. She hugged her stuffed teddy bear to her chest.

Gillian edged forward and peered around her daughter. Said offender waggled his fingers at her. She released a pent up breath. "Morning, Quint."

Heidi's eyes grew huge. Her mouth gaped like fish until she finally formed words. "You *knew* he was here?"

"It was late by the time he got done cleaning up the bathroom."

"So."

"So, he still has some work to do on it."

"So."

"So there is no running water until he finishes." She held her hand up when her daughter opened her mouth. "He has to get a part to finish. *So* it was either he went home and got next to no sleep to then turn around and come back here and we could wait *for*ever long for a hot shower, or I let him stay here and he gets to the store as soon as it opens."

Heidi glared at Quint.

He smiled. "I made breakfast."

The teen sniffed. "French toast?"

"And bacon." He nodded. "And some juice. Hungry?"

"I could eat." She scrubbed at her lopsided ponytail. "Mom can't cook."

"Heidi." Gillian swatted her butt as she hurried to the kitchen.

"Ha, you got the kid calling you out." He tsked. "Hungry?"

Gillian shook her head. "I'll just grab a cup of coffee later."

"Nonsense." Quint walked over to her and took hold of her elbow. "You can't start your day without a well balanced breakfast."

"Did you get that from your mom?"

"No. Dad." He frowned. "One of the few things I agree with him on."

Gillian let Quint lead her to the table and pull out the chair for her. What could it hurt to sit and have a meal? "How did you make all this?"

Quint handed her a plate loaded with food. "What do you mean? I pulled stuff from the cupboards and cooked."

"The cupboards here?"

He chuckled. "Yeah."

"She's just in shock they contained actual food," Heidi said with a mouthful of French toast. She swallowed. "My mom's idea of cooking involves the freezer and a microwave."

Gillian bent her head over her plate and kicked her daughter under the table. "You need to just hush yourself now."

Heidi pointed her fork at her mom and glanced at Quint. "She has set water for spaghetti on fire." She shoved a forkful of food into her mouth. "Three times."

"Don't talk with your mouth full." Gillian took a sip of juice. "Matter of fact, stop talking all together."

Heidi gave her a huge closed mouth smile.

"Tell me about your dad." Gillian wanted to change the subject. Her shortcomings were not fodder for landlord/hunky cowboys. "You two don't get along?"

Quint ate in silence for a long moment. She didn't think he was going to answer until he finally said, "My parents have been together since they were fourteen. My dad has had his life mapped out from the time he was a teen. He knew where he'd go to college, he was even sure he'd end up in the Major Leagues. When that was done he had his next career planned out. Then he wanted to do the same for my sister and me."

"And that's offensive why?" She shouldn't pry, but that didn't sound like a parental-deal breaker to her.

"Not so much offensive as it's annoying." He took a sip of juice. "To have someone tell you what to do and when to do it."

Heidi raised her glass. "Thank you."

"You're a kid. I'm over thirty. It's a little bit different."

Heidi didn't look too convinced, but she didn't comment.

Quint shook his head. "I found it easier to leave than to fight."

Gillian shared a look with her daughter. Not the same kind of fight, but they knew the feeling.

He shifted uncomfortably in his seat. At first she thought it was from their conversation. "How are your ribs?" Working so hard on the bathroom all night would tweak the already sore muscles.

"I'm fine." His tone was just enough clipped to say "drop it".

Gillian wracked her brain for something to say. She eyed Quint for a long moment. He was a handsome man. Strong.

Brave. And a little more than opinionated. How had he stayed single for so long in such a tight-knit community?

Maybe he wasn't single. "I have to say, I am a little surprised there's not some woman knocking at the door this morning demanding to know why you weren't home last night."

Quint shrugged. "No one who cares that much."

"How can that be?" If he were her man she'd care.

Whoa. She didn't like the directions her thoughts had shifted to. She had no right at any kind of proprietary glommings where *any* man was concerned.

He seemed awfully interested in the food on his plate all of a sudden. "I don't know."

Gillian wasn't about to deprive her curiosity. "How long have you lived in Paintbrush?"

"Little over five years now."

"And you're still on the market?" Gillian swiped at her mouth with her napkin. Though the man had all but sucked chocolate off her mouth the night before she couldn't stop herself from asking, "You're not gay, are you?"

Heidi squirted juice out her nose. The teen turned three shades of red and excused herself from the table.

Gillian mopped it up as calmly as you could please. "Gross, hon," she called after the girl.

Quint still hadn't answered her.

"No, I don't think you're gay. I can't imagine what it is, though. I'd have bet money these mother hens here in town have been clamoring to get you hooked up with their daughters."

"I didn't say that wasn't the case." He set his fork down, leaned his elbows on the edge of the table and laced his fingers over his plate. "Just nothing ever came of it."

"How many single women are there in Paintbrush?"

"Over or under forty?"

Gillian rolled her eyes. "Under."

"Fourteen," he answered quickly.

She leaned forward. "That's amazing."

He shrugged. "Like you said, when you're a single guy, you get to learn who all the single ladies are. Pretty dern quick."

"Over forty?"

"Ten, but Ms. Ida just got herself engaged so technically nine. And any one of the esteemed Paintbrush population have eligible female kinfolk within driving distance."

"And how many single guys?"

"Not near enough." He smiled, rose from the table and gathered up all the empty plates.

Gillian was getting nowhere with her line of questioning—though really what she was hoping to garner, she wasn't actually sure. She had no business grilling him on his relationships. Nor did she have any stake in them. She sighed. "That was great." She patted her full belly. "As I see no shower in the immediate future, I should probably go ahead and get in to work."

Quint nodded. "It shouldn't take me too long once I get the part from the store."

"Is there anything I can help you with before I go?"

My incredible hard-on?

Probably not the best morning come-on. Sleeping only a few feet away had been much more difficult than he'd anticipated.

"Nope, I'm good." He shifted behind the counter, straightened himself. He was in a constant state of half-aroused

128

just being in the same room with her.

"Okey-dokey then. I better go get ready."

Her hips swayed the length of the hallway. He'd swear she did it on purpose to tease him, but in truth, it was the way she walked—always. He'd watched. Far too many times.

Quint could use a splash of cold water on his face. Though it wouldn't help much. He needed to dunk his entire body in a freezing cold creek to ward off the effects of Gillian Harwood. He glanced at his watch. He had about thirty minutes until the shop opened up.

"Do you need me to stay and help you finish?" she asked a few minutes later.

If you stay I will *be finished.* "No, I'm good. Headed to the store right now." He crossed from the kitchen to the front door.

Gillian looped a purse over her shoulder and followed him. They stood in the small foyer. "Heidi is headed over to the Cates' ranch to go swimming with Ryder and some friends." She tucked her hair behind her ear. "The Cates' daughter is home from college and they're having some kind of party."

Quint nodded. "Lisa. Haven't seen her in ages." Marti Cates called almost everyone in town personally to invite them to the party when Lisa agreed to come home. Once the girl turned eighteen, she'd hightailed it out of town so fast the dust was already gone before anyone noticed. "Will you be there?"

"I'm not much up for pool parties." She lifted her cast.

He chuckled. "They have a huge spread. Lots to do. There'll be food and half the town."

Gillian nodded slowly. "I'll probably need to pick Heidi up."

"Tell ya what. How about I swing by after work and pick you up at the garage? We can go out there together and you won't have to drive all by yourself."

She narrowed her eyes at him.

"What?"

"I am just trying to figure out your angle."

"Why do I have to have an angle?"

"Maybe 'cause your mom dropped you on your head as a child and it broke your take-it-easy button?" A smile tipped the corner of her mouth.

"It was never proven." He blinked his right eye in rapid session like a tic earning laughter from Gillian. "So, what do you say? Is it a date?"

Date? Did he mean it like the way her stomach fluttered when he smiled? "Sure, why not?"

"Really?" He cleared his throat. "I mean great. What time?"

"Five?"

"Sounds good." Quint stared at her for a long moment. "See ya then." He turned and was out the door.

"Can I use the car?" Heidi came up behind her mother and wrapped her arms around her shoulders and rested her chin atop her mom's head.

"I thought Ryder was picking you up."

"This is the twenty-first century. Girls can drive."

"That's not what I..." She sighed. "Yes. The keys are on the counter. I have to go to work. Have a good time. And be careful please." She patted Heidi's hands and the teen released her.

Gillian walked the few short blocks to the garage. Just around the corner she saw a couple walking toward her. The elderly couple wore matching jogging suits. A little poodle hurried along at their feet with a color-coordinated bow atop its curly head.

She gave them quick smile.

"Morning, Gillian."

She tried to hide a startled look. "Good morning."

How did they know her name? Her step faltered. She'd lived in Mobile for years with her mother, her sister and eventually Heidi. She couldn't remember walking down the street somewhere and passing someone who called her by name. The past year, she and Heidi hadn't stayed anywhere long enough to make even casual acquaintances, much less friends.

But in all of ten minutes in Paintbrush, people knew her by name. They rallied around her to help her find a job, find a home. They accepted her.

Just like that.

No questions asked.

"What put that frown on your face?" Manny handed her a cup of coffee when she walked into the office.

She told him about her walk to work.

"I don't know if it's a sadder comment on the places you've been..." He shook his head. "You going to the Cates' later?"

"As a matter of fact, Quint offered to drive me."

"Did he now?" Manny's eyes widened.

Gillian tucked her purse under the desk. "Why do you say it like that?"

Manny took a huge bite of a cinnamon roll. He took his sweet time chewing. Once he swallowed, and took a sip of his coffee, he said, "Just find it curious. That's all."

She sat behind the desk and leaned back. "Sounds more like some old biddy gossiping over the clothes line."

Manny barked with laughter. "That it does. That it does."

He turned to go, but Gillian stopped him. "Can I ask you a question?"

"Fire away?"

"What kind of guy is Quint? Is he just teasing me? Is he bored and I'm a new target?"

"I've known the boy since he got to town. He's been, hands down, a hard worker. He's never caused a lick of trouble that I know of. And from what I hear—" he winked at her, "—he's one of the most eligible bachelors this side of the Big Horn Mountains."

"Hmm." She sipped her coffee. "Are you going to the Cates'?"

"Naw." Manny squared his ball cap on his head. "I don't socialize too much since my Loretta passed on."

"That's too bad."

"Naw. It'll give us something to gossip on tomorrow."

Chapter Nine

The bell over the door dinged announcing a new customer. Gillian shoved the last of the May files into the large cabinet—only two months to go. It was time consuming work, but Manny needed his files up to date and when she was done, she wouldn't feel like a charity case job offer. Not that he'd made her feel that way. "Manny had to run out. He'll be back in a few minutes."

"I'm here for you."

Gillian glanced up as Quint leaned his shoulder on the doorframe. Her pulse quickened. Hands down the man was hot. The way his hair curled just at the temples. Even the crease lines at the corners of his eyes gave him an air of rustic charm. Add in his southern boy finesse and there was no wonder why he made the women swoon—on the surface, he was a catch. Deep down, he was genuinely a nice guy, which made him the catch of a lifetime.

If the way Ruby glowered at her every time they crossed paths was any indication, that woman was determined to lay claim to him for herself. Add in the other single Paintbrushites and there was a bachelor war ready to erupt. And here he was, for her.

Why was he interested in her?

She gave a quick mental shake. *Snap out of it, girl.* It was a ride to a party, not a declaration on bended knee.

"Five more minutes. I need to close down the computer." She'd planned to check e-mail again. She'd waited until Manny was out of the garage just in case something did come through from Rick—she didn't want to show fear in front of her new friend. But Quint's early appearance derailed her internet forays.

He tucked one hand in his back pocket. "Can I help you do anything?"

"Nope, I got it covered. Sorry I'm not ready."

"No worries. I'm early. You do what you need to do." He leaned up against the doorframe while she ran around and closed down one system after another.

It unnerved her to have him watching her every move—and he was. She ventured a glance his way every now and again and he didn't once take his eyes off her.

She shouldered her purse. "All done."

Quint stepped away from the door. "I have to tell you something before we go."

"Okay."

He cupped her cheek. "You have to be the prettiest woman in Big Horn County." He leaned in and touched his mouth to hers.

Gillian's purse slid from her shoulder and landed at her feet. She took advantage of her free arm and gripped the front of Quint's shirt to pull him closer. She deepened the kiss, with her cast resting on his hip.

Quint wasted no time taking his fill of her. He cupped her butt and pulled her flush against him. His fingers tucked into the back pockets of her jeans and kneaded gently. His erection pressed into her hip.

So many emotions and desires stirred. All new and as exciting as they were scary as hell.

Gillian was way out of her league. Out of her element with this man. She pulled back, gave him one last quick kiss. "We don't want to be late." She patted his cheek and bent to retrieve her bag. "Ready?"

Holy hell, he was ready to explode.

"Yeah." His voice squeaked. "Yeah."

Gillian walked away as calm as you please. He would be lucky if he didn't spontaneously combust right then and there.

If he had any sense, he'd take to her to the house and have his wicked way with her, slack the need that increased every time she came near. He shook his head. If he was smart, he run as far as he could in the opposite direction and leave her the hell alone. The woman had a kid. And with that came needs and responsibilities Quint had never sought. He wavered between not ready to start something he wasn't sure he could handle and diving in head first.

"Should we stop and get something to take to the party?"

The question snapped Quint from his thoughts and he chuckled. "Newbie."

"What?" She smiled up at him.

"A Cates shindig is by far gonna leave you mystified." He tucked his hand at the small of her back. "They'll have enough food to feed a small country. I hope you like barbeque."

"I, I thought you were kidding." Gillian's chin hit her chest. "I mean, I'd heard about some of their parties and assumed Missy was exaggerating, but wow."

Three enormous meat smokers sat side by side puffing out sweet and tangy aromas. There were honest to God stations. One for each food group—and an entire table dedicated solely to baked beans. Gillian's stomach rumbled.

"Ready to eat?"

"Absolutely."

Quint guided her through table after table laden down with an array of breads and veggies. By the time they reached the actual meat, she had little room left on her plate.

"How're you?" An older man with a shock of white hair turned from the closest smoker and smiled. "You must be Gillian. I've heard a lot of nice things about you."

Quint came up beside her. "Gillian, this is Mr. Cates."

"I'd shake your hand, but..." She couldn't move much under her loaded down plate balanced atop a glass of tea as her cheeks heated. "I can't imagine what people would say about me, I've hardly been here two weeks."

He smiled. "That's thirteen days longer than it takes most of us to make up our minds." He winked.

"Thank you so much for inviting my daughter and I to your party."

"My pleasure. She is a sweetheart, jumped right in and helped my Marti get some of the tables set up."

Gillian tried not to show her surprise. "My daughter? Tall, blonde teenager. Usually chomping bubble gum."

He laughed. "That'd be the one. Never got more than a holler away from Ryder Lunsford."

"That sounds more like the girl who I know and love."

"So, what can I get for ya?" He clicked his tongs together.

"Whatever you think tastes best."

Quint nudged her shoulder. "Darlin' it all tastes good."

"Ain't that the truth?" Mr. Cates lifted the lid of the smoker and snagged a huge piece of meat and set it smack dab on top of everything on her plate. He gave Quint twice as much.

"It's a wonder your plate hasn't folded under the pressure." Her stomach growled again.

Quint guided her to a bunch of picnic tables. They sat between his aunt and her husband, and one of the couples she'd seen at the diner.

She stared down at all the food in front of her. She didn't think she'd ever had that much food on her plate at one time—or two. But it all looked—and smelled—wonderful.

The other two couples finished their meals before she and Quint could even start. Jacob and Zan mentioned taking the girls to the pool, and the other couple wanted to wander around and work off the Mississippi Mud pie they'd eaten. Quint and Gillian had a quiet section of the eating area all to themselves.

"If you stop staring at it and actually put some in your mouth..." Quint nudged her elbow with his.

She giggled. "I don't know where to start."

"Close your eyes."

She blinked said eyes several times. "What?"

His hand hovered over her plate. "Close your eyes."

Gillian looked at him for a long moment. Her eyelids fluttered shut on a sigh. And she opened her mouth.

Something moist brushed her lip a moment before a tangy burst of flavor exploded in her mouth.

"Keep 'em closed," Quint said when her eyes opened the barest of slits.

"Mmm." She chewed the brisket, still with her eyes shut. She swallowed. "Wonderful." She darted her tongue out to swipe at dab of sauce on her lip.

"Ready for something else?"

She nodded. "Sure."

Something rough scrubbed across her lip. When she opened her mouth the taste was vastly different. Breaded and woodsy.

"What was that?"

"You've never had fried okra before?"

She smiled. "Can't say that I have."

Quint leaned into her. "I'd love to keep doing this, but I don't know how much more I can take before I combust."

Gillian's eyes jolted open. She glanced first at his face then down to the growing bulge in his jeans. "I, uh, sorry."

"Don't be. I just don't want to embarrass either of us here at the party."

"Good thinking." The plastic fork punctured her plate when she speared another piece of okra. She gave a quick, nervous laugh. "If you stop staring and actually put it in your mouth..." She mimicked his earlier words.

Quint winked at her and took a bite of his own meal. They ate the rest of their dinner in silence. A few of the townsfolk stopped by to say hi. Quint was very popular. Ruby stopped at the table long enough to glare at Gillian before she headed to another table—probably to glare at her from a distance.

"They have a margarita machine over there. Would you like me to get you one?"

Gillian chuckled. "No, but water would be great."

"Alrighty, be right back." Quint took their empty plates to the trash.

"Hey. How are you doing?" Zan sat down next to Gillian and settled her youngest daughter in her lap all bundled up in a towel.

"I'm full." She patted her stomach.

"Willard is the best smoker in the entire county."

"I believe that."

Zan stared at her for a long moment. "Are you okay?"

The brisket sat heavy in Gillian's stomach. "My arm hurts a little."

The woman leaned in closer to Gillian and settled her hand on her un-casted hand. "That's not exactly what I mean."

"Did Manny say something to you?" She pulled her hand free and settled both in her lap.

Quint's nosey but well meaning aunt frowned. "Manny? No."

Gillian closed her eyes and released a heavy sigh. *Learn when to keep your mouth shut.*

"Hon, half the time you look scared to death. The other you look like you're ready to run away as fast as you can." She readjusted the toddler in her lap; the little one had fallen asleep swaddled in the thick towel. "If you ever need to talk... I am a great listener."

Gillian snorted. "Something in the genes?"

Zan smiled and looked down to her daughter. "Something like that."

"I appreciate the offer." It wasn't enough the people had opened their arms and accepted her into the town, but several had offered shoulders to lean on. Hers and Heidi's wrong turn landed them in some alternate universe. That was all she could figure.

"As long as you know you really can take me up on it."

"Take you up on what, Aunt Zan?" Quint came back to the table and looped an arm over his aunt's shoulder.

"She said if I was interested in your deep, dark secrets

she'd give them to me for a night of babysitting." Gillian winked at Zan.

"I'll counter that with two nights of sitting to keep my secrets, secret," Quint said.

"Woo-hoo." The little girl stirred in her lap and she lowered her voice. "I feel a bidding war coming on." Zan toggled her gaze between Gillian and Quint. "If I play my cards right I might finagle a mini-second honeymoon for Jacob and I."

Jacob hurried over to them. "We need to go."

"What's wrong?" Zan stood.

"Emily's not feeling well." He shifted his daughter in his arms. "I think it was the third brownie that did her in."

"I remember those days." Gillian waggled the little girl's foot.

"It's always something." Zan shook her head and laughed. "We'll see you two later." The Bowmans left amid a round of good-byes and quick sugar-OD explanations.

Again Quint and Gillian were sequestered all by their lonesome. Being alone with Quint—even at a party—left her warm in places she didn't want to feel warm. Especially after the cozy tête-à-tête with his aunt. "Um, we should go find the kids. Heidi and I should head back to town. We both have work in the morning." She headed across the lawn toward the pool area Heidi had vanished to.

"I'd bet Heidi's boss would give her a pass if her mother let her stay out too late." He smiled down at her and settled his hand at her back as they crossed the huge yard. "It's summer time. And a party."

Gillian frowned. "Did that excuse work with your parents when you were sixteen?" She hadn't meant to use her stern mom-voice, but slacking was not something she'd taught her daughter up to that point and it wasn't on the agenda to add in.

His hand fell away as did his smile. "Not once."

"And when you got older?"

"There'd been no point in trying. I did my own thing and my parents had no say."

Did he not see how sad and lonely that was? "You're a loner. Plain and simple, huh? No rules. No worries."

"I moved away from my family, didn't I?"

She shook her head. "But you moved close to both your aunts."

"It was to get away from my dad more than anything."

Gillian slammed her hand on her hip. "I don't get that." She paced away from him. They were on the side of the Cates' house, headed to the pool. With no one within ear shot, she pressed the point. "My dad ran off when I was little. I never even got to know him. To talk to him. All I know are the tainted stories my mother told me. Some may be true, some may not. But like I said, I'll never know."

"But what if he smothered you? Treated you like you were still a fifteen-year-old screw up? Constantly." Quint shoved his hands in his pockets.

He couldn't mean that, not really. Did he not know what he had? "Even then I would." Gillian slowed her steps and stopped right in front of him. Would have been nose to nose if he weren't so much damn taller. "I would relish being smothered."

Quint snorted.

Gillian grabbed his elbow before he could walk away. "My dad left when I was three."

His cheeks reddened. "You said that already."

"I don't know where he is or even how to find him. I didn't get to go to the daddy-daughter dances at school. Never had him there to cheer me on or hold me up. He'll never get to walk me down the aisle when, if, when I get married. Hell, he never even got to see his beautiful granddaughter."

Gillian held up her hand when he started to speak. "My sister died when I was just a teenager. She was my best friend. Can you imagine losing your sister? Or Zan? She left me and..." Gillian caught herself before she said too much.

"Then my mother died." Breath caught in her lungs. "She left me all alone to raise a child. All by myself." She pointed her finger at her chest. "I had no one." She'd never had a conversation with anyone about all her losses. Heidi was too young and far too close to the situation to be burdened with this. Gillian had never made close enough friends to share even the most mundane details, much less all of the death surrounding the Harwoods. "I'd give anything to have my family. And you—" she stiffened her spine, balled her fist at her side and looked up at him, "—you do have family who care enough to love you and want the best for you. And you pout because daddy 'expects too much'. Grow up, Quint Walters."

Quint's mouth hung up, unable to string together words as he watched Gillian's retreating back. How had that gone so wrong?

He shoved his hands on his hips, ducked his head and leaned against the house. Mentally, he ticked off all the reasons to let her go. He had just as many reasons to go after her, not let her walk away mad. None of which, though, could spur him into action. He counted to one hundred and then one hundred again. Let his blood pressure even out and even then he stayed up against the side of the house. He wasn't ready to be sociable.

"Whatcha pouting about, cowboy?"

"I am not fucking pouting." His head jerked up in time to see Ruby's smile fade. "Sorry. Didn't mean to speak to you that way."

She held a beer in each hand. "Is everything okay? I saw the new gal and her daughter leave all in a huff and thought maybe you could use a cold one." She held an opened bottle out to him.

"Thanks." He took the brew and sucked it all down in one long drink. "May I?" He held out his hand for the other bottle.

Ruby chuckled and handed him the other bottle. "If it's that bad, we could hit Dominique's. They have something with a little more punch."

He eyed his friend for a long moment. "Why the hell not?" They left the party and he followed Ruby to her house to drop her truck off. He purposely went the long way through town, so he didn't pass his own damn house. The most self righteous woman he'd ever met was bedded down inside.

He gave himself a mental slap when the thought popped into his head. That woman had lost almost every member of her family. But did it give her the right to psychoanalyze his life and tell him what an ass he'd been?

"Why are you letting her work you up like that?"

"What?"

Ruby twisted in her seat toward him. "If you grip the steering wheel any tighter, you're gonna snap it right in half."

Quint held back the growl that bubbled up in his chest. "It's not what you think."

"If you say so." She crossed her arms over her chest. "I just can't see what the big deal is. She'll be leaving before too long."

"What makes you say that?"

"That woman has been in six cities in the last year. I heard her telling Manny about it one day. Sounds to me like someone with wanderlust. And not big on commitment. To anything or anyone."

"But big on telling me off," he said under his breath. Ruby was right. No point in letting Gillian have any more power over him. "I'm buying the first round."

Eight rounds in and he and Ruby had laughed so hard his sides were on fire—sure it could be from the fall the day before, but the Mustang Pale Ale made the world right. Kyle Eubanks, Dominique's owner—and Jacob's cousin—came over and plunked himself down in an empty seat. "What are we celebrating?"

"Freedom." Quint raised his beer mug. Ruby clinked her glass to his and they both slammed back the amber liquid.

Kyle tipped back in his chair. "It's getting close to closing time."

Quint yanked the pocket watch from his hip pocket. It took him three tries to push the button in and pop open the cover. Little good it did as the numbers swam around the face. He snapped it shut and shoved it back in his pocket, then smiled up at Kyle. "I'll take your word for it."

The owner narrowed his eyes first at Quint, then at Ruby. "Who can I call to come get y'all?"

Ruby cleared her throat. "I've only had two."

Quint frowned and counted the empty beer mugs littering the table top. "Two?"

Kyle hollered something to the bartender who confirmed her sobriety.

"I'm fine to drive."

Something about her smile turned the beer in his stomach rock solid.

Kyle slapped Quint on the shoulder. "Y'all be safe."

When the owner was back across the room, Quint tried to focus on his friend. "Why'd you let me drink so much? Alone?"

She shrugged. "You needed to blow off some steam. And somebody had to drive your ass home." She dropped a couple of bills on the tabletop. "Speaking of, you ready to head that way?"

Quint nodded and stood—after three tries. Ruby came around the table and wrapped her arm around his midsection to keep him from listing to one side or the other as they walked out to the parking lot. If her hand lingered on his ass a bit as he opened the passenger door, he'd blame it on the brew making him hallucinate.

In the truck, he leaned his head back and closed his eyes. When the truck rocked to a stop, he was surprised they were back in town already. "Didn't mean to fall asleep."

"No problem."

Maybe he'd had more to drink than he thought. His little one bedroom foreman's quarters had grown to a two-story Victorian. He rolled his head from one side to the other but the dwelling didn't morph into anything different. After a blink or two, recognition came through. "Your house?"

"Well, I, I have work in the morning. I could have dropped you off and drove your truck home, but then you'd be stranded out there until I could get back out and return the truck. This way, you can sleep it off here and head out at first light." Her smile was as big and bold as you please.

In his alcohol soaked brain, it made sense. Maybe.

She pulled the keys from the ignition. "You need help out of the truck?"

"Um, nope. I think I got it." He slid out the passenger side and almost instantly regretted the movement. Lights danced around his head and bells rang in his ears, but he'd be damned if he needed any other assistance.

He only tripped once going up the steps. In the living room he plopped down on the sofa, afraid his legs might not hold out too much longer. "I'm gonna feel this in the morning."

"Naw." Ruby sat next to him and settled her hand on his thigh.

Pangs stirred behind his fly—he was a man, not a eunuch after all—but nothing compared to the tsunami of desire that swept through him every time he even thought of Gillian.

"I know something that will make you feel better." She leaned in and settled her mouth on his.

Nothing. Nada. Zilch. He couldn't even muster the ardor to kiss her back. Too much beer? "I'm drunker than a skunk." He laughed against her lips. "Can't move."

"You don't have to. Let me." Her hand slid higher and her kisses moved to his ear, then neck. Quint tilted his head, rested it on the back of the sofa. He let his eyes slide shut. She tugged on the top button of his shirt.

His arms were too heavy to swat her away. He did want to swat her away, right?

The slow rubbing on his thigh coupled with the feather light kisses lulled him into a calm, relaxed state. Sleep-inducing warmth spread through him. He fought to stay awake, stay cognizant of Ruby.

Or was it Gillian?

He'd been with both women throughout the day, but they merged together in his mind. Two women, one who looked cowed eyed at him, the other who couldn't stand him half the time. One had held him by the heart and the other by a thread of friendship. But which was which? He couldn't remember anymore.

Ruby was his bud, his pal. Gillian, though, he wanted her with a fierceness that ached in the pit of his stomach—and every other area that made him male. He'd do just about anything to steal another kiss or two from her. To feel her warm skin beneath him.

He moaned and let his head role to the side. "Mmm, Gillian..."

Chapter Ten

Quint's tongue had a sweater. A woodpecker had taken up residence in his skull. It took three tries to pry his gritty eyes open—a move he immediately regretted. Bright sun streamed in through the huge bay window.

He frowned. He didn't have a bay window.

Scratching his hand through his hair—hell, even his hair hurt—he glanced around and surveyed the area. Ruby's house. How had he gotten there?

He sat up and a piece of paper fluttered to the floor. His name stood out on it written in Ruby's big, bold handwriting.

Had to leave for work. Your keys are next to the coffee pot.

No mention of how or why he was sacked out on her sofa. He scrubbed his hand over his face. The last thing he remembered was Gillian storming off at the Cates' party. Everything after that was hazy at best.

His unbuttoned shirt fell open when he stood looking for his boots, which sat at the end of the sofa. With his feet shoved into the boots, he checked the clock on the mantle. Half past ten.

"Holy hell." He should have been at work three hours earlier. Ryder and Heidi half an hour after that. Nausea rolled in his stomach and burned the back of his throat. He smacked his lips together and tried to alleviate the dry mouth but it did little good. He couldn't remember the last time he'd had a killer hangover. College maybe. Even then he hadn't drunk so much he couldn't recall a single detail.

Massaging his temple shooed away the woodpecker, but nothing was forthcoming.

The fading aroma of fresh brewed coffee lessened the gurgling in his stomach. He wandered into the kitchen and found his keys next to a half-empty pot. A note up against a mug read: *help yourself.*

He washed down a couple of aspirin with a lukewarm cup of coffee, Mr. Coffee long since off duty for the day. He snapped up the phone on the counter and phoned Jacob.

"Hey. Sorry," he said when his friend and employer answered the phone.

"For?"

He frowned. "Being late."

"Ruby called. Told me it'd probably be noon before you made it in."

"She did? Did she say why?"

Jacob chuckled. "No. But when a woman calls in for a man, you tend not to ask too many personal questions."

Quint groaned and closed his eyes. "And the kids?"

"I had Ryder and Heidi ride out and check fences before they did the feeding. They got done and left about twenty minutes ago. Didn't see any point in keeping them around."

"Thanks." He tucked the phone in the crook between his shoulder and chin, then rinsed out his mug and set it in the draining pan next to the sink. "I have to make a couple of quick stops and I'll be there as soon as I can."

He hung up with Jacob and scooped up his keys.

It took a little snooping from one window to the next to

figure out where his truck was. It sat out right smack-dab in front of Ruby's house, at the curb. He sucked up his pride and headed out the front door into the bright, morning sunlight and wild speculations that would circulate if folks saw him.

Doing the walk of shame at ten-thirty in the morning on the most populated street in town was just about last on his list. Next only to taking his dad up on a job offer and getting all his teeth removed with a hammer. Halfway to a clean getaway, two of Ruby's neighbors looked up from their yards where they stood gabbing over the hedges with one another. Huge smiles split their faces—and he'd just given them fodder for the next day or two.

"Morning, ladies." He raised his hand and waved as he slid into his truck.

A few blocks down, he pulled into the lot at the Paintbrush Motel—time to face up to whatever it was he'd done the night before. His hands shook. He hadn't been nervous around Ruby since... never. Since he'd met her, they'd been easy friends and never had a cross word. Sure they'd rib each other from time to time, but it was all good-natured.

Ruby sat alone behind the register counter. Engrossed in a crossword, she glanced up at him when the bell over the door jangled.

An uncharacteristic pink tinted her cheeks. "Morning." She turned her gaze back to the puzzle and penciled something in before she set her book aside. "You look like shit."

"I feel like shit." He shoved his hands in his pockets. "I, uh..." He lowered his eyes, didn't have the balls to look at her not knowing what, if anything, had happened.

"You passed out cold the second your ass hit the sofa." She crossed her arms over her chest and leaned back in her chair. "If that's what you're wondering."

"I didn't, I wasn't. God, I was afraid of what I might have done to you."

Her eyebrow slashed up. "That repulsive to you, huh?"

Quint pulled his hands from his pockets and gripped the edge of the registration counter. "No. I'm glad to know I didn't hurt you or take advantage."

"Darlin', you were sucking up beer like it was soda. By the time we left, you could hardly stand. I don't think there would have been much trouble of you taking advantage of a hooker."

Something in the sharp edges of her tone skittered up his spine. Again, he fought to recall anything from the evening before. Nothing but a black hole.

Ruby pushed back her chair and stood. "I'd steer clear of the bar for a while though, you knocked over an entire stack of glasses on your way out. Was there anything else? I have some work to do." She grabbed her ring of room keys.

"No." He turned to go. "Thanks for being there."

Ruby just stared at him for a long moment. "That's what friends are for."

"What the hell is wrong with you?" Zan cornered Quint in the diner parking lot. He'd ordered a couple of lunches to-go, hoping food would lessen his boss's ire once he made it out to the ranch.

He settled the bag on his front seat and turned to his aunt. "I beg your pardon?"

Dressed in brightly colored scrubs, she thrust her still-gloved hands on her hips.

"Is that sanitary?" He pointed to the purple latex then leaned back against the truck. "How did you know where to find me? Did Missy call you after she took my order?"

She waved away his questions. "I got no less than three calls telling me you were sneaking out of Ruby's house first thing this morning."

"It was after ten. Hardly first thing. And I was so not sneaking."

She heaved out a sigh. "And Kyle called me to ask how you were holding up after you and the mustang had such a late night."

"Last time I checked, I was a grown man."

"Who lives in a small town where people feed on any kind of gossip."

He crossed his arms over his chest and shrugged. "It's hardly worth repeating."

"No? One of the most eligible bachelors takes one woman to a party—who he has been shamelessly flirty with since she got to town, not to mention moved her into his home."

He rubbed the spot on his chest that started to ache with his aunt's tirade. "Vacant home."

"*And* he leaves the party with another woman and is then seen coming out of her house the next morning." She shook her head.

Anger heated his gut. What he did and with whom was no one's business. "You're sounding remarkably like your older brother."

"And you're acting like a damn college boy." She spun on her clompy nursing shoes and left him standing alone in the diner parking lot. Over her shoulder, she called back to him, "You will have to grow up one of the days, Quinton Walters."

"Come with us." Missy leaned her elbows on the counter at the diner. "The whole town turns out for the picnic, then later we have a spectacular fireworks show." A huge smile crossed her face. "Cade will be here."

"I don't know..." Gillian gnawed on her lower lip. She didn't do well with crowds. Even more, she was afraid of running into Quint. She hadn't seen him since the night of the Cates' party—and that hadn't ended well for them. But oh, how she'd heard an earful from folks seeing him slink out of Ruby's house the next morning.

Gillian might not be adept at matters of dating and romance, but fickle still hurt. Not that she hadn't yelled at him and stormed off. It didn't lessen the ache when she thought of Quint with Ruby. Not that she had any reason for the pangs of jealousy or the sudden urge to rip the woman's hair out handful by handful.

So she'd kissed Quint a couple of times. A little necking does not a relationship make. Whether or not she was looking for a relationship—which she wasn't.

Then there were the gossips, the ladies who were in the diner when she'd come in for breakfast before work all week. They'd all been trying to decide how long anything had been going on between him and Ruby. No one could recall a single instance that would have given them a clue—and as they loved to gossip, it had to have been fodder for a while. Still, if he was coming out of Ruby's house, undoubtedly the pair had progressed past a "little necking".

The women all clammed up pretty quick when they saw her, but she'd managed to come in once or twice and overhear them, and what she missed, Missy was sure to fill in. She'd been part of the speculation as well, Missy had implied, but not outright said what all they'd supposed.

Gillian wanted to tell them how far off they were—the man

hadn't even bothered to call her once since the night of the party. It worked both ways. When the latch on the back door stuck, she'd wanted to call him to come out and fix it. Instead, she'd gone after it with a screwdriver until it was broken for sure. Then she'd called Manny. He'd replaced it in a matter of minutes. Questions had hung in his eyes as to why she hadn't called the homeowner, but he was good at not prying.

After that, she'd set aside part of her check to give Quint as rent. Then, if or when, she needed to have him out, it would be as tenant and landlord. Nothing more, nothing less. There'd be no reason for any awkwardness.

"Pretty please, Mom." Heidi bounced up and down next to Gillian, tearing her from self-pity-dom. "We *should* go. Can we, please?" She clasped her hands together in front of her and poked out her bottom lip.

"Are you six or sixteen?" Gillian glanced over her shoulder and stared out the diner window at all the red, white and blue bunting lining Main Street. When was the last time she and her daughter had done anything celebratory? She turned back to Missy. "Do we need to bring anything?"

Chapter Eleven

The borrowed quilt and pan of brownies she'd made grew heavier with each step. She considered turning back and holing up in the small house until all the town hoopla was finished. One look at the huge smile on her daughter's face, though, kept her trudging down Main Street to the field back behind the community center.

"There's Ryder." Heidi tucked her hair behind her ear. She'd worn it down, even curled it a little. "Can I go sit with him?"

"Sure, you go..." Heidi was gone before Gillian could even finish speaking. "...ahead."

"Teenagers," Quint spoke from behind her. "Need an extra hand? Or two?" He snagged the pan from her hand and lifted up the tin foil. "Mmm. Brownies. My favorite."

"Everything's your favorite," she mumbled under her breath. "Why limit yourself? To anything."

"What's that?"

"Nothing." Gillian followed him to the dessert table. Her insides did somersaults. Now she really regretted coming to the picnic.

"These smell so good."

She pasted on a polite smile. "You're a guy. If it's even remotely edible you think it's good."

"That's true. Quint will eat just about anything." Ruby joined the pair at the table. "Doesn't have a discerning bone in his body when it comes to food. And sometimes other things." The woman's smile didn't quite reach her eyes as she looked Gillian up and down.

If Quint hadn't gone home with Ruby after the party, Gillian might find it amusing. Was Ruby just protecting her territory? For whatever reason, the woman still saw her as a rival.

Quint cleared his throat. "Would you like to join me and Ruby? We have a couple of seats saved over there." He motioned to the other side of the field. Ruby crossed her arms over her chest and raised an eyebrow with a "like hell" expression.

Gillian considered saying yes, to make Ruby squirm, but as fun as that would be, Missy promised to save a seat for her. "Thanks, that would be nice." She eyed Ruby whose cheeks reddened. "But, no." She turned and left without so much as a backward glance.

A smile spread across her mouth, and for the first time, the outing wasn't so horrible.

She made her way through the small crowd, looking for Missy. All she needed to do was look for the largest cluster of people. Cade Holstrom had come to Paintbrush for the Fourth of July celebration. Despite being a break-out star in Hollywood with a couple of "singing cowboy" movies, out behind the community center in Paintbrush, Wyoming, he was a neighbor come home. And everyone wanted to squeeze in and say hello.

Gillian had heard some of the gossip surrounding him. His older brother Dale was in prison for attempted murder—of Quint's aunt of all people. When she'd heard the story it was the first and only tarnish anyone had ever put on Paintbrush. But no one held it against Cade. They all spoke of him like he was some dignitary. Gillian had spied his mother once at the grocers. If the cashier hadn't pointed her out, she'd never have known that woman was once the queen of the town. She was dressed in nothing more than rags.

Apparently, she and her husband had divorced after their son went to prison and the husband took off with the family fortune. Missy told her that Cade sent money, but it didn't look like the woman ever tapped into the bank account. Plus, she was embarrassed to show her face in town—even though folks didn't seem to hold any ill will toward her. But after what her middle child did... It must be hard with the yin and yang of offspring. Rumor had it their eldest son, Bart, was off in Vegas or somewhere living it up, spending what was left of his trust fund.

At least with Cade's return some of the focus on the new girl shifted to talk of why he'd come to town and if he and Missy would rekindle an old romance. Gillian should thank him for taking the heat off her. She snorted. At the Fourth of July picnic, she didn't think it prudent to bring it up. Especially since she'd yet to lay eyes on the man—in person.

"Gillian, come here."

As if she'd conjured up the invite to meet him, Missy called her into the middle of the group. The woman's eyes lit up and a flush colored her cheeks. If the look on her face was any indication, Missy was all for rekindling whatever spark might exist between the pair. She pushed past a couple of people and grabbed Gillian's hand. "Cade, this is Gillian."

The young Hollywood star removed his cowboy hat and nodded. "Nice to meet you, ma'am." His blond hair was cut shorter than it had been in his last picture. It didn't detract from the heart-stopping beauty, though. He was such a handsome man it almost hurt to look at him. But the genuine smile that lit up his cerulean blue eyes made her comfortable, not the least bit uneasy, since he *was* a celebrity.

"How long will you get to stay in town for?" Gillian shifted the quilt on her arm.

"Here, let me get that for you." He shoved his hat back on his head and took the quilt from her then settled it on the back of a chair. "I'll be here a week or two. My agent's working on a new contract, so right now I'm in between projects." He crossed his arms and leaned a hip against the table. "How's your arm? Missy mentioned you'd gotten hurt during the last storm."

Gillian's cheeks warmed with a quick blush, but with the early afternoon heat it would be hard to tell—hopefully. It was surreal having this conversation. "It itches like crazy."

He beamed a million-watt smile again at her. "I'll bet."

"Mom, we're going to go up to the grocer's and grab a couple of things for Hank." Heidi held a slip of paper and dragged Ryder behind her by the sleeve. She didn't so much as drool or swoon over Cade Holstrom.

Gillian frowned. Her daughter was way further gone with her puppy love for Ryder. A scary prospect. Maybe they should go now, before Heidi was too far gone—if it wasn't already too late.

"Cade, can you give me a hand?" Missy's smile hadn't wavered.

"Excuse me." The man tipped his hat at Gillian and hurried over to Missy's side.

Zan, Jacob and their daughters settled in around the other end of the table. They all waved.

"It's nice being someplace where folks are always welcoming." Bonnie Carmichael pulled out the chair next to Gillian and sat.

"Mmm." A non-committal grunt was all she could manage. The tightness in her throat threatened to asphyxiate her. Bonnie Carmichael had voiced her thoughts and, at the same time, her fears. Having people around to watch out for you could also lend itself to someone getting too close and poking their nose into business they had no right to intrude upon. Someone breaking down the wall she'd spent a number of years constructing after her sister's murder and her mother's death.

Gillian glanced over to Quint's table. How many times can someone bang into that wall before it starts to crack and possibly crumble completely? And what might that person think about what they found on the other side? Too much insecurity and damage? Too much past that couldn't be put behind?

Not that he'd be the one knocking on walls. He was otherwise occupied with one protective female.

Gillian shook off her melancholy. It was hard to let her thoughts grow so sad with the wonderful weather and all the folks around having a good time. She sat and just listened while the small group chatted about everything from Jacob's plans for Skipping Rocks Ranch to their opinions on the next job Cade Holstrom should take.

Half an hour later, Hank came over to the table. He shook hands with Cade and made small talk for a few minutes. As he was leaving he asked Missy, "You wouldn't happen to know where that your son of yours has gotten himself off to? He was supposed to be back ages ago."

"No, Daddy, sorry. Do you need me to go find him?"

He shrugged. "Naw. He's gotten himself somewhere. I'll find him eventually." He headed back to the food table.

Gillian scanned the area for Ryder and Heidi. She'd assumed they'd come back already. Panic rose in her chest. She excused herself from the conversation and headed toward the grocer's.

She cradled the cast in her other arm to keep from swinging into anyone as she wended her way through the ever increasing crowd. By the time she turned the corner onto Main Street she was almost at a run and she smashed into a firm, warm chest.

"Hey, where's the fire?" Quint smiled down at her.

She took a step back to keep the man from invading her space. Something he was constantly doing. "I'm, uh." Her voice cracked. "Looking for Heidi."

"Is everything okay?"

"It will be when I find my daughter."

Quint's smile broadened. He glanced over his shoulder and stepped farther into her path, blocking the way. "She's fine. Let's take a walk." He snagged her elbow and tried to lead her back the way she came.

"What?" Gillian pulled free. "What's going on?" A riot of thoughts crowded around her head.

"Nothing."

"Quint, if you don't move so I can find my daughter so help me..." She shook with fear and rage.

His smile fled quickly. "Gillian, darlin', calm down."

"Move." She pushed past him and stopped hard in her tracks.

Standing next to the cottonwood tree in front of the grocer's, Heidi and Ryder were...kissing. Heat flamed through Gillian's cheeks. "Oh."

She retreated until her back came flush with Quint. He wrapped his arm around her middle and guided her back behind the building, out of view of the necking teens.

Laughter rumbled in his chest and vibrated against her back.

"You knew?" she whispered, fighting her own laughter.

Quint ducked his head, his mouth right up against her ear.

"Yeah, about ten seconds before you. Hank asked me to come find Ryder." He paused and his breath feathered her hair. "I didn't want to embarrass them."

His thumb rubbed back and forth over her stomach. His laughter subsided, but his heart beat a steady tattoo against her back. More of a comfort than Gillian thought possible.

He took a deep breath. "You want me to break them up?"

Did she?

Of course she did. While she wanted Heidi to have a normal adolescence, what little was left, she didn't want her to become too attached, for when they had to move again—and it was only a matter of when not if—she didn't want Heidi to pine away for something she couldn't have.

"Yes."

He held her a moment longer, gave her a quick squeeze, then released her. He settled his hand on her elbow and turned her to face him. "Do you want Heidi to know *you* caught her?"

She gnawed her lip. No one ever said parenting was easy. It didn't come with an owner's manual. No instructions for this— and when she was a teen she'd never even come close to a boy to be found kissing.

"Tick tock." Quint tapped her on the nose. He peeked around the corner. "They're getting an extraordinarily long amount of...face time."

She scanned the space between the buildings where they both stood. "One sec." She wedged herself behind a stack of empty crates. "Knock yourself out."

Quint gave a high pitched whistle. "Ryder?"

There was a momentary pause then the teen hollered back, "Yeah?"

Quint's boots crunched on something as he rounded the

corner. "Hey, bud, your granddad's looking for you."

Gillian held her breath as the scuffle of feet grew between the buildings. She didn't dare try to catch a peek of her daughter; she might not be able to keep her mouth shut.

After a minute or two the crates shifted and Quint's hand reached around the stack. "Coast is clear."

Quint waited to see if she would actually take his hand. When she did, he was hard-pressed not to pull her tight up against him again.

Did she know how perfectly she fit to him? Did she know how much his heart raced any time she came near?

Of course not. He hadn't paid her one lick of attention in over a week. He'd acted like the jackass his aunt had all but accused him of being. He'd stayed away from her, hoping whatever lust and want that had clogged up his judgment would pass and he'd be able to get on with his life. The opposite happened. He'd fantasized about her night after night. After a few days, he'd hung around town longer than need be when he came through running errands, hoping to get a glance of her.

Worse than longing for the sight of her was the hunger for conversation. He'd had no pretenses with her, didn't feel any of the demands he did with other folks. She held zero expectations for him. He'd picked up the phone several times to call—only to remember how he'd left things with her. He should have apologized, right away, admitted what an ass he'd been and how he'd messed up things between them. So many things he could say, so many things he wanted to share, but pride kept him away from the one person who pulled his attention.

Plain and simple, he'd missed her.

He sure as hell wasn't going to tell her, though. The look on her face when he'd asked her to sit with him at the picnic... He shook his head.

"Thanks." The corner of her mouth tilted up. "You know, you're a pretty thoughtful guy."

A spark of hope floated around him when she didn't immediately release his hand. "You say that like it's a rarity."

"To me it is." She sighed. "And it's nice."

"Then why didn't you want to sit with me?" Damn. He could kick himself for saying it aloud.

Gillian's gaze shot up to his. "And get between you and Ruby? No thanks."

His short bark of laughter echoed between the buildings as they strolled slowly. "We're just friends."

"She doesn't seem to think so. Any time anyone—any female—comes near, Ms. Ruby all but starts snarling and baring her teeth."

"She's not like that." He ran his finger along his collar, all of the sudden a little tighter than a few minutes before. Sure Ruby had a crush on him when he'd moved to town, but they'd become friends. Nothing more. He'd never intimated anything stronger. Had he?

"She's exactly like that." She glanced up at him. "I may be new here, but I'd bet if you ask anyone in town, they would tell you as much. People around here love nothing more than something juicy to talk about."

Zan was right about the gossip churning through town. Folks had speculated about him and Ruby from the beginning. They hadn't even bothered to do it behind his back. It had died down some. Until the Cates' party. He'd talked to Ruby about it again and confirmed nothing had happened when he'd drunk himself into oblivion. If she was so hot for him why would she lie about *not* doing anything with him? "We're just friends."

"Does she know that?"

"Yes. And hopefully so do you."

She blinked up at him, her forehead pulled down with a huge crease for a brief moment. Then she shrugged and her face smoothed out. "It's kinda cute really. A big strapping thing like yourself and you have your own personal guard dog."

He waggled his eyebrows at her. "You think I'm a big strapping thing?" He jumped at the chance to change the subject.

"Man, your ego does not need any help, does it?"

"Are you offering it up a boost or something?" He pulled on their clasped hands and stopped her. "'Cause you know, I'm always in need of a boost."

"I could go holler at Ruby for ya." She motioned with her cast. A wicked smile curled her lips.

"No, I think I'm good right here. Right now."

"I, um…"

"With you." Quint walked her backward until she came up against the building, hidden from any passersby.

The mischief on her face faded. Her lips parted, but she didn't utter a single word.

With his free hand, he stroked the backs of his knuckles down her soft, creamy cheek. "You're so beautiful."

Slowly he leaned in, gave her a chance to protest or move away. Nose to nose, he waited a heartbeat before he captured her mouth with his.

It seemed like a lifetime rather than only a couple weeks since the rainstorm when they'd first kissed. Or even the week earlier at the garage. It was never enough. He always craved more.

He ran his tongue across the seam of her lips, teasing, enticing. When she opened to him, he let her warmth envelope him as he held her small hand clasped in his. His other hand slid from her cheek up into the hair at the nape of her neck, the soft locks sliding between his fingers.

Quint itched to feel more, to slide his hand up under the light blue T-shirt she wore. But he didn't want to spook her by moving too fast. It took every bit of effort to step back and disengage himself.

Gillian's blue eyes fluttered open. A crimson blush darkened her cheeks. "Wow."

A huge smile spread across his mouth. "I knew you'd know just what to say."

The corner of her mouth tilted. "Yep. Ego the size of Wyoming."

"Don't you mean Montana?"

She frowned. "Huh?"

"That's where you were heading when you got here."

Gillian released his hand and pushed away from the wall so quickly Quint didn't have time to react. He hurried to catch up to her. "Hey. Did I say something wrong?"

"Don't be silly."

"Talk to me." Quint jogged until he could cut her off. "What just happened?"

"Nothing happened." She toyed with the edge of her cast.

"I don't mean to pry." He cupped her elbow. "Okay, maybe I do. Every time anything remotely personal comes up, you change the subject or shut down completely." He tried not to think of the heat seeping from her into him. He'd like nothing more than to go back to kissing her and teasing her. The seriousness that rolled across her face was so intense it twisted his gut. "I'm trying to get to know you. But you're not making it easy."

Gillian frowned. "Why?"

"I'm guessing someone hurt you pretty deep."

She gave a quick laugh. "I mean, why are you trying to get to know me?"

As soon as the words left her mouth a spark of déjà vu flitted through her from her conversation with Heidi after Quint's job offer.

Quint's eyebrows knitted together. "What kind of question is that?"

"A dumb one." She pulled her elbow free. She didn't want him to feel how badly her entire body shook. "I need to get back to the picnic."

"I want to be your friend. I am your friend. Friends get to know each other. Learn about each other. They talk to each other." He reached for her face, but pulled his hand back and tucked his hands into his pockets. "I'm a good listener."

There were a lot of things Quint Walters was good at. Not least of which was confusing her. When he was near she didn't know which end was up. "There's that ego again. Is there anything you're not good at?"

He shifted his gaze up toward the sky for a moment. "Modesty."

Gillian shook her head.

"Tell ya what." He started walking and led her back to the rest of the picnickers. "Come sit next to me during the fireworks tonight."

She scoffed. "Uh, no."

"Come sit with me."

"And have your guard dog nipping at my heels?" Gillian shook her head. "No thank you."

"We can talk. No hanky-panky. No judgment. Just someone to listen to whatever you want to talk about. Or not talk at all." They came to her table and stopped. "What could it hurt?"

What indeed? Again, the wall's integrity threatened to disintegrate. She sighed. "I'll think about it."

"You do that." He tapped the tip of her nose and left to find his table.

Gillian sat heavily in her seat. She wanted to go bury herself under the covers of the huge bed and block out everything. Except the feel of Quint's lips on hers. And the tender way he caressed her cheek. Whether he wanted to admit it or not, he was a damn nice guy and it *was* a rare thing.

"Mom, I was looking for you. Where have you been?" Heidi plopped down beside Gillian.

"I was out looking for you."

The teen's cheeks pinkened. "I've been here and there."

And under the tree with Ryder Lunsford. Gillian wouldn't bring it up at the picnic, but later, they'd talk for sure.

"Can I get you a plate?" Heidi stood and pulled at the hem of her short shorts.

"No thanks, hon. You go on ahead."

The rest of the afternoon blurred into early evening. Food disappeared as fast as it hit the tables. People talked and laughed. Gillian managed to relax in slow degrees, but just before dusk as the sun slid being the Big Horn Mountains, her nerves tightened. Quint and his offer to "talk" taunted her.

Maybe he forgot. He was sitting with Ruby. And no matter what he said, that woman had a proprietary hold over her friend. It wasn't even just Gillian. Ruby crossed her arms over her chest and frowned at any woman under sixty who dared come within eyelash-batting range of the man.

"I think I'm going to head back to the house." Gillian stood from her chair and lifted the quilt.

"Are you okay?" Missy swiped at her mouth with a napkin. A smudge of chocolate sat on the corner of her mouth.

"You have a little, right—" Gillian motioned to her own mouth.

Cade leaned back in his chair. "I got it." He slowly ran his thumb over Missy's lips and wiped off this chocolate.

The intimacy between the two was too much to bear so Gillian slipped away while they were distracted.

She found Heidi, Ryder and a group of teens setting up seats with Hank. She motioned her daughter over. "I'm heading back to the house. My arm's bothering me." True enough. She tried not to ever lie to her daughter and it *had* been aching all day, though really she was running from a man who wanted to be her *friend*.

"Do I need to...?" Heidi volleyed her gaze over to Ryder.

"No, sweetie. You stay. But be home right after the fireworks show, okay?" She gave Heidi a quick hug. "Get back to work before Hank comes looking for you."

Heidi flashed a quick smile. "Aw, he's a big old teddy bear. Love you." She ran back over to the small group and grabbed another chair from the stack.

"Not trying to sneak away, are you?"

Gillian almost stumbled at Quint's words. She pivoted slowly around. He stood, leaning up against a stack of chairs.

"Who me?" She pasted on a bright smile. "Wouldn't think of it."

"Yeah." He straightened. "I have us a spot over here. Follow me."

"Where's your guard dog?"

He glanced back over his shoulder at her and smiled. "Ruby had a late check-in and had to go in to work. Then she has to run up to Sheridan to see her mama."

"And she let you stay here all by yourself?"

"Be nice or I won't share my popcorn with you." He stopped at a dark, plaid blanket with a huge bowl of popcorn, a bottle of wine and two fluted glasses.

The little voice in the back of her head screamed at her to leave, but the warmth that spread up from belly rooted her in place. "This looks a little more than watching some fireworks."

"And talking." He rocked back on his boots and tipped his hat back. "Or not talking."

"Quint."

"Nothing more. I swear. Cross my heart." With his index finger he made an X on his chest. "I have a couple of pillows to prop your cast up on. So your arm doesn't hurt." His smile broadened.

"Were you eavesdropping on me?"

"Who me?" He patted his chest and rounded out his eyes all innocent-like.

"Now you're mocking me." Gillian couldn't help but smile.

"Wouldn't dream of it." Quint held out his hand to her. "Sit?"

He helped her get comfortable, stacked a couple of pillows up for her cast and poured her a glass of wine before he joined her on the blanket.

"Cheers." He held his glass up.

Gillian clinked her glass to his. "Cheers."

Townsfolk milled about for a few minutes until the mayor announced the show would begin soon.

"Would you believe this is my first time ever watching

169

fireworks?"

Quint paused while tossing a piece of popcorn in the air. The kernel bounced off his forehead. "Are you serious?"

Maybe it was the wine or maybe just the fact that when she was with Quint but a comfort she'd never known before washed over her. She wasn't sure she wanted to talk to someone. To unburden herself. She'd confided in Manny, but only about what made them leave, not what made her tick. No one had heard that story. Explaining her lack of pyrotechnic gazing was an easy one though. "Growing up, it just wasn't something we did. It was just my mom, my sister and I. As I told you before, dad was gone early on. When we spent time together—if we had time together—we'd always end up just talking and never get anything done."

Gillian ran her finger around the edge of the wine glass, remembering. The Harwood women had many a late night talking about anything and everything. God, how she missed her mom and Becca. "Then once Heidi got here—" she shrugged, "—I never had time for much of anything."

"With your mom and sister both gone—" he shook his head, "—is it hard? Raising Heidi all alone?"

"Yes and no." She took a long drink from her glass. "I don't really have anything to compare it to. It's had its bright spots and its difficult moments." One in particular that she didn't think she'd ever get out from under.

"That's rough."

"You have no idea," she said under her breath. "What about you? I know Bonnie and Zan are close by. Do you miss not having other family around here?"

Quint leaned back on his elbows and crossed his legs at the ankles. "Thank God, no."

Gillian jumped at the first explosion in the sky. Green and

blue light shimmied over Quint's face.

"Why don't you get along with your dad?" She scooted closer to him to hear over all of the noise. "Are y'all too different?"

She saw rather than heard his huge sigh as his chest rose and fell highlighted with the neon flash of light.

"It's not that. I got tired of letting my dad down."

"I can't believe that." She frowned. "How could you have let him down? You're the most conscientious, selfless person I've met."

"You don't know my dad." He tilted his head toward her. "Or maybe you do. Jeffery Walters."

Gillian shook her head and shrugged.

"From the Texas Rangers and—"

"Like Chuck Norris?"

His teeth flashed white with a quick grin. "No, like baseball. He played for the Rangers for a bit. But he spent most of his career with the San Diego Padres."

"Gotcha." She wished he smiled more when he spoke of his father. Instead, his mouth turned down and his eyes squinted around the edges. "But you followed in his footsteps, playing ball."

"For all of five minutes." Quint frowned. "How did we start talking about me?"

Gillian shoved a handful of popcorn in her mouth and shrugged.

"You're not going to tell me anything are you, despite my magnanimous offer to listen?"

"Uh-uh."

"I should just sit back and watch the fireworks."

"Uh-huh."

"Pass the popcorn, please."

Gillian set the bowl between them. The pair ate in silence and watched the show. When the bowl was halfway empty, they both went in and their hands tangled.

Quint didn't let go. He pulled her hand up to his mouth and stuck her index finger between his lips. "Mmm. Salty."

Gillian closed her eyes.

The man did *things* to her. Things she never thought she'd experience—maybe not never, but someday in the distant future when Heidi was grown and on her own, assuming they could get from under the trouble they were in... With Quint however, she lost fear, lost inhibitions she'd developed early on. She could breathe and tension eased from every fiber of her being. She was so relaxed, she shifted and her cast slid off the pile of pillows and hit on the hard-packed ground under the blanket.

"Ow." Her eyes shot open and she ripped her hand from his to cradle her throbbing arm.

Quint sat up. "You okay?"

"Hurts." Tears welled up.

"Take a deep breath. Now another." He rubbed her back. "You want me to walk you home?"

She nodded. Quint helped her stand. Colors danced across the sky as they wended through the seated crowd. She should go back and sit, watch the show. The pain would subside, but so many emotions raged through her she needed the quiet of the house to think. To digest the way Quint stirred the want in her.

They walked the few short blocks back to the house in silence. By the time they pushed through the front door, the pain had in fact subsided and guilt took its place.

"I'm so sorry." Gillian stood in the doorway.

"For?"

"Making you miss the rest of the show."

Quint tucked a loose lock of her hair behind her ear. "Don't worry about it."

"You should go on back. Catch the end."

He removed his cowboy hat and scuffed his fingers through his hair. "I like where I am right now just fine."

Chapter Twelve

Gillian stared at him for a long moment. Her heart hammered so hard it rang in her ears. Indecision danced all through her. Without time to talk herself out of it, she shoved the door open wider. "Would you like to come in?"

"Thought I'd have to stand out here all night, mooning away."

Gillian snorted. "Like you've ever mooned over a woman."

"I could moon." He tossed the hat onto the end table. "I've just never had cause to. Before now."

She led him into the middle of the living room. "I never know when you're being for real and when you're trying for charming."

Quint tilted his head to the side. "Maybe they're one and the same."

She nodded. "Charming." She crossed the room toward the kitchen. "Can I get you something?"

"No. Sit. I should be asking you that." He motioned her over to the sofa.

He settled his hand at the small of her back and guided her across the room. Then he fluffed up two pillows for her cast and—with a smile—ordered her to "park it". Her cheeks heated as she sat.

Quint crouched in front of her. "Is the pain unbearable?" He lifted the cast in his hands, ran his thumb carefully over the backs of her fingers just peeking out from the end. "It doesn't look swollen. You want me to call Dr. Hambert?"

"No, actually it's feeling better." Gillian ducked her head. "I didn't want to tell you."

"Why? That's good."

She looked up and held his gaze. "I feel bad for making you leave the fireworks."

He chuckled. "There's plenty of sparks going on right here." He released her cast and set his hands on either side of her on the sofa. He leaned in and placed a soft kiss on her lips.

Gillian savored the moment. Wanted not to forget a single moment spent with Quint. She was afraid it might end far too soon. She committed the touch of his lips to hers to memory for those dark and lonely nights yet to come. She ran her fingers through his hair, desperately wanting to let the softness lull her into complacency. Too many thoughts, though, danced around her head. Not the least of which was her self-appointed rival. She pulled back. "What about Ruby?"

Quint shifted to sit next to her on the sofa and took her face in his hands. "Gillian, I swear to you, there is no other woman in my life. And hasn't been for a very long time."

And he hadn't cared one way or the other about his lack of companionship until Gillian came crashing into his world. She made him think things, made him contemplate the future. What he wanted to be when he grew—hell, *if* he wanted to grow up.

It was odd that his father had harped on him to make decisions and make "plans" for the future. All it took was one lost soul accidentally thrust into his life that helped put things into perspective, and to know it was time that he took charge of what he wanted. Unfortunately, his dad still wouldn't be happy with anything he might come up with. It wasn't *his* plan. Top of the "to do" list though was to figure out how and where Gillian Harwood fit into everything.

Gillian frowned up at him. "You look so serious."

Quint held her gaze as he slid his hands into her hair. "You are so damn beautiful." A blush crossed her cheeks and crawled down her neck. It was sexy and powerful all at the same time—to know she reacted so...so...much to him.

And it was mutual. There were so many things he wanted to say to her—so many things she *made* him want to say—but all he could think of as he settled his lips on her ear was, "I have wanted you since you ran me over."

"I did not..." Gillian trailed off in a whimper as his teeth nipped the tender lobe. "I didn't *mean* to run you over."

"Semantics." He needed to feel her. He slipped his hand up under her shirt, flattened his palm on her back.

"Do you always get what you want?" Gillian settled the clunky cast on his shoulder, wrapped her other arm around his neck and pulled his mouth down to hers.

The long, intense kiss made him momentarily forget the question she asked. "Do I get what I want? When I'm lucky," he said against her mouth.

"Are you feeling lucky?" She snuggled closer to him.

Quint scooped up her legs and draped them across his own. "When I'm with you? Always."

Her breath tickled when she sighed against his throat. He shifted, hoping to relieve some of the pressure in his jeans.

It didn't work.

Especially when she wriggled her ass against his erection.

The pressure that built inside him was so intense, to the

point of painful—a good painful—but painful nonetheless. "We need to get more comfortable." He leaned her back until she lay under him on the small sofa. He wedged himself between her thighs, and settled against her warmth.

Quint loosened his grip slightly and stoked her thigh in slow, meandering strokes, stopping just at the edge of her shorts.

Every second, every kiss he expected her to call a halt to it. Not that he wanted her to, but he sensed wariness in her, almost inexperience. Which was silly. She was well into adulthood. And had a child for goodness sake. It was an innocence, though, that added to her appeal. She had no pretenses. She didn't push or rush; she let him take charge even though she set the pace.

The whine and pop of the fireworks outside played an eerily similar soundtrack to the one going off in his head as he shifted his hand beneath her and kneaded her supple, round—spectacular—ass.

She was perfect. Soft where she needed to be soft, curvy in places that set his pulse to racing for more, to explore the parts hidden by clothing. It took every ounce of will not to strip Gillian bare then plunder her right there on the sofa.

He moaned as she deepened the kiss and let his tongue in to mingle with hers. She was so sweet, so warm, it set every part of him on fire.

Heat pooled in her stomach and worked out in every direction while he kissed her senseless. Thoughts of wanting his hands elsewhere, unencumbered by clothing, tumbled through her.

Gillian reached for the buttons on his shirt. Instead she grazed his ear and clunked his shoulder. "Damn cast." She flopped her head back and tears threatened the corners of her eyes. "I'm sorry." For smacking him with her cast. For not knowing what to do. Every new emotion swirled through her, fought with the fear and trepidation of going where she'd never been before.

"It's okay, darlin'." He sat up and yanked the shirt over his head, forgoing the buttons altogether.

God, he was beautiful. She'd seen him shirtless during the rainstorm, but she'd been otherwise preoccupied with the electricity shooting at them from the sky. He was all tan skin and not an ounce of flab. Sandy blond hairs covered his well-sculpted chest. She ran her fingers from his neck down to his waist and back. Too tempted, she leaned up and licked his collar bone. Salty and musky.

Quint groaned and slid his hand under her shirt to cup her breast. He ran his thumb across the tight peak coved in lace. When she looked up at him, he said, "If you want me to stop, say so. But soon, before I combust."

Instead of complaining or pushing him away, she covered his hand with hers. "Don't stop." She slanted her head back and closed her eyes, reveled in the feel of him touching her, caressing her. She'd never in a million years imagined the fire that raced through her. She'd like to think it was from sheer inexperience, but what did she have to compare it to? No man had ever touched her as intimately as Quint Walters.

The fabric of her shirt slid up, but she didn't dare open her eyes. Not even when he kissed her through the lacy bra. Before she could stop herself, her hips gyrated against him in rhythm to the kisses and the need to be closer to him grew until it hurt. "What are you doing to me?"

He nudged her chin with his lips. "You like?"

She peeled her eyes open and held his gaze. "Very much so." She turned her face to his and ran her lips greedily against

178

his. She traced the seam of his lips until he opened and let her sweep her tongue up against his. A moan rumbled the back of her throat.

Quint shifted and all but fell off the small sofa. He broke the kiss and stood with her in his arms then walked down the short hallway to the master bedroom and settled her on the middle of the bed. He gave her a pillow to put under the cast. "How's the arm?"

She gulped. "Fine."

"Are you sure?"

"Yes."

He cupped her cheek, ran his thumb over her lower lip. "Are you okay with this? Me and you?"

"Um, yes."

He gave a nervous, nasally laugh. "You don't sound too convincing."

"It's not that." Gillian wasn't sure what to say. A few pertinent details had been left out. She sighed. "The thing about Heidi... Once Heidi came along..." She smoothed back his hair from his forehead. How do you tell someone you've been lying to them? From the moment you met them. Her hands shook as she debated what to say, how much to say.

Quint leaned forward, set his lips to her to her forehead and kissed her softly. "I can leave."

It would be the hardest damn thing he'd ever done, but for her, he was willing to go as slow—however maddeningly—as possible.

Gillian stared into his eyes. "No, I want this. I want you. More than I can tell you."

Quint's heart pounded as all the blood rushed to his dick

179

and made him harder than he thought feasible.

"I want you too, darlin'." He coaxed her back onto the pile of pillows. "First order of business, you have too many layers of clothing." He helped her undress; her cast made it necessary for *him* to strip her down to all her glorious, creamy skin. He quickly undressed, too and joined her back on the bed.

Her gaze was transfixed on his dick. He'd be damned if it didn't swell even more.

"You're so...big." She gulped.

How would she take it if he stood on the bed and beat his chest? He wanted to.

Tentatively, she reached and touched the tip. He sucked in a quick breath as all thought fled.

She frowned. "Did I hurt you?"

If Quint wasn't so damn horny and almost ready to explode he might start to question her past sexual experiences. Did the guys she'd been with just wham-bam-thank-you-ma'am and not give her time to explore and enjoy? Now was not the time to ask. But he'd be damned sure to give her all she needed.

He rolled to his back. "Touch me all you want."

She ogled him with a mixture of wonder and awe before she wrapped her hand around him. He covered her hand with his and drew it up and down his rigid cock. Up and down, and again.

Tension crackled through his nerves. He let her stroke him until he couldn't take it any longer. He stilled her hand. "Okay, okay, okay."

"Not good?'

"Too good." Again he wanted to question her, but another time. He slid his hand over her hip, then eased between her thighs. He swept his fingers across her clit and teased the small bud until her eyes slammed shut and her mouth parted on a shuddered sigh.

He fondled her until she was wet and ready for him. "Almost forgot." He leaned over the edge of the bed and snapped up his jeans. He dug through his pocket until he found the little foil packet.

"You're awfully sure of yourself." Something between anger and hesitation laced her words.

He shook his head. "A habit my daddy impressed upon me in high school. Better to be prepared than staring down the barrel of a shotgun."

"I..." She chuckled. "I don't know quite how to respond to that."

Quint slid the condom on. "No need." He leaned forward and kissed her deeply, and wedged himself between her thighs. He glided the tip of his cock along the edges of her folds. Back and forth. Until she was writhing against him. He stopped kissing her and watched her as he slid inside her. There was a moment of resistance and her eyes jolted open briefly, but he was so wrapped up in the moment he could have hardly slowed down.

Gillian turned her head to the side. If he wasn't mistaken a tear or two slid down her cheeks, but before he could explore it further, she matched his thrusts and it brought him right to the edge again. He was so close right there, but he wanted her to come first.

He squeezed his hand between them and teased her clit, rubbed the nub until she shuddered beneath him and warmth surrounded him. Only then did he allow himself to trip over the edge and join her.

Quint's breathing evened out. For a moment Gillian

thought he'd nodded off. When she was about to get up and let him sleep, he ran his hands over his face and through his hair. He shifted up on his elbow and regarded her with wary eyes. He opened his mouth twice, closed it again until he finally said, "Why didn't you tell me? That you were a virgin."

"Not really a conversation starter. 'Oh, by the way, you're the first guy I've ever slept with.'" She took several deep breaths, tried to steady her nerves. "I got caught up in the moment." What else could she say? That she'd *wanted* him to be her first. That she was actually afraid he'd stop if he knew the truth.

A deep frown creased his forehead. "Wait a minute. How is Heidi...if you're...?" He sat up so quickly, Gillian couldn't hang on to the sheet. She covered her bare breast with her crossed arms; the rough cast abraded her sensitive skin.

"I think you need to explain."

The harsh tone to his voice cut through her gut. "I *am* Heidi's mother."

Quint shifted his feet off the bed and turned his back to her. "That's not possible."

"My sister Becca gave birth to her. When Becca...died, I adopted Heidi."

There was a long moment of silence before he asked, "How old were you, when your sister died?"

"Eighteen."

"Man." Quint ran a hand over his neck. "How old were you when Heidi was born?"

"Fourteen."

His shoulders stiffened. "So you're thirty?"

Gillian narrowed her eyes at his back. "What does it matter?"

He turned and looked at her. "I'm wondering how many other things you've lied about."

"I never lied about my age. No one ever asked me. If you assumed something, that's not my fault. I *am* Heidi's mother legally, emotionally and anyway that matters. Anything past that is none of your damn business." She hurried from the bed and scooped up her T-shirt. "You know, you have a lot of nerve. I have a child I have to take care of, to protect. If I neglect to give you information that will keep her safe..." She shook with anger. "When have you ever had to be accountable for anyone other than yourself, been responsible for any damn thing?"

"Who are you to judge me? I didn't come waltzing in to town pretending to be all these things that I'm not."

"I have not pretended..." All the fire and heat of anger drained away from her. Why was she fighting? Whether the intent was not the same, he was right. She'd lied through omission. She'd deceived him. She expected him to accept it as no big deal, when her way of dealing with it was to ignore it. He was entitled to his anger, but she didn't have to sit there and let him lecture her.

In an almost whispered voice she said, "I think maybe you should leave."

"I think maybe you're right." Quint rummaged around the room until he was fully dressed.

Once he walked out and down the hall, Gillian flopped back onto the bed. She cried, but only for a minute. She had never wallowed in self-pity and had no plans to start now. She scrambled around the room and gathered up her clothes then dressed. The front door slammed and she sat heavy on the bed. A moment later, Heidi popped her head around the corner of the bedroom door.

"You sleeping already?"

Gillian's cheeks flamed. "I, uh..." How was she going to explain Quint's leaving?

"You look funny. Do I need to call someone for you? Missy? Quint?"

"Quint?"

"He's probably still out at the field. Do you want me to go find him?"

How had he gotten out of the house without her daughter seeing him? Gillian scrubbed her hand over her face. "No. I'm fine."

"Are you sure? You look terrible."

"Thanks." She smiled and patted the bed next to her. "So tell me, how was it?"

Heidi smiled broader than Gillian had seen in well over a year. "It was so cool. I have never seen so many fireworks in my life. Well, I've never seen any in person before anyway."

Gillian's chest tightened. Just chalk it up to another way she'd failed. Tears threatened again, but she would not let them fall in front of her daughter.

Heidi continued talking. "Then Ryder walked me all the way home."

"Did he kiss you good night?"

"Mo-om."

"What?" Gillian sighed. "I know we had 'the talk' when you were twelve, but it doesn't cover what it's like when your heart is involved."

Heidi frowned. "What's that?"

Gillian chuckled. "Don't change the subject."

"No, look." Heidi pointed to the window.

An orange light emanated from the backyard.

"Fireworks?" Gillian rose from the bed determined not to look back at the rumpled sheets and the reminder of what she'd shared with Quint and how quickly it had turned.

Heidi snagged the back of Gillian's shirt. "No. They ended fifteen minutes ago."

Gillian pulled the curtain aside. The little shed in the backyard was on fire. Embers rained down within feet of the back of the house.

"Call the fire department." Gillian ran through the house and out into the yard in her bare feet and turned on the backyard hose but the deficient water pressure did little to battle the flames. It was difficult to hold the hose with her cast behind her back, but she did manage to soak the grass pretty well. But if any of the embers floated up to the roof of the house...

"They're coming." Heidi ran up beside Gillian. "What can I do?"

"I want you to run down to Missy's house and stay there until I come get you."

Heidi grabbed Gillian's shoulder and pulled her toward the house. "Mom?"

"Just go." Gillian jerked free and motioned Heidi toward the back gate. "Now."

The teen left with no more argument. A few minutes later the first of the fire department arrived, hoses, axes and all. Quint led the charge.

"You need to get out of here. Let us take over."

Though he was in fireman mode, his matter of fact tone might as well have been a slap across her face. She handed him the running hose and hurried around the house to the front lawn. A couple more of the fireman showed up and joined Quint in the back. Hank arrived a couple of minutes later. "You okay, girl?"

"Yes."

He nodded and rushed to the back with the other men.

Time passed in slow motion as neighbor after neighbor joined her on the front lawn. Missy ran down the block with Cade right behind her. "Hey, hon."

"Is Heidi okay?" Gillian tightened her arms around herself.

"She's fine. I wanted to come check on *you*." Missy looped her arm over Gillian's shoulders.

"I'm fine." She said the words, but the trembling throughout her body screamed otherwise.

She couldn't shake the fear that Rick had found her, but he couldn't have. There was no way he could possibly find her and Heidi in Wyoming. Even if he'd tracked them to Montana, her little accident that put them in a town she'd never heard of and should make it impossible for him to find the Harwoods. But as he'd already proven, he was quite the resourceful man.

Still she didn't think a fire—of her shed—was his style. The man had torched the home of his girlfriend after he murdered her knowing full-well her daughter was somewhere inside. If he'd gotten this close to them, there would be no doubt. It still didn't explain what was going on.

Her knees shook. "I need to sit down."

Missy steered her to the curb and sat with her. "I'm sure it'll be okay." The woman rubbed her back assuming the fire had knocked the wind out of Gillian.

"How?" The question applied to so many things. She hadn't meant to say it aloud.

Missy answered, "There's no telling. Maybe a stray firework."

A stray spark that managed to avoid three blocks of homes

and land on her shed? No, that was as far-fetched as Rick being near. Before she could say anything, Quint and Hank walked out onto the front lawn.

"Fire's out." Quint swiped at his damp forehead. "I need to speak with you for a minute."

Quint guided Gillian to a semi-private patch of yard. He couldn't name the emotions that ran rampant through him. He'd left the house and all but ducked behind some bushes so Gillian's daughter wouldn't catch him—catch him sneaking out of his own damn home.

His brain couldn't even wrap around the fact the woman was a virgin. On the one hand, his chest wanted to burst because she'd chosen him to be her first. But the lies that went with it all... He was so damn confused. Deception was deception no matter how you twisted it, but as she'd said, it wasn't really a conversation starter. He wasn't even sure he had the right to feel betrayed.

Then the damn fire. He'd barely made it to Main Street when the call had come through. Had he not been within earshot of the station he wouldn't have been one of the first on the scene. Every fiber in his being screamed with fear for Gillian and her daughter. And she'd been standing there with a damned garden hose trying to control the blaze. So many things had run through him: pride, fear, lingering anger and not the least of which was the fact the woman was crazy to battle a fire by herself. Too many emotions to put together and make sense.

"Did you get your cast wet?"

"What?" She frowned and glanced down at the hot pink cast. "No. It's fine."

He nodded. "Can you tell me what happened? With the fire." He had questions about what happened between them and what didn't happen, her telling him the truth from the beginning. Not to mention he couldn't shake the feeling there was much more to the story. Now was not the time though. He needed to focus on one thing: the fire.

"Um, Heidi came home. We were talking about the fireworks." Her cheeks reddened and her gaze shifted away from his. "Next thing, we saw the glow of the fire through the window." Gillian cradled her cast. "I don't know anything else. How did it start? Can you tell?"

Quint stared at her for a long moment. Two fires since she'd come to town. He rubbed his chin with the back of his hand. There'd only been three fires in all of last year. None suspicious. Until the Harwoods arrived. He ran through the possibilities of how or who started it. Again, he'd just barely made it out of the house before Heidi came bouncing down the walk with Ryder in tow.

The teen wouldn't have had time to set something so quickly. For the most part neither would Gillian. From the time he left until he'd gotten the call, he shook his head, it was too engulfed. It didn't make any sense. It'd almost had to have been set while he was still there.

His stomach rolled.

"We'll investigate." In daylight, they might find the point of origin. The little shed was mostly empty, only a few hand tools he'd used to work on the gate and in the yard otherwise the fire might have been fiercer. If the winds had been much stronger it could have jumped to one of the neighbors' yard and spread.

"Was it an accident?" Gillian glanced around them.

Strange question. Paranoid almost.

"We'll investigate. Until then." He shrugged. "I can't say one way or the other."

She nodded and hugged her arms to her chest.

Quint wanted to grab and hold her, but he was still too confused from all he'd learned earlier. "Okay. Bye." He left her standing there. He made it to his truck when a hand landed on his shoulder.

He sighed and stood with his shoulders straight. He didn't have to turn to know what was coming next. "Hi, Aunt Zan."

When he didn't move, she walked around to squeeze in front of him. "Why did you just walk away from her like that?"

He held her gaze. "What do you mean?"

"You acted like..."

"Like I'm doing a job."

She frowned, shook her head and left him standing next to his truck. "Like an ass."

Chapter Thirteen

Once Quint got back to his small house at Skipping Rocks Ranch, he hadn't shaken Gillian's odd behavior. He wasn't sure why, but he knew deep in his gut she hadn't started the fire; still, she'd been too jumpy, scared almost. And he'd left her standing there. Alone.

He shook his head. He hadn't handled one thing right with that woman since she got to town.

Too wired to sleep, he got on the computer to see what he might turn up on her on the internet. Googling her name didn't come up with any hits on the first couple of pages for her. He was about to shut down his computer but a link at the bottom of page caught his attention: Gillian and Heidi's names.

It was a year-old link for a Mobile, Alabama newspaper. The article referenced a ten-year-old trial where a man named Richard Damon was convicted on several drug charges despite the prosecution's key witness, Becca Harwood, being gunned down in front of her four-year-old daughter. The house was then set on fire.

"Holy effing shit." Quint scrubbed his tired eyes.

He read on and his stomach churned. It was speculated Rick Damon did the deed himself, but with all the charges he already faced, the prosecution wouldn't make the daughter testify, assuming she hadn't been so traumatized from the whole event in the first place and could have ID'ed him if pressed. The man served his time and was released. The prosecution was considering charging him in the murder of Becca Harwood, but according to the article they didn't have a strong case against the man.

Quint tried to remember everything Gillian'd said since he'd met her. They'd lived in several states. And were on their way to Montana—they were getting as far away from Mobile as possible.

The argument they'd had at the Cates' party popped in his head. She'd railed at him for being a whiner about his dad. She'd lost all of her family and didn't have the option of self-appointed distance. It was down to Gillian and Heidi and no one else.

He groaned. Add another point to the *Quint sucks where Gillian is concerned* column. The tally grew leaps and bounds every time he came in contact with the woman.

Gillian lost her sister, her home and became an adoptive mother all during the summer after she graduated high school. The most difficult thing he'd ever had to deal with when he was eighteen was picking what college to attend. And even then he applied solely to the one on the bottom of his father's list.

His admiration tripled for Gillian—hell, every little piece of information gave her more character, will and determination than any other person he knew. He couldn't imagine having to make the choices she did. Though she didn't really have a choice. Motherhood was thrust upon her—she'd taken it willingly. She never complained, never bemoaned anything.

It explained so much. Her reluctance to share her past. The fact that he was the first man she'd ever been with. She hadn't lied about the reasons. They just didn't make sense. Until now.

He couldn't help but wonder. For the last twelve years, had she had anyone to help her? Anyone to give her support?

Not once had she mentioned a friend.

How could she not go insane with loneliness? Despite not wanting to be under his father's thumb, when he'd chosen to move, he stayed close to family, needing that connection with his aunts. That had been his reason for coming to Wyoming.

But Gillian was there by accident.

He leaned back in his chair and watched the screensaver dance around his laptop.

So many more things fell into place.

No credit cards. Manny had mentioned it one afternoon; he thought she'd made a great life-choice to live debt free. Quint would bet it was to limit any paper trails.

Her reluctance to give up any information. She'd been running for over a year. Had that man threatened them in some way; was she protecting her daughter? Heidi's safety was first and foremost on her mind. She said so herself. Being sequestered out in the middle of nowhere by accident wasn't in her plans, but it also put her ever further off the grid, in a place you didn't find without a reason. If he hadn't broken her arm, she'd be somewhere folks were expecting her. In Paintbrush, she was hidden in plain sight.

He'd always wondered why she hadn't moved on—broken arm aside. So many answers and he didn't even know there were questions. It made sense. The way Gillian went about things. She just *did*. Did what needed to be done.

Quint propped his feet up on the corner of his desk. She was right. He'd never had to be accountable for anything. Sure, when he'd quit the Dallas Fire Department, he'd given up his spot so one of the older guys didn't get cut and lose their pension benefits. He'd like to think it was a magnanimous decision but truth be told, he didn't care that much about the job and it had been easy to walk away.

Same with baseball. When he'd gotten sent down to the minors and then hurt his knee for the third time that season, calling it quits had been easy. He'd started playing ball to please his dad. Stopping pleased only him. Then he'd up and moved to Wyoming.

"But five years later and I'm still hanging on here." He tucked his hands behind his head and let his eyes flutter shut.

Working with Jacob had been the best decision he'd made to date. Working on the ranch he didn't feel hemmed in to a life that he hadn't picked. Not to mention, clean, fresh air all the while doing something he loved.

To him, ambition was doing something you enjoyed, not something your daddy had handpicked for you from the moment you were born.

And again if he could kick his own ass for being a whiner, he would have.

Gillian didn't have the chance to piss and moan about what was thrown at her. It came with all too real consequences. If he wasn't already half in love with love her... His eyes jolted open.

Love?

His heart hammered against his ribs. He stared at the ceiling for God knew how long. He did love her. He loved her strength, her commitment to her daughter. Hell, he even loved the way she rolled her eyes—just like her daughter—when he flirted with her. She was knockdown gorgeous, even if she didn't know it. And he'd been her first lover. Ever. Some strange proprietary hold came over him. She was his and nobody else's. He hardened again and shifted in the computer chair.

His eyes closed as he remembered her soft skin under his hands. She might have been inexperienced, but she hadn't been lacking in any way. He'd have done more to make sure it was as enjoyable and memorable as possible had he one inkling she

193

was *that* inexperienced. If nothing else, he would rectify it the next time he made love to her. And he was damn determined there would be a next time—as soon as possible—if she ever spoke to him again after the way he'd treated her.

She was everything he hadn't realized he'd been missing. Now if he could just convince her...

Gillian shoved her purse under the desk and flipped through the receipts Manny had left for her to file. She hadn't slept well. Between making love to Quint and then all but being accused of yet another fire... Her stomach had been up and down more than when she'd taken Heidi to Six Flags in Missouri and they'd ridden that damn roller coaster three times in a row.

If she'd had a little more money saved up, she and her daughter could move on. The thought seized her chest. For the first time in years, they had friends. People who cared about them. And there was Quint. She didn't know how to categorize what he meant to her. He held onto the little part of her heart she'd been saving. And regardless of what happened, when they left, he'd always have it.

He'd hurled some nasty—however not entirely incorrect—accusations at her. She'd given back just as much, telling him he didn't know what responsibilities were. Heat crawled through her cheeks. Once Quint left the fire he was probably thanking the fact he got out when he did. She had piles of baggage and he wouldn't even know when or where another load would be added to the heap.

She sighed and snagged the tire pressure gauge from the desk drawer and stuffed it into the end of her cast to get at an itch.

"You're not supposed to do that." Quint stood in the doorway holding two steaming cups of coffee.

She dropped the gauge back down to the desk. "I can't help it. It itches." Her pulse raced. The man was hands down sexy. Despite how things ended the night before, she wouldn't be opposed to a repeat performance—maybe they could leave off the for-real flames at the end. That could get old.

"Thought maybe you could use a pick-me-up." He held out one of the coffees to her.

"Thanks." She took the cup and set it in front of her. "Is it that obvious?" She ran her fingers under her eye. Still puffy. *Great.* "Sit?"

Quint shook his head and lowered himself to the guest chair in the corner. "You look fine, but you were a little harried when I left. I'll bet you didn't get any sleep." He took a sip of his coffee then scrubbed at his neck and right shoulder.

"You okay?"

He grunted and his cheeks reddened a bit. "Fell asleep at my computer. Neck's killing me this morning."

She set her coffee down. "You want me to take a look at it?"

"Can you? I mean with your arm all jacked up?"

"One's better than a tight shoulder all day." She smiled.

"Knock yourself out then. Where would you like me?"

Spread over the desk. The second the words popped into her head she banished them. Last night was probably a fluke not to be repeated. She cleared her throat. "You're fine where you are." She stood and walked around the desk and behind Quint's chair. "Where exactly?"

He pointed to his right ear and motioned to his shoulder. "All the way down."

She stood at his side and settled her hand on his neck.

"Dang, you got yourself a pretty good knot there." Her fingers itched to work more than a knot out of the man's shoulder. She tried to ignore the want burning in her belly, but just being near Quint, breathing in his unique musky scent, feeling the warmth of his skin through the denim shirt, all of last night flashed through her mind.

Gillian was in deep, deep trouble.

After a few minutes, he stilled her hand. "Good enough." When she went to go sit down, Quint held fast to her hand. "I need to talk to you."

Whatever burning had sprung in her belly turned leaden and crashed with a hearty thud that jellified her knees. He'd been angry and had called her a liar—which she was, but it wasn't deliberate. "About last night." She swallowed hard. "I should have told you before...before we...I'm sorry. I hadn't meant to deceive you. And once we started, it seemed too late to bring it up."

Quint, still holding on to her hand, shifted in the chair as he set his coffee on the desk. "I'm sorry I overreacted." He clasped her hand in both of his and kissed the back. "If I'd known, I would have been much gentler, made it more special."

Gillian sighed and pulled her hand free to cup his face. "It was perfect. I wouldn't have asked for anything different." Emboldened she leaned forward and placed a gentle kiss on his mouth. His hands snaked around her waist and pulled her down to his lap.

Against her lips he said, "I can't tell you what you do to me." He deepened the kiss.

Quint tasted of coffee and a hint of cinnamon. His hands were everywhere all at once. Touching her. Teasing her. Her body quickened at the memory of the night before. He'd been everything she'd always imagined. And more. So much more it scared her to the very core.

She hadn't "waited" to have sex for any particular reason. Well, she had in high school because she'd seen how torn up Becca had been and the consequences of one careless moment. She couldn't fault her sister entirely—she'd been in love with her boyfriend, and vice versa. From that Heidi came to be. If Heidi's father had been too immature at the time to handle everything, it was his loss.

Once Gillian had settled into a rhythm for motherhood, raising a child—one who went through years of therapy after witnessing her mother's death—wasn't conducive to dating. Too many questions were asked about ages and timeframes. It became easier to avoid it all together. It was surprisingly easy to not date. She had her daughter and she had a job she enjoyed. Then the years had slipped by so fast and truly she didn't feel as if she'd missed anything.

Until last night.

Had she ever known the passion she'd experienced with Quint existed for real... It shook everything she'd walled up inside herself. Shook her to a core she'd buried so deep behind the walls of never-will-happen. He'd given her many firsts. First awakening of passion. First sense of having power over a man. Even her first hickey. She'd discovered the abrasion on her breast as she'd showered that morning.

She giggled against his lips.

"Something funny about my kissing?" His hand tightened over her butt.

"Nope. It's perfectly perfect." She delved her tongue inside his mouth and threaded her fingers into his hair. Let the soft curls pull through her fingers. He was rock hard against her hip and she wriggled in his lap. His groan fired up her remaining self control.

Gillian slid her hand down between them and cupped him through his jeans.

He bit down on her lower lip; let his kisses trail across her chin and over her neck to nuzzle at the hollow where neck met shoulder.

The peal of the bell alerting of a vehicle entering the empty garage bay broke the pair apart.

"I have to, um..." Gillian fought to catch her breath as she stood and motioned to the doorway. She moved quickly, too quickly, almost tripping over her own feet as every inch of her blazed with want. She patted her lips, still swollen from his intense kisses. She glanced back at Quint. "You okay?" He had a bewildered look on his face.

Quint nodded. "Fine." He cleared his throat. "Fine. I'm gonna sit here a minute." He snagged his cup from the desk and raised it. "Have a drink." He grabbed an auto magazine and thrust it over his lap with a sigh.

She didn't have time to examine what had just happened. She turned and walked into the garage. "Good morning, Mrs..."

Gillian's voice faded as she walked out of the small office. Quint had come to confront her—bearing coffee to soften her up before he demanded some answers. Demand, no. He'd try to cajole, pry the truths from her that she didn't seem inclined to share. He'd ask her to let him in, to let him help her. It scared him shitless to think of what she and her daughter had endured. He couldn't do anything about what had already happened, but he'd damn sure do anything and everything in his power to help her from here on out.

Her haunting words the night he'd played nursemaid became crystal clear after his internet search. She'd asked him to protect her daughter, keep her safe, if anything should happen to her. He'd blown it off as the drugs and the accident talking. It was, on the surface, a simple request but in light of Richard Damon's release and her running for the past year...

His hand tightened around his coffee up and almost crushed the paper cup—hot coffee and all.

His intentions were to get her to talk, but merely seeing her sitting there, his desire had spiked. His resolve wavered. Then, when she had touched him, any and all thought fled. All he wanted to do was drag her to him, make her his all over again and block out the rest of the world.

No woman had ever driven him to distraction. Then again, no woman had ever tempted him to get down on bended knee and commit to happily ever after.

He took a long, hot sip of coffee hoping to ward off amorous thoughts. Good thing, as Mrs. Edwards came in and sat in the chair next to his. "Morning, ma'am."

"Good morning, Quint." She set her little leather purse in her lap and smiled at him.

"Car trouble?" The last thing he wanted was small talk.

The beehive atop the woman's head bobbed as she nodded. "The Cutlass has a knocking noise under the hood. I asked my son to look at it next time he's up from Cheyenne, but with this summer heat, I didn't want to take any chances. Can never be too careful." Her wrinkled smile grew as she leaned forward. "I've been meaning to call you. My granddaughter is coming up for a visit next month. I was hoping to have you out to supper."

Coffee roiled in his stomach.

The women of Paintbrush had been trying to fix him up from day one. He'd happily gone along and had free meals here and there. Most of their granddaughters, nieces, and friends of friends hadn't been any more interested in dating than he'd been. No harm no foul. At the same time, his heart had never been fully vested in any one person. Until recently.

Not that he and Gillian had a "relationship". Truth be told, he'd learned more about her from the internet search the night before than anything she'd shared with him.

"She's the sweetest thing." Mrs. Edwards wrinkled up her nose. "Much better than that old biddy Red's granddaughters. She's had you out four times in the last year. My Shelley makes those girls pale in comparison." She held tightly to the purse in her lap and waited for a reply.

As non-committal as possible he said, "You do make the best apple dumplings in all of Wyoming."

"Alrighty then." Gillian skirted her desk and sat. She never quite made eye contact with Quint as she snapped up a pen from the desk and tapped it repetitively on the fake wood top. "Did you need anything else, Quint? Or did we finish covering the services rendered?"

The frost to her words sat Quint up straighter in his seat. *Where the hell had that come from?* He frowned and tossed his half-empty cup in the trashcan next to her desk. "Yeah, we're good. For now."

He bid his goodbyes to Mrs. Edwards and headed out to his truck. Manny pulled into the lot next to him.

"Hey, Quint." The mechanic eased his heft from the truck. "You having trouble with your truck?"

"No." He flipped the keys over in his hand. He blew out a breath, and tried to relieve some of the tension that had settled in his chest after Gillian's cold words.

Manny eyed him for a long moment. "You're sweet on her." He didn't ask a question.

"I don't—"

"I've seen the way you look at her. I don't blame you one bit. If I was thirty years younger, I'd give you a run for your money, son." He shut the door to his truck. "Just be careful with her. She's more fragile than she'll ever let on."

Quint didn't respond. He only stared after the man as he

walked into the garage. Had Gillian opened up to him? Had she confided in Manny? A powerful jolt of jealousy rocketed through him. He had no claims on the woman. If anything he should be relieved she'd let at least one person in to her life.

It scared him, though, how much he wanted that person to be him.

Chapter Fourteen

Gillian kicked off her shoes and had just lain on the sofa when someone knocked on the door. Heidi was out with Ryder and Hank, gone to ride at the Bowman's ranch. Gillian snagged a pillow and put it over her face. Whoever it was could just go away.

The knocked sounded again. "Gillian, I know you're in there. Your car's sitting in the driveway." Quint's voice softly came through the front door. He rattled the knob. "I have a key."

She groaned and sat up. "I'm coming. Hang on." She tossed the pillow onto the sofa and got to the door as Quint was inserting his key into the deadbolt. "I told you I was coming."

The corner of his mouth turned up. "Yeah, but I wasn't sure if you actually were." He tucked the keys back into his pocket. "May I come in?"

"It's your house." Gillian waved her arm in a sweeping motion.

He shook his head and laughed as he looked around the room. "You'd never know two people, much less of the female persuasion, lived here. I've never seen two more tidy, less frilly gals in my life."

You tend not to unpack much when you're ready to run at any moment. She wanted to say the words. Felt them burning the back of her throat trying to get out, but then there would be many questions she wasn't ready to answer. "That reminds me. I have something for you." She walked over to the kitchen table and rooted around the stack of papers she'd left on the corner. She turned back to Quint and handed him an envelope.

"What's this?" he asked as he opened it. "Money?"

"Rent." Her stomach balled with nerves as she waited for his response. When he did nothing more than stand there she continued. "It's not much. Yet. We don't have many expenses here so I am hoping to have more to you by the end of the month. Manny pays really well." She rambled on and shifted from foot to foot.

"I don't want your money."

What a shock. Nothing she did meshed well with Quint— except when they made love. She turned and walked back over to the sofa then plopped down. She lifted her feet to the edge of the scarred wooden coffee table. "My feet hurt too much to stand there and argue with you."

He tossed the envelope next to her propped up feet. "There's nothing to argue about." He sat at the other end of the sofa. "I didn't ask for rent. I will not accept rent." He ran his hands through his hair. "Like I said when I offered you the house, you're doing me a favor staying here. It doesn't do the house any good to sit empty all the time."

He patted the cushion between them. "Here. Give me those feet."

"I don't..." Gillian scrunched up her nose. "Thanks, but no."

"C'mon. What are you afraid of?"

She snorted. "You don't scare me." She shifted on the sofa and plopped her feet into Quint's lap. *Scared of Quint Walters?* Terrified was more like it. He made her think things and feel things she hadn't given herself permission to feel. But for just a little bit, it was nice to be tempted.

Quint slid off her shoes and dropped them to the floor. "Manny's working you pretty hard, huh?" He rubbed her feet.

Gillian fought back a moan. She'd given more massages than she could ever try to recall, but no one had ever given one to her. She didn't want to explore the different emotions whirling around and through her. After the cold shoulder she'd given Quint that morning she was surprised he showed up on her door step at all. Between that and the town trying their darnedest to settle him down with one of their relatives, she couldn't imagine why he wasn't busy having dinners and romancing the different Paintbrush generations.

"You didn't answer me." He shifted under her legs and propped his own feet up on the coffee table. "Is Manny working you too hard?"

"Naw. This is a piece of cake." She leaned back and closed her eyes. "I've had some pretty crappy jobs."

"Huh. Like what?"

"In high school, I worked at the movie theater and got to clean the floors after every movie. Do you know how nasty that is?"

Quint chuckled. "I can only imagine."

"I doubt it." Gillian settled her casted arm over her stomach. "I had really long hair back then. Like down to the middle of my back. No one bothered to tell me I should wear it up." A shudder ran through her. "My second night working, there was something stuck to the floor. I shoved at it with the broom but it wasn't going anywhere. I bent over to get it and..." She trailed off as a yawned ripped through her.

"And?" Quint wiggled her foot.

She peeled one eye open and looked at Quint. "My hair

stuck to the floor."

"Ugh."

"I yanked it back up but had no less than three pieces of gum stuck in it. Got a nice new bob." Gillian slid her eye shut again.

"How long did you work there?"

"A little over a year. Then I went to work at a grocery store for a while. Had to clean the bathrooms every other day. Much cleaner than the theater floor. Let me tell you."

Quint's laughter rumbled through him. The vibrations tinkered through her. More than anything, she wanted to recapture what they had before the fire. Something in Quint had changed though when he'd learned he was her first. And then when Mrs. Edwards started matchmaking... The jealousy she had no right to feel scared and angered her.

As he rubbed her feet, the rhythm could lull her into the sleep that had escaped her the night before. As much as she'd like to sleep, she didn't want to waste a minute with Quint. She pulled her feet away.

"What did you do after your sister died? For work I mean."

"Secretarial work." She sat up and let her feet fall to the floor then leaned forward with her elbows on her knees. "My mom was still alive. She couldn't work, because she was too sick, but she watched Heidi. I worked during the day and went to night school to get my masseuse license. It was hard after my mother died. But we got through."

Quint settled his hand on her back. The warmth from his hands seeped through her thin shirt. "You are remarkable."

"No. I just did what I had to do."

"Which is what makes you so remarkable." He leaned forward and mimicked her position. "I admire you."

"Great. I've always wanted to be admired." Gillian stood and tugged at the hem of her shirt. "Don't you have a dinner date to get ready for?"

Quint frowned as he stood, too. "What?"

"Mrs. Edwards's niece or granddaughter or cousin. Friend of a friend. I can't remember." *And I can't believe I just blurted that out.*

He grabbed her shoulders and turned her to face him. When she didn't meet his gaze, he tucked his hand under her chin and raised it up. She had no choice but to look at him. "I want you to know, I didn't make a date with her *granddaughter*. I haven't made a date with anyone in a long time. I do have hopes for my next few dates, but that all depends on whether you say yes."

Her heart beat a rapid tattoo. "Me?"

"Yes, you." He leaned forward and gave her a quick peck on the lips. And then another. All damn day long all he could think about was Gillian. And how long it would be before he could touch her again, feel her up against him. So much so it'd hurt. He'd considered going into town for lunch just to get a quick glimpse of her, but then he'd have been behind and he wouldn't have been able to get to the house just as she got off work.

He peppered her with light, quick kisses. He was determined to take things a little slower. And not get so carried away as they had the night before.

But Gillian had different ideas and leaned up on her tip toes. She snaked her hand around the back of his neck and deepened the kiss. A little groan echoed in the back of her throat as a shiver raced through her, both of which ignited every fiber of his being.

Quint slid his hands up and down her back, slowly at first

then his hands wound their way up under the hem of her shirt. He had to feel her again.

But it still wasn't enough. He slid his hands down and cupped her ass and lifted her until she could wrap her legs around him. Her warmth cradled his rock-hard dick.

"Where's—" he breathed in deeply, "—where's your daughter?"

"Out. Won't be back for hours." Gillian nipped at his earlobe and then his neck. "We're all alone."

He carried her back to his, her—God, it was getting so jumbled up in his mind, it was hard to think straight anymore—back to the bedroom. He leaned her against the footboard to give her support as he ground his hips into her. He fumbled with her shirt—awkwardly tugged and pulled until together they finally rid her of it. He lowered his mouth and laved at her taut peak through the pink lace. He worked the clasp of the bra loose until it gave and fell away affording him all her sweet skin. He tugged gently at the rosy peak.

Gillian buried her fingers in his hair. "Holy Christ, Quint." She yanked his head back and kissed him hard, her tongue thrashing with his.

"Hang on, hang on." He stood up straighter, cradled her to him, and walked around to the side of the bed. Before she could so much as breathe he tossed her onto the bed and ripped off his own shirt. Then he shucked his boots, jeans and boxers, standing before her naked as could be.

They both reached for her pants at the same time, their hands colliding.

"Let me." He pushed her hand aside and unfastened the button. His fingers eased under the cotton as he lowered the zipper. Her smooth belly teased him, taunted him with what was to come. "Lift up." He pulled at her pants to slide them off.

She shifted this way and that until she was as naked as he.

His hands shook as he positioned her with her legs hanging off the bed.

Quint couldn't remember the last time nerves got the best of him when he was making love to a woman. Had he know the night before she was a virgin, he'd have been a hell of a lot gentler if not a little hesitant—and nervous as hell. He was damn glad he hadn't known before. But now that he did, he wanted to be sure to give Gillian something to remember forever.

He knelt in front of her.

Gillian leaned up on her elbows and looked down at him. "What are you—"

"Do you trust me?"

She held his gaze for a long moment then bit her lower lip and nodded.

Quint skimmed his hands up her thighs and back. When she laid back on the bed, he wedged her legs open. He kissed his way up one leg, stopped just at her hip and worked his way down the other. Gillian's fingers dug into the comforter.

A slight smile spread across his mouth. God, she did things to him, stirred places low in his gut he didn't know he was capable of feeling. Never thought he ever *wanted* to feel.

She stiffened slightly when he draped her legs over his shoulders, but she didn't stop him or push him away. Her eyes were squeezed tightly closed making him smile wider. Her gasp echoed through the room when he dipped the tip of his tongue into her sweet folds. He laved her clit, enjoyed the warmth that surrounded every last suckle.

It didn't take long before her hips lifted from the bed and met him stroke for stroke. He slid one finger inside her and about lost it when she contracted around him. But it wasn't about him, it was about Gillian and loving her like he should have the night before. If he couldn't find the words to tell her yet, he was damn sure going to show her how he felt about her. How he was making her his and only his. In a way no other man ever had. And if he could figure out how, never would.

"I don't think... I can't...you have to stop." Gillian's hands were clamped tight on her thighs.

Quint stopped long enough to answer her. "Yes, you can. Come for me, Gillian." He eased another finger inside her and stroked his tongue across her swollen clit. Faster and faster, he guided her higher and higher. She writhed beneath his ministrations.

He was getting a cramp in his knee, but he couldn't stop. Not with Gillian so close.

She moaned, almost growled, and came around his fingers with a hearty shudder.

Carefully, he slid out from under her legs and snapped up his pants to grab a condom. He rolled it on. The damn thing broke, split right up the side. He cursed under his breath. He only had one in his pocket. He hadn't exactly thought he'd need it, but he'd hoped.

He could stop, despite what teenage boys had said for years, he wouldn't die if he didn't follow through to completion—it hurt like hell, but didn't kill a guy.

"Hurry, Quint." Gillian rubbed her foot along the back of his thigh.

He could delve in for just a moment, pull out before he came. He was back between her thighs before she'd even opened her eyes. Hands on either side of her on the bed, he leaned forward and kissed her softly as he slid between her wet folds, embedded himself down deep inside her. The moisture and the warmth made it damn hard not to come right then and there.

Gillian stalked her fingers up Quint's chest as he rocked against her—in and out, he focused on little else. Held himself at enough mental distance to keep up his composure. He wanted to make her come again, feel the rush of her orgasm as it surrounded him.

The peaks of her taut nipples brushed against his chest with every beat of his drumming into her. He tempered his breathing, but she was meeting him thrust for thrust and rocking his concentration. The little mewing in the back of her throat was growing more distracting.

She slid her fingers up into his hair and pulled his head down next to hers. A shiver wracked through her and she came around his cock. "So good." Her breathy, lustful voice drew his balls up tight. She bit down on his earlobe then traced her tongue over the contour.

He couldn't hold off any longer and spilled himself into her.

"Oh, Jesus." He panted and tried to catch his breath. What the hell had he just done?

"God, Quint. I've never..." She hugged him tight to her chest, the cast scratched across his back. "Thank you."

He all but groaned. *Yeah, you're thanking me now...*"I'm sorry."

She released him and let him put some space between them. "For?"

"The condom broke. I should have stopped, but damn it you make me crazy. I lost control."

She blinked rapid fire at him and swallowed hard. "Broke?"

"Yeah." He slid from her.

"How could that happen?"

Quint scrubbed his hands down his face. "I..."

Gillian climbed down from the bed and ran to the bathroom. Quint heard the shower turn on. His heart hammered against his chest as much from the heartiest orgasm he'd ever had and the fact that he'd had unprotected sex for the first time since he was seventeen and thought he knew everything.

He hadn't moved so much as an inch by the time Gillian emerged from the bathroom draped in a towel. She had some sort of plastic bag wrapped around the pink cast and wouldn't—or couldn't—hold his gaze.

His stomach rolled as he said, "What's done is done. You can't wash it away."

She toyed with the edge of the towel and shrugged.

"I'm sure it'll be fine. But if not—"

"I'm sure you're right," she said as she nodded. "But if not, we'll be miles away from here when it matters. You don't have to worry one way or the other."

"What? Why?" He shot up out of the bed. His heart hammered triple time. "When were you going to tell me?"

Gillian frowned. "Not that I owe you any explanations for what I do, one way or the other, but you didn't think we'd stay here permanently."

"Actually, I thought the town had grown on you. Hell, I thought I'd grown on you."

She picked at the plastic bag covering her cast and sighed. "Paintbrush is great, I guess, but once my cast comes off, I can go back to work. There's not a big market here for a masseuse. We'll move on when we're ready."

"You act like it's no big deal to just pick up and go time after time, but it sounds to me like you're running. Is it because of me? Or Richard Damon?"

Gillian's knees shook. "I beg your pardon?" She sat heavily on the edge of the bed. Water dripped off of her onto the quilt. That she could focus on. She could not, however, focus on the name that just came out Quint's mouth. He had no reason to know it, much less hurl it at her.

Quint slipped into his jeans and squatted in front of her. "I didn't mean to drop that on you like that."

"How?" Her voice eked out just above a whisper.

"After the fire last night..." He cupped her cheek. "The way you were acting, I put your name into a search engine." He relayed some of the more horrific details that all the papers had run at the time of the murder. When Gillian did nothing more than sit there he lifted her chin until she met his gaze. "Why didn't you tell me?"

"I've never told anyone." She swallowed hard as her nerves hummed. "Heidi doesn't even know some of why we left. She was so young, Quint." She shivered. Quint stood and gathered up the quilt around her. "It was years of therapy before she could sleep in her own room and more still before she had any semblance of a normal life."

"Tell me what happened that made you leave Mobile." The mattress sank beside her as Quint sat. He draped his arm over her shoulder and pulled her into a cocoon of his arms.

"Rick had been released from jail one day—one damn day— before he started calling. He wanted to see his 'Huggie Bear'."

"Is he her..."

"No! Heidi's father was a boy who went to school with Becca. When he found out my sister was pregnant his parents moved him to Little Rock to finish out his senior year." She finally managed to get the remainder of the plastic bag off her cast. "Last I heard he was attending Auburn." She shrugged. "Neither side tried to stay in contact. Rick was a man Becca got involved with when Heidi was two. They were together for two years before she...before she died.

"When the calls started, I spoke with the prosecutor and they still hadn't made a decision whether they were going to go after him from Becca's death. They know he killed her, I know he killed her and Heidi saw it, though thankfully she blocked that day out, but all the evidence they had wouldn't sway a jury one way or the other." Her shakes had subsided slightly. "Day after day he kept calling. I had the numbers changed and he'd find it again. I couldn't understand the almost obsession. He had no affiliation with her really. He could barely tolerate her when he was she was around. I can't tell you how many times Becca left her with me. Once he got out of jail though... I was in the process of getting a restraining order when I came home early from work one day to find him sitting on my front porch."

"Jesus." Now it was Quint's turn to shake.

"I snuck in the back of the house, grabbed a few essentials and grabbed Heidi, and we took off for parts unknown. That was a little over a year ago."

"The job in Montana?"

"I was referred by a friend of a friend. No one who knew us would think to look there. When we ended up here by mistake it seemed a good enough place to stay."

"Why would you leave then?"

"It's getting complicated."

"Because of me?"

Gillian nodded. "And Ryder. And the fires." For this first time she looked up at Quint. "She was trapped in a fire until a neighbor heard her crying and pulled her out. Her mother's body was decimated in the same fire. I swear to you on my life Heidi did not nor could not start those fires."

"I never..." He shook his head but blanched slightly.

Gillian nodded quickly. "The fire at the motel, you most certainly entertained the thought it was her. I saw the way you were looking at her." She shook off his arm and stood, letting the quilt fall to the floor. "I'll be honest, I thought maybe Rick had found us, but whatever he is, subtle is not it. One or both of us would be dead if he knew where to find us."

"What does he want from you? Why would he keep coming after you?"

"I haven't the faintest clue."

Chapter Fifteen

Quint slept maybe two hours once he'd left Gillian. The pair had talked and talked until Hank brought Heidi home from horseback riding. Then he'd offered to run up to the diner to grab dinner for everyone. He'd hoped the longer he hung around the better chance of her asking him to stay the night, but she wasn't even close to that point. Once he'd gotten back to the ranch, he'd done a little more research. As best as he could tell—all the goings on of a released suspected killer was big news in Mobile—Rick Damon was well east of the Mississippi River.

Quint'd broken down and called his aunt and Jacob. He needed someone to talk with to help him sort out the tumble of emotions running through him. Plus, it didn't hurt to have a couple extra set of eyes watching out for Gillian and Heidi. He'd also sworn them to secrecy. He didn't want to spook Gillian any more than she already was with the fact that he knew so much about her.

It killed him to think of her having to deal with anything alone much less something so traumatic as well as potentially lethal... Not anymore, though. He'd be there for her when she needed him.

To top off his lack of sleep, he'd had to attend to an early morning fire out near the edge of town. An abandoned house had flamed up just before dawn. It hadn't taken long to put it out thankfully, but it was troubling nonetheless. Especially when he found a pink hair band near the point of origin. One similar to a band that Heidi had worn when she'd come to town.

Gillian's claims of her daughter's innocence the night before rang in his ears. He'd like to think the teen didn't have anything to do with it, if for nothing else, Gillian's sake, but the evidence piled up more and more against the newcomer with every blaze.

"Boy, you need to get the lead out or we'll be raising fence posts for the next three days." Hank lifted his straw hat from his head and swiped at his brow with a green bandana.

Quint gave a quick mental shake. There was no point in worrying over the "what ifs" when the "happening nows" grew with each day. "Sorry."

"If your ass was dragging any lower you'd get skid marks on your hide." Hank slapped the hat back on his head. "You want to talk about it?"

"Not right now."

Hank scoffed. "That's the same thing Ryder said this morning. I don't know if I should feel bad the way folks keep pairing off. First you and Gillian, Ryder and Heidi and now Missy and Cade. I never thought I'd say it, but he's good for my girl. Even though that boy is a Holstrom."

"He's a good guy." Unlike Rick Damon. Damn, why did his thoughts flip back to that man any chance he got? He'd found a photo of him online and memorized the face. He'd even sent the picture to Jacob and Zan. New people in town stuck out anyway but this way he'd have a harder time getting to Gillian.

"And I'll be running off with Clara."

"That's super." Quint frowned and set the posthole digger down. "Running off to where?"

"I was just seeing if you were listening. Boy, talking to you's like talking to this pole." He smacked his hand atop the four-by-six-post.

"Sorry, just have a lot on my mind."

"Gillian?"

"Among other things, but yeah."

Hank shook his head. "Something not quite right with her daughter."

Quint paused after he slammed the digger into the ground. "Why do you say that?"

"The other day when that fire started in her back yard, her momma sent her down to Missy's to stay safe. Ryder said she balled herself up on the sofa and shook something fierce. Never would say what was the matter but that's just a little much for a shed fire."

Unless you'd been caught in one yourself as a child. Sure, Quint had toyed with the fact that maybe Heidi had been starting them. It wouldn't be the first time trauma led to mimicking actions, but if that was how she reacted... "Funny thing that fire. Do you have any theories?"

Hank shook his head. "Not a one. It's strange. They started when those two got to town, but you know what, it seems more like it's aimed *at* them rather than *by* them."

"How do you figure?"

Hank peeled off his gloves and grabbed up two water bottles. He handed one to Quint and took a long sip before he continued. "All the fires were in the proximity of where they were at, but small enough to get help there before it got outta hand. If I had to guess, I'd say someone was trying to make it look like one of the Harwoods were up to it."

"Why?"

"To run them out of town? Scare them?" Hank shrugged.

217

"Could be any reason. Folks around here don't always take to having new people."

Or one person in particular. But Quint couldn't wrap his brain around Ruby setting the fires. Shoot, one of them was at her motel. If it had gotten out of hand she'd have lost her entire business. He rolled the water bottle across his forehead. That fire, though it was a fast burn, probably would've burned out before it could reach the backside of the motel.

"I need to go into town at lunch."

"Why don't we break now? Then maybe you'll have your head screwed on right."

"Maybe."

Quint juggled the sack of meatloaf sandwiches and the sodas as he pushed through the door of the Paintbrush Motel.

"Hey, Quint. What are you doing here?" Ruby scooted back from her computer and stood.

Quint held up the paper bag. "Lunch." He didn't really have a plan how to proceed. In his gut though, he suspected Ruby may be the key to the fires. They hadn't started until Gillian and Heidi's arrival. The only person he could think of who was put out by the pair of Harwoods was Ruby.

"Wow. I wasn't expecting to see you today." She fussed with her hair as a smile spread wide across her face.

He cursed himself for being three kinds of ass leading her on this way. But if Gillian's comments at the picnic were any inkling, he'd been doing it unknowingly for years. "I brought a couple of Clara's house specials."

Ruby shifted some papers from her desk and motioned for Quint to sit. "How have you been? It seems like forever since

I've seen you." She took the sacks from him, opened them and set the contents onto the desk.

"It's only been two days."

"Has it?" she asked around a bite of sandwich. "Been keeping yourself busy?" It was almost accusatory. Had he been back in his oblivious world of a few days ago, it would have passed without the slightest register, but now, now that this strange unshakable notion that Ruby was neck deep into trouble...

Quint nodded. "I've been putting out fires. Figuratively, and unfortunately, quite literally."

He watched her as she shifted in her seat. It wasn't so much what she did that made his suspicion grow, but what she didn't do—like ask questions. Paintbrush was a small town and gossip was standard currency. Anyone who could get a little extra knowledge was golden until the next big thing came along. The fact that she didn't pump him for information... Damn, he'd hoped he'd been wrong at the turn of his thoughts.

"No one got hurt this time, but it seems something funky is going on. Sheriff Reese is going to send out the findings to the Sheridan fire marshal and get his take on things."

Ruby blanched slightly but still didn't give anything else away. "Strange."

Without coming right out and asking her if she'd done it—and he still had enough doubt to keep his thoughts to himself for now—he hoped the news that it was going to be reviewed would harness whatever motives pushed her to do it and compel her to admit it—or at least stop.

They ate in silence for a while. He'd like to say it was like old times, comfortable and relaxing, but he was so tense that the slightest movements came across as jerky and clumsy. He knocked over his soda bottle three times and shot ketchup onto his jeans.

"So, have you started thinking about the Founders' Day dance next month?" Ruby balled up her napkin and tossed it into the empty sack.

Little else. He was hesitant to ask Gillian to something so far away. Afraid she would say no because she was leaving. Afraid she'd say yes and *still* end up leaving. The first weekend every August, the entire population met out at the old Harper ranch twenty miles east of town. The property had fallen by the wayside many, many years before, but folks would go to the first settlement in Paintbrush to pay homage to the town's first family. One summer in the mid-eighties, a barn had been erected to hold a dance and later that fall an auction for the local charities—or whatever was needed. "Is that next month?"

Ruby nodded. "I hear that Cade Holstrom may stay on until then. Something about his agent using it as a promotional opportunity or some hokey crap like that."

"Hmm." Quint shoved the last bunch of fries into his mouth. He mumbled something incoherent and liked to have choked in the process.

Ruby jumped up and pounded his on the back. "Can't take you anywhere, Walters."

When the worst of the coughs subsided he held up his hand in surrender. "Stop, now."

"Sorry." The woman blushed. She sat back down. "If you think you might go to the dance, maybe we could ride up there together."

"Sure, we'll see."

Gillian paced the length of the living room. For more than a year, running took up her every waking thought. Wherever she and her daughter landed, she was halfway out the door before the dust ever settled. Ready to go when she felt threatened or scared.

Rick was not above ignoring a restraining order. And as he'd already proven once that he was less than worried what his actions brought down on him, his interest in Heidi was too worrisome to wait around and see what he might do next. She didn't think he'd hurt her daughter—why would he, he had no reason to. Heidi had never spoken a word to prosecutors and the papers were quick to point this out each and every time the story came to light again—but she'd never thought he'd kill her sister either.

If she knew that he was in Mobile, she could relax.

Think. Think. Think.

Gillian paced again and again. "I could call Brenda and see what she may have heard." Her friend Brenda had been a rock for her and she'd definitely missed her, but she had not once wanted to risk any information getting to Rick.

She stopped at the phone, picked up the receiver and set it back down. She did this three times. "It's not worth the risk."

She was all torn up inside about her growing attachment to Quint—worse was Heidi's growing attachment to Ryder.

She dropped onto the sofa. "Do I keep her bodily safe from Rick or heart safe from Ryder?" She scrubbed her hands over her face.

The phone rang and jarred her upright. "He-hello?"

"You okay?" Manny didn't bother with small talk.

"Um, yeah."

"I wasn't sure when you didn't come in this afternoon."

Gillian glanced at the clock. Half past one. *Darnitall.* It was her half-day at the garage. "I am so sorry. I don't know how it slipped my mind." She jumped up and ran toward the back of the house with the phone tucked at the crook of her neck. "I will be there in ten minutes tops."

"No hurry, hon. I just... Get here when you get here." Manny hung up.

Gillian turned off the phone and dropped it onto the unmade bed. She ran around the room and snapped up the clothes she'd left strewn everywhere. "This day is already crap; what else could go wrong?"

"Crap." Gillian yelped when she smashed her finger in the stapler. So far, she'd managed to knock over a stack of tires, burn the roof of her mouth on nasty coffee, and catch and rip her pant leg on the edge of a beat-up car.

"Gillian, can you bring me the socket wrench I left in the tool box?" Manny hollered from just outside the bay door where he was working on Clara's car.

"Sure thing." She pushed away from the desk and went in search of said wrench. She scooped up the tool and stepped out the bay door just as a dark sedan drove by slowly. The late afternoon sun shone in her eyes blocking out the view of the license plate. "Did you see that car?"

"What? Where?" He raised out from under the hood of the car.

Gillian pointed the direction the car went that was nothing but a pinprick of taillights.

Manny stared at her for a moment. "Probably someone just passing through. There's a big cattleman's auction up in Sheridan this weekend. We get people passing through now and again coming from Jackson Hole."

Gillian nodded and handed him the socket wrench. She wanted to chalk it up to the auction but some sort of unease stirred low in her stomach. She tried to shake off the feeling. "Back to work." She patted Manny on his shoulder and he hunched under the hood of the car again.

Gillian went back to her small office and turned on the computer. She put Rick's name in a search engine but nothing past the trial and his subsequent release came up. There was nothing indicating what he was doing now or where he was. As far as she knew, when he was released, he was free and clear to do anything and go anywhere as there were no further changes pending. He could be anywhere. But could that be in Wyoming?

"What do you mean you need time off?" Jacob slammed his coffee mug down on the scarred wooden table. "This is the busiest we've been in well over a year. I have two new clients bringing their horses up for boarding at the end of the week."

Quint was toying with the idea of flying down to Alabama to see what Rick Damon was up to. "It was just a thought. Sorry, I can do it another time." The more he considered it, the more he realized he risked the chance of alerting the man to Gillian and Heidi's whereabouts if he went snooping around.

Jacob gripped the back of his chair. "You've been having a few weird thoughts the last little bit. She got to you, didn't she?"

Quint nodded. "More than I thought possible."

"What are you going to do about it?"

"What is there to do about it? She's already talking about leaving."

Jacob scoffed. "Are you kidding? Make her stay. Make her *want* to stay. If you want her badly enough you'll figure out what to do."

"It's not that easy." Quint shook his head.

"Nothing worth having is."

It would be hard to stay. The more and more it rolled around her mind, though, it would be harder to leave. Despite trying to keep her heart disengaged, she was head over heels in love with Quint Walters. Throw in Missy, Ryder, Hank, and Manny, and she'd found an entire family from one wrong turn.

If they stayed though, could she ever truly feel safe and comfortable? Would she ever stop looking over her shoulder? If there was some way she could get a message to Rick to assure him they had no intention of ever causing him problems, would his threats go away?

The doorbell rang and made her pause in her thoughts.

Ryder stood with his hands shoved down in his pockets. "Hi, Miss Gillian."

"Hey, come on in. I'll go get Heidi." She shook her head and scooped up the basket of clean laundry. If she let it, all the thoughts and fears would drive her crazy. She needed to block it out for a bit and run through her routine for normalcy. She walked in to Heidi's room. The teen thrust something under the covers and jumped up from the bed. Gillian pretended not to notice as she set the laundry atop the dresser. "Hon, Ryder's in the living room."

"What? Why?" Heidi bolted toward the closet. "He's early. I'm not ready." She flipped through the rack of clothing.

"For?"

"We have a date. A for real, for real date." Heidi raised her arm and sniffed. "Ugh. Shower. Mom, tell him ten minutes." She jerked the shirt over her head. "Can't believe he's early." She dashed into the bathroom.

Gillian leaned her head out the teen's door. "Be right there, Ryder. Make yourself..." she trailed off.

The shower ran and Heidi was singing. Gillian hurried to

the bed to see what was so important her daughter had to hide it.

She pulled back the covers. And just stared. A cell phone. It vibrated as she watched it. Sierra Hill's face popped up on the screen. The room pitched and nausea rolled Gillian's stomach.

Heidi emerged from the bathroom wearing tan shorts and a pink tank topped off with a towel on her head. Gillian had no idea how long she'd stood there staring at the small device.

"I didn't have time for a deep conditioning but I'm sure..." Heidi pulled up short when she saw her mom. "What are you looking at?" Heidi's gaze shot to the bed as the phone vibrated again. "I, uh..."

Spots danced before Gillian's eyes. She snapped up the phone and rushed down the hall. Heidi was fast on her heels.

"Mom, let me—"

She stopped so fast that Heidi slammed into her back. "Not one word." Gillian took several deep breaths. She tried to remain as calm as possible, but with the ringing in her ears it was growing more difficult.

"Ryder." She had to clear her throat.

The teen stood from his perch on the edge of the sofa.

"Ryder, I need to you to leave. Now."

"No, Mom." Heidi pulled at Gillian's sleeve.

Ryder swallowed hard and volleyed his gaze between the two Harwood women. "Is everything okay?"

The doorbell rang before Gillian could answer. Not that she had enough breath to tell him that no, nothing was okay. Her breath came shorter and shorter as her chest burned.

"I think your mom's gonna pass out." Ryder took a step closer as the bell chimed again. "I'll get it." He all but tripped over his feet and grabbed the door.

"Hey, guys." Quint sauntered in and removed his straw cowboy hat.

"I'll... uh..." Ryder looked like he wanted to bolt, but he stood his ground.

Quint frowned. "What's wrong?"

Gillian grabbed Heidi's arm. She tried in vain to get a deep breath, but she was able to find her voice finally. "How long?"

"Mom, it's not that bad." Heidi blanched.

"How long?" She held the phone with the fingers of her casted hand. A cramp built.

Heidi lowered her gaze to the floor. "Since before we left."

The ringing in Gillian's ears increased as her grip tightened. "How is that possible?"

"Sierra added me to her plan a couple of years ago. It's only an extra ten bucks a month. She has unlimited texting. Her parents didn't care."

"And you've been doing this the whole time we've been gone? The whole damn—"

"It's okay, Mom. I never did tell her where we were. Even when she asked. And I used babysitting money when we were in Alabama. I've paid her back some since we moved here. I used the money I earned from Jacob."

"You what?"

"I mailed her some money."

The spots before Gillian's eyes were in full-blown River Dance mode. "When?"

Heidi shrugged. "A few days ago."

"You're hurting her." Quint came up behind Gillian and pried her hand lose. "Ryder, take Heidi into the kitchen."

Gillian sank down to the edge of the sofa and bent her head between her knees to level her breathing.

"Take a deep breath. Now another." Quint stroked her back. "Want to talk about it?"

She shook her head. After a few minutes, her fight or flight kicked in. She pushed Quint's stroking hand away. "I have to pack. We need to leave."

"Why the hell do you have to leave?" Quint settled his hands on her shoulders to keep her from getting up. "Let me help you."

Gillian looked into his eyes. "You can't." She loved him too much to put his life at risk. "There's nothing you can do." Nothing she could afford to let him do. If something happened to him, because of her... She couldn't live with that. Plus she only had enough strength to protect Heidi. She didn't have one extra ounce to give to Quint no matter how much he thought he was willing to help her "fight" whatever darkness came after them.

Sure he said he was willing, but he didn't know what Rick was capable of.

And if she could help it, he never would.

Gillian sniffed back tears and swiped at her runny nose. "You want to help? If anyone comes looking for us, pretend you don't know us. Forget we were ever here."

"I can't do that." Quint spoke quickly.

She pushed herself up from the sofa. "You have to."

"Don't go." His voice cracked. "Please, let me protect you."

Gillian turned, stood up on her tiptoes and gave him a gentle kiss. "You're a good man, Quint Walters. You take care of yourself. I, uh..." She almost told him she loved him, but she didn't want to hear what he said in return. If he shared that feeling she wasn't sure she could actually walk away. If he didn't... She didn't want to know everything she felt and shared with him was all in vain. "Good bye."

Quint watched her walk down the hall. His gut burned with anger and hurt at the same time the rest of him numbed. He could protect her and her daughter if she would just give him a chance. But she would rather run. Alone.

It was the worst kind of rejection he could have ever gotten.

He snapped up his hat off the coffee table and slapped it on his head. When he slammed through the front door, Ryder jumped up from the front porch to his feet. "Heidi told me I should leave. I went out the back door. I didn't want give Miss Gillian anything else to get all upset about." He glanced back toward the house. "Did I do something wrong?"

"No, son. Family stuff."

The teen stuffed his hands into his pockets. "We had a date tonight. Me and Heidi. I really like her," he said the last little bit almost to himself, like he didn't realize he said it aloud. "I was planning on asking her to the Founders' Day dance next month." He tilted his head up to the darkening sky. "Maybe tomorrow?"

Quint didn't have the heart to hurt the boy. "Maybe."

Ryder nodded and hopped off the steps. His shoulders were slumped as he scuffed his way down the sidewalk to the street. He glanced back over his shoulder once, looked toward Heidi's window.

"I feel your pain, boy." Quint shook his head and dug his keys from his pocket.

Gillian had sworn him to secrecy—and he'd kept that promise, sort of. Zan and Jacob had been good at keeping quiet. At the time, he didn't think it would be an issue. Once the Harwoods were gone he'd sit the boy down and explain to him why they left. Some of it anyway.

Something had spooked Gillian and she was doing the only

thing she knew how to do. Run away.

If she could leave him so easily, then screw her.

He scrubbed his hands over his face. He instantly recalled his thoughts. He didn't mean it. He didn't want her to leave, didn't want her to leave him. How could he convince her she was safe in Paintbrush?

Maybe he needed to have a little talk with Sheriff Reese. Apprise him of any potential trouble headed to town.

He needed to give Gillian a little time to calm down. Surely she wouldn't up and leave in the middle of the evening. Paintbrush had wormed its way into her heart. He knew that as he knew he'd have to follow after her if she did leave.

"I left my bag up at Manny's garage yesterday." Heidi slumped in her seat. Gone was the happy teenager. In her place was the sulking, miserable girl who had made the trip from Mobile across the U.S.

Gillian gripped the steering wheel so tightly her knuckles whitened. "We can run by there and grab it on the way out of town."

"Why do we have to leave?"

"Because, despite you lying to me, I love you, and I'd like to keep you alive a little longer."

"Aren't you being a little dramatic? It's a cell phone. This isn't fair."

"Life is not fair." Gillian smacked her cast on the steering wheel. "Do you think Becca thought it was fair to die because her stupid boyfriend has anger management issues and killed her? Do you think it's fair that I became a mom when I was barely old enough to vote?" She ground her teeth. "You'll get over it and thank me for it later."

"I doubt it. I hate you."

"Well, I love you." Gillian straightened her shoulder. "And I will do anything I have to, to keep you safe. Even if that means making you hate me."

They rode in silence the few short blocks over to the garage. Gillian pulled into the lot out behind the small building and set the gear to park. When Heidi tried to get out of the car, Gillian grabbed her hand.

"I'm sorry. I shouldn't have said what I did. I know it's not fair for you, but I don't know what else to do."

Heidi kept her eyes downcast.

Gillian turned in her seat to face her daughter. "I have loved you as if you were my own child since the day you were born. You were three weeks early. I don't know if I ever told you that. You came out all squawky and pink. Took great exception to being thrust into the world so quickly. Had a very strong opinion since day one." She tucked a loose strand of hair behind Heidi's ear. "And I fell instantly in love with you. I'm not ashamed to admit, too, I was a little jealous of Becca."

"Why?"

"She had you. You were hers. And she was so terribly lucky. I know that your mother would be proud of the way you've grown up. You are a special young woman." Gillian cupped Heidi's cheek. "It's not fair that you don't have the life you should at your age. I am especially sorry for that. But again, I will do what I have to to keep you safe."

"I get that. I really do. But why does me having a cell phone mean we have to leave again? Rick is in Alabama."

Gillian sighed. "Because he can trace that cell, the envelope with the money or anything you might have told Sierra straight to us."

"Aren't you being a little paranoid?"

Quint had once accused her of lying. He didn't know the half of it. "Even though you're sixteen, I didn't want to burden you."

"I'm not a baby." Heidi crossed her arms over her chest.

"I know, sweetie." Gillian looked away from Heidi and took a deep breath. "There are a few things I may have neglected telling you. But only to keep from scaring you."

Still in an arms-crossed slouch, Heidi turned toward her mother with a raised eyebrow.

Gillian gave a short sad laugh. "You don't know how much you look like your mom right now. I miss her so much." A tear eked out the side of her eye and ran down her cheek before she could stop it.

Some of the attitude left the teen as her eyebrow lowered and she loosened her arms.

"A week before we left, I got a call from the prosecutor. They were thinking about re-opening your mother's case. See if maybe they could get some new evidence. Specifically about what you saw the day your...that day."

Her eyes rounded. "But I was only four. I don't remember anything. I swear to you."

"I know. And that's what I told him. He was quite persistent, so I told him I'd think about it. He said he'd subpoena you if it ever came down to it." Gillian shrugged. "I had my mind half made up to run at that moment."

"But we didn't?"

Gillian shook her head. She had to tell Heidi. Tell her everything. The girl needed to know why they'd left the world they knew behind. "Rick called. Often. Maybe once a week trying to get me to let him see you."

Heidi blanched. "Why?"

"He said he was like your father. He missed you. He missed Becca and could remember her through you." Gillian cut the engine of the car. She wouldn't be able to drive right anyway. "I'd actually started the process to get a restraining order against him. That same day someone slashed all my tires."

"Rick?"

"I don't know. It would be one hell of a coincidence if not. After the prosecutor told me of his potential plans, the calls came three, four times a week. He was being persistent."

Heidi grasped Gillian's hand. Her eyes were big and round. "But you wouldn't have, right? You wouldn't have made me go see him."

"Oh, honey, no. There was no way in hell I'd let him get within ten feet of you."

Heidi relaxed in small degrees. "What changed? Why'd we run?"

Gillian beamed inwardly. Such a smart child. "You remember that day you twisted your ankle and we had to go to the emergency room?"

"Of course, we left that night."

Gillian took a deep breath. She kept her hands clasped tight in her lap so her daughter wouldn't see them shaking. "I'd run out of the house so fast when I got the call from the school, I left my purse with the insurance, wallet, everything sitting on my desk. While you were getting X-rayed, I ran home to get it."

"And?"

"And..." She licked her lips, tried to swallow away the lump in her throat. "Rick was sitting on the front porch."

Heidi reached out and grabbed Gillian's hand again. "Of our house?"

"Yes." She could still picture like it was yesterday. He'd

been sitting on the top step like he had all the time in the world and he was right where he needed and wanted to be.

"W-what did you do?"

"I parked around the corner, snuck into the backyard and grabbed our stuff." She cupped Heidi's cheek. "I cleared out the bank account before I headed back to the hospital and you know the rest."

"I'm so sorry."

Gillian barely heard the whispered words. "Hon, you have nothing to be sorry for."

"But if it weren't for me—"

"If it weren't for *Rick*. He, *and he alone*, is responsible for his actions. You didn't do a damn thing wrong. I want you to always remember that. Do you understand me?"

Tears streamed down Heidi's face. She sucked in a huge sob. "Okay. Okay." She sniffed a couple more times and swiped at her eyes. "Where are we headed this time?"

Gillian opened her car door. "I have no idea."

Chapter Sixteen

She opened the back door to Manny's garage and was knocked down by a blast of heat.

"Mom, are you okay? There's smoke." Heidi pulled Gillian back up to her feet.

"Stay by the car," Gillian said and pushed the teen back, but Heidi followed her around to the front of the building where they found a small group of people, Missy and Ryder right at the front.

Gillian ran up to her friend as she asked, "Missy, what happened?"

"There you both are." She pulled Heidi into a tight hug. "I've been looking for you."

"Is anyone in there? Manny?" Nausea rolled Gillian's stomach.

Missy shook her head. "He's up in Sheridan, something about an auction. I fixed him up a sack dinner before he left."

Gillian settled her hand on her stomach. "Good."

Missy lowered her voice. "Ryder said y'all had had a fight. Is everything okay?"

"Yes." Heidi glanced toward the building and groaned loudly. "My bag."

"We'll get you another bag." Gillian patted Heidi on the

shoulder.

"But, Mom, I need it."

Gillian frowned.

Heidi dragged her mother off to the side. "Ryder gave me a bracelet. I took it off and set it in my bag when I was helping Mr. Manny unpack boxes. I looped it on the rack of windshield wipers and forgot about it."

"Hon—"

Heidi squeezed her mother's hand tighter. "It was his grandmother's bracelet. He said it was special. That I was special."

Gillian ran her hand though her hair. "Where again?"

"I'll go get it." Heidi took off at a run before Gillian could stop her.

"Get your ass back here." Gillian ran after her, but Heidi was too quick and was in the small office door next to the closed bay doors. The heavy metal door slammed behind her before Gillian could get to it. "Heidi!"

The sirens of the fire truck wailed over the noise of the blaze.

Quint and Hank jumped out of the truck and ran up behind her a moment later. "Missy, get those people back away from the building." Quint turned to Gillian and lowered his voice. "You need to get back. Any number of things could blow."

Breath caught up in her lungs. "Heidi ran inside." Gillian grabbed the door knob and the heat seared her hand. "Ow." She pounded on the door with her fist. "Heidi!"

"Gillian, move." Quint swung his ax at the wooden doorframe as soon as she stepped aside. Flames shot through the gap and Gillian's stomach pitched.

"Back door." Hank ran around to the back with Gillian only

steps behind him despite the cumbersome cast. Adrenaline pushed her toward her daughter. The door swung open as they reached it. Ryder held Heidi in his arms.

"Where the hell did you come from?"

"Ran around back after her." Soot covered his face. "She's not breathing good." Heidi coughed in his arms with her bag clasped tight to her chest.

Quint hurried up to them. "We need to get as far away from the garage as possible in case one of the tanks ignites." He grabbed Gillian and dragged her behind him as Hank steered his grandson. They were halfway down the block when they stopped. Quint gazed at Gillian for a long moment, but didn't say anything. Then he ran back to the building.

"Set her on the ground, son." Hank removed the oxygen tank off his back and strapped it over her Heidi's face. "Both of you stay here with her. I have to see if Quint has the fire under control."

Gillian held onto her daughter's hand and nodded just as a loud explosion shook the ground.

"Quint!"

Gillian grabbed Ryder's shoulder. "Do not leave her side. Do you hear me?"

She waited long enough for the teen to nod and ran back down the block to Manny's garage.

Hank was getting up to his knees as she whipped past him. The crowd of onlookers scurried in every direction to get away from the falling debris.

"Quint!"

"He went around the side." Missy motioned toward the back of the building.

Gillian was breathing heavily when she rounded the garage

to find Quint lying on his back with a large piece of charred wood on his chest. She shoved the plank aside and dropped to her knees beside him. "Quint?" She checked for a pulse.

"He's over here." Cade Holstrom ran up to Gillian's side. "Is he breathing?"

"I think so." She lowered her ear to his mouth. A warm breath tickled her lobe. "Yes, he's breathing."

Quint moaned.

She leaned in closer. "Quint, can you hear me?"

"Yes."

If she hadn't already been down on the ground when he spoke she may have gotten there pretty darn quickly as her legs shook even beneath her.

"Where are you hurt? Do you have any pain?"

"Yes. My hand."

She looked at the hand lying on his chest. With greatest care, she lightly touched the back of his hand. There was no apparent damage or wounds.

"No, the other one. Under your knee."

"Oh jeez." Gillian shifted. "I'm so sorry."

Quint chuckled then coughed slightly. "I'm fine." He pushed himself up to a sitting position.

"You most certainly are not. You were unconscious when I got over here."

"I was resting my eyes." He scrubbed at the back of his head. "How's Heidi?"

"Hank put his oxygen mask on her. We need to get her to the hospital."

Quint nodded. "Cade, do you have your truck here?"

"Yes."

"Gillian, go with Cade. Take Heidi to Dr. Hambert's ASAP. He can get started on her."

"What about you?" She gripped his turnout coat. "You need to come with us, too."

"I need to help Hank get this fire under control. I'll be there as soon as I can."

"Promise?"

"I promise." He looped his hand behind her neck and pulled her in for a quick kiss. "Now go."

Missy, Cade and Ryder accompanied Gillian to Dr. Hambert's office while Quint and Hank put out the rest of the fire. What of the population that hadn't come with the initial fire, was drawn out by the explosion. Thank goodness it was him that took the brunt of the blast, some of the older folks— shoot, even Hank would have been down for the count had he been much closer—would have been much worse for the wear. As it was his ears were ringing something fierce and he doubted he'd ever forget the stench of the hair burnt off his forearm.

Ruby popped into his mind immediately. He hadn't seen her milling about the crowd, but he'd also been a little preoccupied. He couldn't rule her out. Especially since the office area burned most. Had it been an accident or workplace mishap, with all the flammable materials and equipment Manny had, something in the service area would have been the point of origin, but with the help of a couple of other hands they'd gotten the fire out and discovered a trashcan under the desk that looked like the culprit, as well as possibly a smaller fire in the corner next to the filing cabinet. He had no choice but to give the fire marshal in Sheridan his suspicions about Ruby.

Quint needed to get over to the doctor's house as soon as

possible. He was worried about Gillian and Heidi. But confused, too. So many other things were fighting for attention in his head. Like why Gillian and Heidi were still in Paintbrush. Several of his neighbors had called when she'd packed up the car and driven off. He couldn't have been more surprised when Gillian came running around the building. He figured they'd be halfway to Bozeman. And why in the hell had her daughter run into a burning building.

Once Sheriff Reese got everyone to head back home, Quint and the sheriff gave a quick debriefing to the mayor and the councilmen—who consisted of the grocery owner and Willard Cates. Reese had Manny's contact information in Sheridan and was calling as Quint ran out of the mayor's office then headed to the fire station.

He'd found Ruby waiting outside the fire station. "I heard what happened. I wanted to go with you to the doctor's. For support."

Quint fought back a frown. It wasn't that she was cold hearted, but she was one of the last people he'd expected to come forward to give Gillian support—especially if she had even the slightest thing to do with the fire. "Sure. Give me a minute to put up all this stuff." He raised his turnout coat and hurried past her. She hadn't so much as moved an inch by the time he got back outside. "Ready?"

She nodded. "How...how bad was it? Is Heidi..."

"I don't know. She was having trouble breathing when they took her to Dr. Hambert's. I don't think she got any other injures in the fire."

They hurried up the few short blocks toward the doctor's house/office.

"Someone told me you were hurt. When something exploded." Her words came out choppy with their quick pace.

"I'm fine." He glanced over his shoulder at her. "But it could have been so much worse. The fire was only a few feet away from Manny's main gas tank." He stopped at the door to the doctor's office, kept his hand on the handle. "It could have leveled half a block had it gone off."

Ruby's cheeks paled. Quint needed to let the sheriff know, but he didn't actually have proof that Ruby did anything to set the fire. No proof with any of the fires other than the burning in his gut that something was off with her. As soon as he had a minute alone, though, he would phone the sheriff. He opened the door and ushered Ruby in then followed her into the quiet room.

"How is she?" Quint removed his hat and held in his hand.

Tears streaked down Gillian's face. "I don't know yet. The doctor hasn't come out." She stood and walked over to him. "I can't lose her, too."

Quint opened his arms. Gillian walked in to his embrace without hesitation. He stroked her back. "She's strong, she'll make it. And Dr. Hambert is one hell of a doctor."

She nodded against his chest, her tears soaking the front of his shirt.

He glanced over the top of her head. Missy had Ryder tucked up under her arm like a momma hen protecting her chick. Soot covered the boy's pale cheeks. "You okay, Ryder?"

The boy met Quint's gaze as tears hung in his eyes. "I'll be okay." Cade paced the floor with his cell phone at his ear. When he flipped it shut he turned to Quint. "The ambulance from Sheridan's almost here. May be another fifteen minutes."

Gillian shook against him. "She was so pale."

"Your daughter is a fighter. She is strong like her momma." He kissed the top of Gillian's head. "Why'd she run into the building? It had to be burning when you got there."

"She left something inside."

"Nothing is worth risking your life over."

Gillian squiggled loose and looked over at the Lunsfords then she leaned up on her tip toes and whispered into Quint's ear. "Ryder gave her his grandmother's bracelet. She couldn't leave it inside."

His heart twinged. Heidi and Ryder were so young but driven by such powerful emotions. Yet he and Gillian had danced around each other from the get go. He gave himself a mental shake. Once Heidi was out of the woods—and she would recover, he had not one ounce of doubt in his being that she would—he would find a way to make Gillian stay in Paintbrush and become his wife. He hadn't waited all these years to find the right woman only to let her run off.

Cade and Missy were whispering to one another as Gillian walked over to Ryder. "That was the bravest thing anyone has ever done for Heidi. I will be in your debt forever." He stood and she took the boy into her arms despite him towering over her several inches.

Ruby paced the length of the waiting room floor. Almost to herself, she mumbled, "No one was supposed to be inside."

The room quieted. Gillian released Ryder and sucked back a sob. "Excuse me?"

"The garage was supposed to be empty. You'd left work hours before. I saw Manny lock up and leave."

Gillian stepped in front of Ruby, halting her pacing. "Did you do this? Did you hurt my daughter?"

"I didn't mean to. No one was supposed to be inside. Quint was starting to suspect that you were the one setting the fires. I figured you'd run if you thought he was going to blame you outright."

"Bitch." Gillian launched herself at the woman. Cade Holstrom snagged her around the waist and kept her from pouncing on Ruby.

Just then, the door to the doctor's office opened. "Gillian?"

Ryder jumped up from his seat. "How is she, Dr. Hambert?"

"She'll be fine, son. She's breathing easier now. But I want them to do a thorough examination up at the hospital in Sheridan. They may want to keep her for observation for a couple of days too. She took in quite a lot of smoke." Dr. Hambert tucked his hands into his pockets. "The hospital has a team ready for her once the ambulance gets her there."

"May I see her?" Gillian was already walking past the doctor. She paused before she completely crossed the threshold and turned to narrow her gaze on Ruby. Her heart beat heavily as heat flooded her cheeks. Tears stung her eyelids. "I'm not done with you. You won't get away with putting my daughter in danger this time or any of the times."

Her hands shook when she turned her back on Ruby. She had to take several deep breaths and count to ten before she was composed enough to approach Heidi's bed on the other side of the room.

"What was that all about?" Heidi's raspy voice clinched Gillian's heart harder.

"Nothing for you to worry about, hon." Gillian stroked Heidi's soot-covered hair away from her face. "Just so we're clear, you're grounded for the foreseeable future for running into a burning building. I'm thinking maybe when you turn thirty, we'll talk and I might consider waiving your punishment."

The teen laughed which then turned into a coughing fit. Tears streamed down her cheeks and she fisted her hands in the blanket surrounding her.

"You're okay, hon. You're okay." Gillian tried to soothe Heidi. It was several minutes before she was calm and breathing slightly better.

Once she could speak again, she looked up at Gillian. "Ryder?"

"He's out in the waiting room. Hang on."

Ryder stood just next to the door when Gillian went in search of him. "She's asking to see you."

He rushed over to her bedside. Gillian pulled the doctor aside. "How is she, really?"

A slight smiled curved the corner of his mouth. "She'll be fine. Honestly. She took in a lot of smoke but there shouldn't be any irreparable damage. Had she been in the building much longer..." He shrugged. "But no use worrying over what didn't happen." He patted Gillian's shoulder.

She understood what he was saying. Her daughter was fine and would be. She would never have been in the fire in the first place, though, if Ruby had not been a petty, vindictive bitch. Gillian scanned the waiting room. Ruby sat in the corner with Quint standing watch. "The funny thing, Ruby." Every eye in the room turned and looked at her. "If you'd have waited maybe an hour, you'd have had Quint all to yourself. We were on our way out of town. We just stopped at the garage to pick something up."

Ruby blanched. Missy gasped. And Quint hung his head.

Cade looked out the front window. "Gillian, the ambulance is here."

"You want me to drive you to the hospital?" Quint flashed back to his conversation with Gillian hours earlier before everyone had left for the hospital in Sheridan. He'd offered the

one thing he could at the time—his support. He hadn't known what else to say to her.

She hadn't quite looked him in the eyes. "No, thanks. Missy and Ryder will take me."

Missy and Ryder jumped to the task and in a big hustle and bustle, left just behind the paramedics. And left a void in Quint. He'd wanted to be there for Gillian, but she hadn't wanted anything from him. At all.

At least with him staying behind, he could explain everything to Sheriff Reese. Cade gave a quick statement and told the sheriff that Missy and Ryder promised to give their statements corroborating Ruby's confession at Dr. Hambert's office when they got back to town.

He and Cade stood by the front door of the sheriff's office waiting for the Reese to get back from the crime scene. He needed to get photos taken before it got too dark.

"She'll be all right." Cade slapped him on the back.

"Sure." He nodded.

"The Harwood women are made of some stern stuff. Missy can't stop talking about them. And don't get Ryder started." Cade smiled.

"That they are."

Cade spoke again but Quint wasn't paying attention. So many thoughts tumbled through his head. He was confused and turned around. The only place he wanted to be was with Gillian and she didn't want him. She'd decided to leave him and Paintbrush behind.

Like she told Ruby, if she'd waited an hour, the Harwoods would have been long gone from their town and their lives. Ruby'd have had no cause for any of her actions. He glanced over at her. She sat in the small jail cell with her head in her hands.

Quint's throat constricted as he asked, "Why?"

"I love you," she didn't hesitate to answer.

"So you set fires to frame Gillian? Because you love me." Quint scrubbed his hand through his hair. "Since she got here?"

"Yes."

"And you hoped to accomplish what?"

"To get her to leave. Or for you to stop looking at her the way you do." She glanced up at him. "I hated the way you looked at her."

"Ruby, you and I, we were only friends."

"We could be so much more. If it weren't for her."

He walked over to the cell and gripped the bars so hard his knuckles whitened. "We would not have been anything more than friends. Before she ever got here I knew that. Now that I've met Gillian... I love her. So much it's painful and she's leaving because of those fucking fires."

Ruby shook her head slowly then faster and faster still until her hair swung with the momentum. "She would have left anyway. Without you." She swiped at the tears on her cheeks. "Did you know that Heidi's not even her child? Did you? She's her..."

"Niece. Yes, I know."

Ruby frowned in disbelief. "She told you?"

"I know everything about her. She told me everything." Once he'd discovered a good portion of it online, but once she'd had someone to confide in, she'd told him.

"He said she's a liar. Lies about everything."

"*He* who?" Heat raced up his spine. Who would be talking to Ruby about Gillian? There was only one person who came to mind. "What are you talking about?"

"Heidi's father. He said Gillian ran out of town with her and he's been looking for them."

His stomach dropped and he waved Cade over. "When did you speak with him?"

"This morning. He said he found out she was here in Wyoming from one of Heidi's friends. He was coming here to get Heidi."

"He said that?" His hands shook and he released the bars. "Cade, I need you to go get the sheriff. Tell him it's an emergency."

"What's wrong?"

"I'll explain in a minute." He turned back to Ruby. "Did the man give you his name?"

"Rick."

Quint closed his eyes and his breath clogged in his lungs. "Please tell me you didn't give him any information."

She nodded. "I told him where she's staying. He had every right to know. He's—"

"That's NOT Heidi's dad." He ran his hands through his hair. "He killed Heidi's mom. In front of her and tried to kill her too. He's been after them since he got out of prison."

Ruby blanched. "I didn't..."

"Of course you didn't. She was fucking hiding."

The sheriff came hurrying in his office with the camera still around his neck. Hank was hot on his heels and asked, "What's wrong, Quint?"

Quint all but launched himself across the sheriff's desk to the phone. "She needs to be warned." He knocked over a coffee mug. It crashed on the floor with a deafening crackle.

"Look at me, son." Hank set his hand on Quint's shoulder. "What's going on?"

"Gillian's in trouble. The reason she came here was to hide from the man who killed Heidi's mom."

"You're not making any sense." Hank's wrinkled face pulled down in a weary frown. "Take a deep breath and start over."

He did as instructed then gave them a condensed version of what all he'd learned.

"Relax. She ain't here. The girl's up in Sheridan at the hospital with her daughter." Hank walked Quint over to the chair at the Sheriff's desk. "Sit. Who else knows what's going on? You prolly told your aunt, right?"

He nodded. "I asked Zan and Jacob to help me protect Gillian. Manny may know. I think Gillian told him some of it."

"Good deal, son." Hank squatted his wiry frame in front of Quint and held his gaze. "I got a hold of Manny fifteen minutes ago. He was headed over to the hospital to check on them. He'll keep an eye on them."

Quint breathed in then out slowly, tried to calm himself. "Sheriff, he's coming for her. Ruby told him where they were staying."

Everyone turned to look at her. Tears streamed down her face as she huddled in the corner.

"He'll probably have no clue they're in Sheridan, but can you call the hospital and the police chief there and give them a head's up?"

"No problem." Reese snapped up the phone receiver and dialed. He gave the police chief the same abbreviated story Quint had given him. Then he called the hospital and gave the staff there a description of Rick from Quint. He asked that security be put on her room until they could get someone from the police department over there. "Can you connect me to Heidi Harwood's room please?"

The sheriff shifted and held out the receiver to Quint.

"Here, talk to Miss Gillian. You'll feel better once you talk to her."

Missy answered on the third ring. "Hey, Quint."

"How is she?"

"Doing real good. She's sleeping now."

He breathed a sigh of relief. "Can I speak to Gillian?"

"What? She's not here. She left a while ago. Said she needed to pick up something at the house. Some stuffed bear Heidi forgot to grab. If you ask me, Heidi did it on purpose so they'd have to come back. But then the fire happened and everything went haywire. Manny's here now. Did you—"

He hung up the phone. "Gillian's not there. She came back to Paintbrush."

Chapter Seventeen

"Left that damn teddy bear." Gillian had borrowed Missy's truck and driven the long, lonely miles back to Paintbrush to get the bear. She couldn't really blame Heidi for trying to thwart their leaving; she didn't want to leave either. She just couldn't take the chance that Rick found out where they were—her ire over the cell phone faded away when Ryder pulled Heidi's limp body from the garage.

She shook off her thoughts as she parked the truck in the driveway of her—no, it was Quint's again—house. She'd left the keys Quint had given her on the kitchen table. Luckily though, the spare key was still hidden under the potted plant on the front porch.

The phone was ringing when she let herself into the house. She debated just letting it ring, but was afraid it could be Missy calling from the hospital.

"Hello?"

"Thank God you're there. Come to the sheriff's office right now." A slight noise echoed in the background—like a bunch of people talking.

Gillian's body shook. "Who is this?"

"Cade Holstrom. You need to come to the sheriff's office now. Is Quint there with you?"

"Quint? No. I just walked in the door. What's going on?"

"Rick knows where you are."

Numbness leeched all her strength and she wavered on her feet. "What?" She leaned her hip against the back of the sofa and gripped the phone so tightly her fingers ached.

"It's a long story. Come here. To the station. The sheriff has men coming in from other towns but it's taking time."

"I..." The phone went silent. "Cade? Are you still there?" When he didn't answer, she pressed the disconnect button several times but got nothing.

A cold sweat beaded over her face and arms.

"Who's Quint?"

She closed her eyes. *Rick.* Behind her. The receiver fell from her hand and clattered to the floor as she turned. Rick stood at the edge of the hallway with his shoulder casually leaning against the wall like he owned the world. He looked exactly the same as he had fourteen months earlier on her front porch.

He wasn't a very big man, maybe five-foot-eight. But what he lacked in size he made up for in the hollow, soulless gaze in his dark brown eyes. He'd scared the crap out of her when she was sixteen and he'd just started dating her sister. Now, after spending years in prison and twelve years older, he scared the ever-loving shit out of her.

"Is he some shit-kicking cowboy with curly hair and a pretty good right hook?" Rick stood away from the wall and rubbed his jaw.

"What did you do to him?"

"Left him bleeding all over the kitchen floor."

Every ounce of Gillian tensed. She looked toward the kitchen. A pair of boots poked out just at the edge of the doorway. "Jesus." She darted for Quint. He lay motionless up against the cabinet. A dark red stain spread across his denim shirt. "Quint!"

Before she could drop down to his side, Rick grabbed her by the hair and yanked her back. "Not so fast." He pulled until she was standing again.

"Ow." She swatted at his hand but only ended up clunking herself in the head with her cast. She needed to get Quint help, but damned if she had the faintest idea how. "How did you find us?"

"It's easy when you know where to look. Heidi's little friend was easily swayed in telling me what I wanted to know."

Images of Sierra floated before her eyes. "You didn't hurt her, did you?"

"Didn't need to. Yet. Once I got here it wasn't easy figuring out where you were. These yokels avoid new people like the plague. However, I did find one woman who seemed to know a Gillian. She thinks you are, in her words, a boyfriend-stealing hussy. I never knew you had it in you. Maybe I had the wrong sister all along."

"You bastard." Gillian tried in vain to kick him but she ended up only making him tighten his grip and yank her harder. "What do you want?"

His hot breath feathered her ear. "Where's Heidi?"

Gillian flinched as a trace of spit landed on her cheek. "She's not here."

"I can see that." He shook her. "Where is she?"

"I'm not about to tell you."

"Really?" A gun came up beside her face, pointed right at Quint.

"Wait, wait, wait. Please don't shoot him." She grabbed at his wrist but the way he held her hair, she couldn't get any leverage to disrupt his aim.

"Where is she?"

She could tell him partial truths. He'd never be able to figure out where. "She's in the hospital."

His grip loosened for a moment. "Why?"

"There was a fire in town." The less she struggled the more lax his hold became. "She got caught inside the building."

"When did this happen?"

"A few hours ago."

He tightened his grip again and shook her. "Why aren't you with her?"

There had to be some irony that Rick was affronted that she wasn't at the hospital with Heidi. "She needed a couple of things from the house." No point in telling him they'd packed almost everything up before the fire. "She wants her stuffed bear."

His hand released her so suddenly she fell to the floor. Laughter echoed off the walls as she crawled over to Quint. He was breathing, but it wasn't deep. She grabbed a dishtowel hanging from the stove handle and pressed it to the wound on the side of his stomach.

"Can you hear me, Quint?" Gillian whispered. "Please stay with me. Please don't die."

He didn't acknowledge her in the slightest. Didn't even twitch at the pressure applied to the gunshot wound.

"Hang in there. I love you and can't lose you. I just can't."

Rick laughter stopped abruptly. "It's here? The bear is here. I could have had it and been gone?" He shook his head and waved the gun at Gillian.

Gillian swiveled her gaze toward Rick. *What the hell could he want with Heidi's toy?*

"Get up. Go get it," he yelled at her.

She ran down the hall and into Heidi's room with Rick hot

on her heels. She didn't see the damn bear anywhere, but she knew it would be here. Heidi had begged her to come back and get it.

"Where is it?"

"I don't know." Her hands shook. "But it's here, I swear to you."

"Find it."

"I'm trying." She looked under the bed and in the closet. And found nothing. Where would Heidi stash it? She rubbed her throbbing temple. *Think, think, think.*

Wait. The bed was made. The entire time they lived in Quint's house, the bed had never once been made. She ripped at the pillows and found the bear under the stack. "Found it."

Rick yanked it from her. With way too much ease, he tore the off bear's head and produced a small cassette.

"What..."

"Becca thought she was so smart, trying to blackmail me into leaving her alone." He shoved the cassette into his pocket. "She was still alive when I started that fire. I bet you didn't know that. I wanted the cassette back and she wouldn't tell me. No matter how many times I shot her. She was tougher than she looked."

Gillian's covered her mouth with her hand as the bile burned the back of her throat.

"It wasn't until I told her I'd go after Heidi that she finally admitted she'd stuffed the cassette in that damn teddy bear." He pointed at the decapitated bear on the floor with the gun. "She hid it, though, too well. By that time, the fire had engulfed too much to keep looking for her. I figured the fire would take care of the bear and Becca's threats."

"You bastard." Gillian lunged at Rick, but he was faster than she anticipated. He backhanded her with the butt of the gun, right across her cheek. She screamed out in pain but still she punched at him. Her cast glanced off his shoulder and he yelped.

"Bitch." He shifted his stance and pointed the gun at her forehead. Her cheek had already swelled and blocked the left side of her vision. Not that she necessarily wanted to see the bullet before it entered her brain.

She'd always feared Rick catching up to her and killing her. The fear had been cloying at times and she'd jumped out of her skin at the slightest provocation. Coming to Paintbrush had been the best mistake she'd ever made. She'd been able to breathe and to just...live. And she'd lived so much. Fell in love for the first—and last—time. Watched her daughter blossom and fall in love as well. It wasn't enough, but she wouldn't trade it for anything. She didn't regret one moment since the wrong turn landed her in the right place. She only wished she and Quint could have had a chance. Him offering to protect her from this nightmare was the best gift anyone had given her since Heidi.

She *did* have one regret. She never told Quint she loved him. If she had a chance to do it over, that was the one thing she'd have done differently.

It was too late, though. She held Rick's gaze. If he was going to end her life she wasn't going to go down as the coward who ran for so many months. Before Gillian could so much as pray for a swift death, the wail of sirens accompanied red and blue strobe lights pouring in from the front of the house.

"How the hell..."

"The police knew you were close. If some dumbass hadn't cut the phone line while I was getting warned..." She shrugged. "It's too late for you now too, I guess."

He growled at her and dragged her back into the kitchen but the momentum of his shove made her trip over Quint and fall heavily on the floor. He scrambled over Quint himself and grabbed at her. "Get up. Get up now, dammit."

His hand landed on her shoulder but she shied away from him. "You're not going to get out of here."

"If I don't neither will you." He pointed the gun at her. "Or your boyfriend."

For the first time since she learned of her sister's death by Rick's hand, a peace came over her. "As long as you can't hurt Heidi then I can live, or die, with that." He couldn't scare her any more. He couldn't make her lie awake at night worrying that he might sneak in and hurt either her or Heidi. Her daughter was safely tucked away in Sheridan.

"You crazy bitch." Spit flew from the corners of his mouth.

"Rick Damon we have the place surrounded. Come out with your hands up." Sheriff Reese's booming voice crackled through a speaker.

"Come here." Rick finally managed to grab a hold of Gillian's shirt. "How many police work in this town?" He fisted his hand in the material and yanked her to her feet.

"I've only met the sheriff. I think he has a deputy or two, but I've never seen them."

"Two?" He scoffed. "Move to the back door."

He pushed at her until she stepped past Quint and across the kitchen floor to the back door.

"Open it, you bitch."

Her hand fumbled on the knob, but she did get it open. She hated leaving Quint, but if by getting Rick to vacate the house then someone would be in shortly to tend to him—as soon as they realized Rick had gotten out.

When they pushed through the door, a row of truck floodlights came on and blinded Gillian. Rick pulled her flush against him and shoved the gun into her neck.

"No need for that. Let the woman go." It was Hank. Gillian couldn't see where he was with the glare, but knowing he was there—that he could help Quint—was enough to give her the strength she needed.

"Let us pass by or she's dead." Rick spit on her as he hissed out the words.

"I can't do that, son."

"I'm not your son. And I'm not messing around." Rick's entire body vibrated against her. He might be a cold-blooded killer when it came to helpless women or unarmed men, but the man was a big, old weenie when it came to facing down someone ready for him.

"I understand. But I don't want anyone getting hurt. You okay, girl?"

"I'm fine. Quint's hurt though, Hank. Real bad."

Rick put his mouth on her ear. "You know this yokel?" When she nodded he continued, "You get him to give us his truck and maybe your boyfriend might make it if they even have a doctor in this shit-for-nothing town." He shook her. "Do you understand?"

"Yes."

The sheriff was once again yelling from the front of the house at Rick. He pushed the tip of the gun so hard against her neck it choked her. "You better make him give us the keys. He takes too long to decide and lover-boy dies. You yell too loud and you die. Do you get me? Make it convincing."

"Hank, I need your truck," she rasped out the words.

"I can't do that, girl."

"Hank, let us go and you can get in there and help Quint. I don't know how much blood he's lost already. He needs attention *now*. Before it's too late." Her voice caught on the last sentence.

"Touching."

"Fuck you, Rick."

"Gillian..." Hank wavered.

He was close to giving in. He needed to give in. "Hank. *Please*. Don't worry about me. Quint needs you."

"Fine." A dark figure disengaged from the truck.

Rick shifted to point his gun at Hank. Gillian leaned back into him, made his arm move. "If you shoot him, the sheriff will come running around the back with whoever he has out there. You won't make it to the truck."

"Shut up." Rick lowered the gun to her side and barked out orders. "Leave the keys in the truck. Open the gate and come this way."

Hank did as he requested and walked slowly across the backyard toward them. "Over to the side, old man." Hank shifted to get right up next to the house as Rick tandem-walked Gillian to the truck.

"Gillian?" Uncertainty laced Hank's voice.

"It's okay, Hank. Please tell Quint I love him."

"You can tell him that yourself." Hanks voice quavered.

"Don't count on it, old man." Rick hurried her the rest of the way to the truck and shoved her inside through the passenger door. "You drive."

Gillian got behind the wheel. She gripped at it with her right hand then laid the casted hand on her thigh. "You're going to have to start it. I can't." She wiggled the cast at him.

"Useless bitch." Rick tucked the gun at her side and leaned for the keys. "You better know a way to get us out of here."

"I know how I'm getting out of here."

Rick's gaze darted to her. "What?"

Gillian swung her cast square at Rick's face. He was too stunned to block the blow. At the same time, she pushed down on the horn with her other hand. Rick screamed out in pain as he brought both hands up to his face. In the process the gun went off and deafened Gillian. A burning spread from her shoulder, but she was not to be deterred. She swung at him again and again.

At some point he dropped the gun completely as he tried to protect his face, but that was okay with Gillian. She smashed her cast against his fingers over and over, ignoring the searing pain in her shoulder and her forearm until a pair of strong arms pulled her from the truck as someone grabbed Rick from the other side. "Hey."

"Calm down. The sheriff has him. You're okay." Cade spoke in slow deliberate tones as he pinned her arms down to her sides and cradled her to him. "Gillian, can you hear me?"

Her breath heaved in and out of her lungs as she nodded.

Rick was still screaming on the other side of the truck as he was placed in handcuffs.

"Wait!" She broke Cade's hold and rushed around to the other side of the truck. She ran up to Rick and shoved her hand in his front pocket and retrieved the cassette. "Dickhead." She kicked him hard in the knee. The sheriff pulled Rick away before she could dislocate the other kneecap.

"Girl, you got gumption and then some." Hank came up beside her.

"*OHMYGAWD*, how's Quint?"

"The doctor's in with him now. He's lost a lot of blood but the boy's a fighter." Hank frowned. "Gillian, you're bleeding."

"I am?" She glanced at her shoulder. A dark red stain blossomed. "Hmm." The lights suddenly shut off, blackening out the world.

Quint's side was on fire.

Machines beeped around him and a stringent odor irritated his nostrils. Hospital was the first thing that came to mind.

Then the man's face flashed through his memory. "Gillian." He tried to sit up but it burned worse and stole his breath.

"Shh. You need to take it easy." His dad's voice was quiet and a little tense.

"Dad?"

"I'm right here."

A hand settled into his. He tried to open his eyes but grit abraded with the movement. Finally, he pried one eye open. He was, in fact, in a hospital. "What happened?"

"You were shot." His dad squeezed his fingers. Quint's mother patted his arm and smiled with a watery smile. "But you're doing good now."

His dry mouth pulled down. "Shot?" He didn't remember anything after walking into his home and finding that man— Rick.

"Where's Gillian?"

"She's fine. Her daughter was released this morning so she had some paperwork to fill out." His dad draped an arm around his mom's shoulder.

"Dad, you have to go find her. Don't let her leave."

"I'm not going anywhere." Gillian came into his peripheral vision. A dark purple bruise puffed her cheek and swollen eye.

"What happened?"

She laughed tightly. "You should see the other guy."

Quint's parents moved away and Gillian took their place. Her right arm had a purple cast and was trussed up in a sling. "What did I miss?" His eyes darted to the new cast.

"This?" She raised her arm slightly and grimaced. "I color coordinated it with my shiner. Though once this thing starts to turn it might clash." Her other hand gingerly settled on her cheek before she took his hand in hers. "How are you feeling?"

"Confused." Again he tried to sit up but the pain was too much. "Is Heidi okay?"

"Right as rain." A warm smile tilted her mouth. "What do you remember?"

What *did* he remember? Ruby admitted to talking to Rick Damon and then he went to his house. "Not a lot. Rick was in town and we couldn't find you so I went to the house in case you showed up there then... I got nothing."

Gillian nodded. Her mouth pulled down. "Rick was there already and he shot you."

Pain pricked his chest.

"I got there a little later." She glanced away. "You were bleeding. I didn't even know if you were alive or not." Her hand tightened in his. "He wasn't after Heidi. Just a toy bear she had back then when he and Becca were together."

"Why?"

"Becca hid a video cassette in it. She'd been more aware of his business than I ever knew. She secretly videotaped him. I don't know what she planned to do with it, but she didn't anticipate him turning on her and killing her when tried to use it as leverage."

"How did he know she still had the toy?"

Gillian shrugged. "I can only guess he was watching her and saw it at some point. That bear was the one thing she was never without as a child. He may have been just making sure he'd tied up any loose ends. I don't know. I never knew about it."

"Where is he now?"

"Sitting tight down the hall cuffed to the bed." She wiggled her cast. "I kinda broke my cast over his face—several times."

Quint smiled. "I knew you had it in you." He groaned when he shifted too much. "Hey," he whispered. When Gillian leaned closer to hear him, he asked, "What're my parents doing here?"

"Are you kidding me? The minute they heard you were hurt they hopped on the first plane to Wyoming. They were here before you even got out of surgery. Had the staff making sure everything was right and ready for you. Makes your aunt look like a slacker. And your mom... Your mom and Heidi hit it off like you would not believe." She leaned in closer and kissed his cheek. "He's not such a bad guy, your dad. He loves you a lot."

Quint snorted and instantly regretted it. He groaned with the sharp pain.

"Shh. You're a tough guy, but you need to relax." She kissed him again then stood.

She released his hand. He grabbed for her. "Don't go."

"I'm not going anywhere far. I have a job to get to. My boss is going to be doing a little remodeling and he's asked me to help him design my new office. Not to mention my daughter has high school in the fall."

"Really?" The zip that shot through him was anything but painful.

"Plus, my boyfriend is going to need some rehabilitation so I am going to be busy here for some time to come." She kissed her fingers and waved. "I'll see you in a bit. You need to talk to your dad. I love you, Quint."

He smiled. "I love you."

He wanted to bask in what Gillian said, but she looped her arm around his mom's waist and the two were gone too quickly. His father was back at his side.

"You gave us a huge scare, son." His father looked years older with his day-old stubble and dark rings around his eyes.

Quint couldn't remember the last time he'd seen his dad anything less than completely put together. "I'm sorry."

"Don't be. You have nothing to apologize for." His dad ran his hand through his silver hair. "If anyone owes an apology it's me."

Jeffery Walters apologizing to his son. For a moment Quint toyed with the possibility that he was, in fact, dead. Luckily, the pain kept that thought on the outer regions.

His dad slid a chair up to the side of the bed and sat. "I, uh..." His voice cracked. "I was so afraid that when we got off the plane I'd get a call telling me we'd lost you. It was the worst few hours of my life."

"Dad..."

His dad shook his head. "I love you, Quint. I know I haven't acted like it over the last few years, but I do. More than you may ever know. If I was too hard on you it was *because* I loved you so much. I wanted you to be able to have anything and everything you wanted. I thought by having a job like mine it would afford you those things. But I can see now that you earned it your own way. And I am damn proud of you." Tears rimmed his eyes. He swiped at his nose. "You are an exceptional son. And I wouldn't change you for anything. However, we need to discuss you bullet-stopping ability."

Gillian's new cast itched like a sonofabitch. She was stuffing a straw down inside the end of it when Jeffery Walters walked into the waiting room. She yanked the straw out and tossed it into the trash. "What did the doctor say?"

She'd felt in the way when the family gathered with the doctor to find out about Quint's injuries and the prognosis for his recovery time.

"He's doing great. Nothing irreparably damaged." He tucked his hands into his pockets.

Gillian stood. "I am so glad to hear that." She headed for the door. What did you say to a man who nearly lost his son because of the madness that followed you? "I want to apologize. To you. I never meant for Quint to get mixed up in any of this. In fact, that's why we were leaving town. I couldn't risk anything happening to him."

"It's not your fault."

"It feels that way." Tear pricked her eyes.

"Miss Harwood, Gillian, the only person to blame is the man who pulled the trigger. You can't blame yourself."

But I do. She'd been strong when she was with Quint but it was all she could do to hold it together. Sure, she'd packed up her daughter and was hightailing it out of town, but not because she wanted to leave. As she told Jeffery Walters, the risk to Quint, to anyone in Paintbrush, was too much to deal with. She'd never expected to fall in love with Quint, or the rest of the town for that matter.

"I may not have been around my son much lately, but I know for a fact that he gladly took that bullet if it meant keeping you or your daughter safe. He will lay down his life for those he loves." The man bent his head. He looked so much like Quint. The two were more alike than either was willing to admit. "How's your daughter?"

Gillian smiled. "She fine. The hospital was a little much for her, so she went back to Paintbrush with friends of ours." *Friends.* It was odd still that in such a short time she and Heidi made themselves at home. Found actual friends—family. If she hadn't already knocked Rick over the head with her cast she'd have had to do it again for making her almost lose the world she and Heidi had found.

Jeffery Walters nodded. "You should go on over and see Quint. He was asking about you again."

"I don't want to intrude on your family time."

"Nonsense." A shy smile tilted up the corner of his mouth—much like Quint's. "Go on over."

Gillian glanced back over her shoulder as she left the waiting room. Quint's father had such an odd expression. She couldn't quite place it but best guess...he looked like he had a secret. She shook off her speculations as she walked down the hallway to Quint's room.

The lights were dimmed when she'd pushed through the door. She started to back out when he called to her.

"I didn't mean to wake you."

"You didn't." His bed was elevated slightly and he had his head tilted toward her. "Come in. Sit." He patted the bed beside him.

Gillian walked over but stayed standing. "How are you feeling?"

He snorted. "Like I've been shot."

Breath backed in her lungs. "That's not funny."

He reached out and took her hand. "Hey. I didn't mean to upset you. I kind of feel like I have to joke about it to keep from letting it get to me."

"Letting what get to you?"

"The fact that you or Heidi could have been killed. All because I let him get the drop on me."

Gillian squeezed his hand. "As a wise gentleman told me,

it's not your fault. The one who pulled the trigger is the only one to blame for this."

"Been talking to my dad have you?"

"Guilty."

Quint frowned. "What else did he say?"

"Not much. Just what I already knew. That you're the bravest, most heroic person I've ever met."

"Do go on." He batted his eyes lashes.

"Some things never change."

"Some things do, though."

Cryptic talk from a man on morphine. Gillian chuckled.

Quint sobered. "Will you tell me what happened? With Rick. The sheriff came by to see me, but didn't tell me what all had gone on."

"Do you really want to know? He's in custody and will be locked away for a very long time. No need to rehash it all."

"I'd like to know. I think the scenarios playing through my head are worse that what may or may not have happened."

"I doubt it," Gillian mumbled. She glanced around the room and snagged the chair and dragged it over to the bed. When she sat, she laced her fingers through his again. "I came back to Paintbrush to get Heidi's bear." She scoffed. "Oddly enough the same thing that brought Rick to town."

Quint frowned but didn't comment.

"Back when Becca was dating Rick, she had videotaped them...well, let's just say during an intimate moment smack dab in the middle of his pool table." Watching the tape only to discover Becca and Rick doing it was an odd mixture of missing her sister and disgust to see the man who killed her all over her. "When they got done she fiddled with the camera and left the room. I don't know if she left it on on purpose or not—

there's no way to know for sure." Gillian shrugged. At this point did it really matter which scenario it was—dead was dead regardless of the intent.

Quint squeezed her fingers and shifted in the bed. "What else was on the tape?"

Gillian sniffed. "For twenty minutes or so there was nothing. Then Rick comes in with two men. I don't know who either of them are. Rick accuses one of the men of stealing from him. Before the man can even comment, Rick pulls out a gun and bam. Pops him in the head."

"I don't get it."

"Becca hid the tape in Heidi's bear. It's been in there for twelve years and neither of us ever even knew it. That's why he was sniffing around Heidi when he got out of prison. The only thing I can figure was since the prosecutors never tried to go after him for that man's death he assumed that the tape never surfaced."

"So he had to try and make sure that he got that tape back?"

"Yep. But we ran. And he was convinced then I had it."

"What happened at the house?"

Gillian took a deep breath. "The phone was ringing when I walked in. It was Cade calling to warn me Rick was in town. The phone went dead. Rick was already there."

A muscled in Quint's jaw ticked.

"Once I knew what he was after, I did everything I could to get him out of the house so someone could get to you. Of course, Cade notified the sheriff when the call was lost and he showed up at the same damn time."

"Reese is nothing if not punctual."

"He is that." She held his gaze as she skimmed over the

rest of the details. "When we got in Hank's truck, I smacked him square in the face with my cast. Never thought you breaking my arm would come in handy but I'll be damned if I could have gotten away from him without it."

"Glad I could help." He looked away from her. "If that was the only way I could help."

"I thought we covered that already." She wiggled his hand until he met her gaze again.

"You're right." He brought her hand to his lips and kissed the backs of her fingers. "Did you mean it when you said you were staying in Paintbrush?"

"Yes. Heidi likes it here. I have a good job—assuming Manny does rebuild the shop. And..." She leaned forward and kissed him gently on the mouth. "I have a boyfriend to look after."

"About that." Quint squeezed her fingers quickly then let go of her hand while he looked away. "I don't think you should go around calling me your boyfriend."

Her stomach plummeted. "Oh. Sorry. I, uh, just... Sorry I just..."

Quint chuckled then groaned.

"You think that's funny?"

"Not so much funny. I was actually thinking you should refer to me as your husband seeing how I plan on marrying you as soon as I get out of this bed."

"Your level of cockiness... What did you say?" And her stomach rolled the other way. Nerves tingled and goose pimples popped up on her arm. "Repeat please?"

The smile at the corner of his mouth broadened. "I would much rather be on bended knee, but I don't know that my legs would hold me up with all this morphine. Will you, Gillian Harwood, do me the honor of becoming my wife?"

"How do I know it's not the morphine talking now?"

"Do you remember when I came over to your house yesterday afternoon?"

"Yes." She nodded slowly.

"I was going to ask you then."

"But I was running away."

"Your words, not mine." He shifted and reached under the blanket. "I had this." He held a small velvet box.

"How did you..."

"It was still in my pocket at the fire and later at the house."

She opened the small velvet box and gasped. A solitaire diamond sat above two rows of smaller diamonds. "Beautiful," she said in just above a whisper. "I can't believe... I never suspected..."

"Having trouble finishing a sentence? That's not like you."

"It's been a rough couple of days." She popped the ring from the foam, but she didn't put it on. It was almost too pretty to be worn. It needed a case so people could come by and fill their gazes. It sparkled like crazy under the florescent hospital lights. "Can you marry someone who's such a coward? Who would run away from someone she loved?"

"Someone who would go to any length to protect her child? Absolutely."

"Are you ready to be the father of a teenager?"

"I never half-ass do anything, so yep."

"What about more children?" Gillian smiled. Warmth ran all through her.

"The more the merrier."

"I have one condition." She handed him the ring and settled her hand in his. "You have to promise to love me forever."

"That is one promise I can guarantee you I will be happy to keep."

"Then, Mr. Walters, you have found yourself a bride."

About the Author

Denise Belinda McDonald started her writing career at the tender age of eight. Her stories have changed over the years, but not her love for telling tales. An overactive imagination and a propensity to embellish have kept her books rich with lovable characters and interesting twists. A member of RWA, she belongs to several chapters.

Denise lives in Texas with her husband, four boys and two dogs where she juggles her time between writing, carpool, Cub Scouts, sports galore and a multitude of crafts.

If you would like to learn more about Denise, please visit her web site: www.denisebelindamcdonald.com or you can e-mail her at denise@denisebelindamcdonald.com.

And for a Chica good time, visit her blog with authors Amie Stuart, Melissa Blue, and Tanya Holmes as well as fellow Samhain authors Vanessa Jaye and Raine Weaver at: www.southernfriedchicas.com.

Be careful what you ask for.
It might come with spurs—and baggage.

Second Chances
© 2008 Denise Belinda McDonald
The Paintbrush series

After catching her boyfriend with his pants around his knees while a walking, talking cliché takes "dictation", Suzanne Walters quits her job, quits her man, quits Texas and moves to Wyoming to find the woman she used to be. Unfortunately, her first five minutes in Paintbrush finds her facing down the town bully in the local diner—and running smack into the one thing she's not looking for: a wet dream in cowboy boots, Jacob Bowman.

Jacob excels at two things—flying under the radar, and saving his pennies in hopes of running his own ranch someday. He can't stop thinking about the fantasy in tight Wranglers who nearly mowed him down exiting the diner. The curvy, vivacious spitfire makes his mouth go dry. She's got her eye on him, as well, but her determination to prove her independence is just as strong as the sexual pull between them.

Life's knocks have given them both strong hearts, and even stronger wills. As danger looms, that stubborn pride could cost their one chance to discover if there's something more between them than great sex.

Will they swallow their pride, or will they lose it all?

Warning: Cowboys and horses and bullies OH MY! Sweet, sweet loving and a little rowdy behavior.

Available now in ebook and print from Samhain Publishing.

CPSIA information can be obtained at www.ICGtesting.com
Printed in the USA
LVOW041520290911

248440LV00002B/94/P